BILLINGS BETTER BOOKSTORE

AND

BRASSERIE

FIN J ROSS

Clan Destine
PRESS

First published by Clan Destine Press in 2020

Clan Destine Press
www.clandestinepress.net
PO Box 121, Bittern Victoria
3918 Australia

National Library of Australia Cataloguing-In-Publication data:

 Ross, Fin J.

Billings Better Bookstore and Brasserie

 ISBN: 978-0-6488487-1-4 (pb)

 ISBN: 978-0-6488487-3-8 (hb)

 ISBN: 978-0-6488487-2-1 (eb)

Cover & illustrations © Judith Rossell
Cover type: Willsin Rowe
Design & Typesetting: Clan Destine Press

Clan Destine Press
www.clandestinepress.net

BILLINGS

BETTER BOOKSTORE

AND BRASSERIE

'If you enjoy wonderfully written historical fiction, or if you want to be reminded of the marvels to be found behind the doors of a bookshop, you'll love *Billings Better Bookstore and Brasserie*.'

Meg Keneally

Fidelia Knight is clever and delightful and, after you've walked the streets of colonial Melbourne with her, the Brasserie in Billings Better Bookstore would be the perfect place to take tea.

Kerry Greenwood

For Mum
Wish you were here.

This recommendation of fteadinefs and uniformity does not proceed from an opinion, that particular combinations of letters have much influence on human happinefs; or that truth may not be fuccefffully taught by modes of fpelling fanciful and erroneous: I am not yet fo loft in lexicography, as to forget that *words are the daughters of earth, and that things are the Sons of heaven.* Language is only the inftrument of fcience, and words are but the figns of ideas: I wifh, however, that the inftrument might be lefs apt to decay, and that figns might be permanent, like the things which they denote.

Samuel Johnson A.M.

A

*Amelia Audacious Admonished an Amateur Abecedarian
and Absconded with an Antediluvian Aardvark,
After Adjourning for an Arousing Absinthe at
Billings Better Bookstore and Cafeteria.
Did she Absolutely? She did indeed!*

Melbourne, March, 1875

She was roused from her sleep by the sound of a chair scraping on the floorboards. Was someone there or had she dreamed it? The floor was as hard as a gravestone and her ear hurt from being squashed against Samuel Johnson. A pale flickering glow filtered through the lace cloth of her refuge – a side table adorned with photographs set around a loudly-ticking casement clock – casting dancing shadows onto her bare arms like an old zoetrope. She was not alone. She sat up, silent as a settled moth, and drew her knees up under her pinafore. She had been holding her breath since she heard the sound and now exhaled ever so silently.

She peered through the veil of cloth and discerned the silhouette of a man – definitely a man – seated just four yards away. It was the exhalations of his breath which set the candle-flame aquiver.

Was the man affected? Why was he here at near one in the morning? He sat at the desk writing, surrounded by books, spasmodically duffing his forehead with the palm of his hand as though inside his mind he had discovered a new intricacy of the universe.

'C, C, what else starts with C?' He spoke out loud. She stifled a gasp with her hand. 'Hmm. Aha! Cross, Cutting, with C?'

She thought these words prosaic. He had a dictionary there beneath his elbow – the one, in fact, that she had been poring over earlier – but never once did he open it. She was almost bursting. What about *coscinomancy*? No, people mightn't understand it. The art of divination by means of a sieve seldom came up in conversation. What about *cachectick* or *crapulence*? Perhaps not. But *cross*? *Cutting*? So ordinary. So banal. She sighed. Not audibly mind, lest she betray her sanctuary; dispel her camouflage.

She could not fathom what he was doing. Sitting there talking to himself like a lonely parrot. *Hooty as a madgehowlet.* She hoped he couldn't hear her thinking and she was glad that he hadn't come while she had been reading in that very spot. Glad also that the smell of tallow from the candle she had burned at the desk had long since dissipated and that he was unaware it was a good inch shorter.

'Aha!' he exclaimed. 'Christopher Crabstick was Cross, Captious, Cutting and Caustic, whenever he could not get a book brought from Cole's Cheap Book Arcade.' He paused. 'Ish dat so? Yaw.'

She furrowed her brow. He was definitely a sailor short of a crew. Did he mean 'brought' when it should have been 'bought'? Yes, the man was patently mad, answering his own question, even. Mother always said that talking to oneself was a surety of malaise. Looseness of the mind. But sometimes one had no other option. Mother never knew how it was to long for someone to talk to, like she had after Ninian and Permelia were gone. Now Mother was gone. And Father too. And the little brother or sister who might have filled the gap left by the untimely deaths of her younger siblings.

She was alone.

How she missed Father reading to her at night by candlelight. How she missed his vocabulary and grammar lessons. Ninian and Permelia wouldn't have missed them. They never shared her fascination with words. She was always alone in her wonderment of language. And now she was truly alone. Oh, except for this nincompoop who spoke in alliteratives. Daft as a dingleberry, yet spellbinding. He interrupted her thoughts again.

'D, D, hmm. Dolly Dumpling…ah, danced, yes, danced…'

She rolled her eyes heavenward, noticing for the first time the cobwebs gathered in wisps on the underside of the table. She crinkled her nose. She didn't like the thought of sharing her sleeping quarters, such as they were, with spiders.

The man was mumbling to himself again. Was he writing a nursery rhyme like the ones Mother recited to her and her siblings as she prepared their porridge in the mornings? Mother Goose Rhymes she called them.

Birds of a feather flock together,
And so will pigs and swine.
Rats and mice have their choice,
And so will I have mine.

She put her hand to her mouth. Had she spoken out loud? She peered through the lace. Not a whisker of his substantial beard had budged. He hadn't heard her.

She truly wanted to call out some more imaginative D words – daggledtail, dallop, dewbesprent, dandruff – admittedly not verbs, but nonetheless much more interesting than 'danced', but she bit her tongue.

She would go on pretending she wasn't there. He would never know he had an audience.

Sometimes she wondered if she really *were* here. Nobody ever paid her any attention. Could they not see her? Was she a will-o'-the-wisp, unseen by those who didn't venture out into the darkness? She seldom saw her reflection in another's eyes; or in the windows; or in the polished silver or crystals of the epergnes on the tables in the store beneath her.

Was she a figment of her own imagination? Could she sit out there, in the open, and read all day? Would anybody notice her? She might try it. Tomorrow. Maybe she only existed to be the thing overlooked, lost, misplaced – but never found. It was helpful when she didn't *want* to be seen but what if, one day, she did?

She especially didn't want to be seen by Mr and Mrs Exon or anyone else from the orphan asylum. They might make her return there. She would never go back. She didn't belong there, refusing to believe as she did that her parents were truly gone.

She only had the awful Mr Bartholomew's word on that score and he had horridly told her never to speak of it. And so she hadn't. Had not, in fact, spoken to anyone since. Speaking about such sorrowful things might only make them real.

Nor had she belonged in steerage. Father had paid a small fortune for a handsome cabin aboard the *SS Great Britain*, yet she had spent the last week of voyage with those poor souls who could afford only the cheapest fare. She had spent much of that week avoiding one particular man, hirsute as a harvest mouse, who leered at her and brushed his tongue suggestively through his bristly moustache. He made her cringe.

His beard was not unlike this man's. But that was where the similarity ended. She did not get the impression that this man would harbour lecherous intentions. He looked too respectable for that. Who was this night owl who sat talking blather and balderdash? Was he, like her, a stowaway in this edifice of knowledge and learning?

Could one stow away in a building? She had heard the expression on board the ship. A young lad, not much older than herself, was discovered hiding, three days out of Liverpool. The ship battled heavy weather in those first days of the voyage and she and her mother, heavy with child, both succumbed to seasickness. During a brief spell on deck for fresh air, she witnessed the discovery of 'Stowaway Sam'. The wretched boy's eyes pleaded as he crouched on the deck, surrounded by half a dozen crew. A startled fox set upon by hounds. While the men called for the captain and discussed, debated and deliberated what to do with the young interloper, he tilted his head at her and smiled. She was not mistaken. She could see it clearly despite the dirt on his face. His matted hair clung to his forehead like the dags on a sheep's bottom and he licked his lips constantly. She could see that the boy was starving and lusting for water to quench his thirst. She dashed to her parents' cabin to retrieve her tin cup and reappeared shortly, having filled it from the water cask below decks. She parted two of the crew members, pushing between their hips, to proffer the cup to the boy.

Was this man like Stowaway Sam? Was he aboard this stone boat to nowhere for the promise it held? She wondered if Mr Cole, the proprietor, knew of this man's midnight escapades. He looked dowdy and sleep-tousled. Did he, like her, have nowhere else to be in the night than in this candle-lit edifice? No bed in which to drive away the thoughts that swirled and competed for supremacy in his head? Maybe, like her, he had a mind which couldn't switch off even in the depths of darkness.

Or maybe, like her, he was on a quest to expand his mind – by sneaking into Cole's Cheap Book Arcade in the middle of the night. She had done this many times in recent weeks, but never before had she had company. If one could call such a strange, self-absorbed person company. He was perplexing. He was odd. Yet he seemed a kindred spirit.

The bearded man kept her awake for another two hours. He penned, pored and pondered over his peculiar alliterative verses until he reached the letter N.

Nelly Neat Never Neglected her Nice New Needle,
Which she bought at a shop just above Cole's Cheap Book Arcade.
Ish dat so?.........Yaw.

She was tired of his musings and certain that she could do better, yet sleep was not forthcoming. He was tiring too; the words not coming freely now. He startled her at three o'clock by abruptly standing and rolling his strange verse into a cylinder, which he placed under his arm. She knew it was three o'clock from the chiming of the myriad clocks in the building, all contrived, she decided, to deprive her of more than an hour's sleep at a time. He pulled a silver candle holder from his pocket and lit the candle from the one on the desk which he then snuffed with his fingers. He paced silently towards the staircase, illuminating the austere paintings on the panelled walls as he passed. She waited a minute, crept from her hiding spot and peered down through the balustrades encircling the store's mezzanine. It was dark as a cave but she could see the man's candle flicker as he ventured through the door. He locked it from the outside, with a key. *He had a key.* Curious. He must be employed here, she concluded.

She was glad he was finally gone. It meant she had the place to herself again. She was hungry. It had been hours since she had had a pilfered bite to eat. She threaded her way, with arms outstretched like a blind person, back to the desk and rummaged around the mess of books and papers for the candle and matches. Once lit, she clutched its holder and tiptoed downstairs and towards the entry. Early yesterday, she had seen a young boy place something wrapped in paper into a large Chinese urn. She plucked it out and unwrapped it. Just as she hoped, it was the remnants of a slice of bread plastered with lard. The boy had evidently found it unpalatable. Dry though it was, she stuffed it into her mouth and relished the prospect of it quietening her carping stomach.

The flickering light danced in the mirrors before her and pirouetted off the brass wall fixtures and sconces. She glimpsed herself in a mirror and reeled at her ghoulish appearance. A trick of the light. Her face cast in amber glows, her hair a quandary of shadows. She wandered around the vast emporium, ran her fingers across vellum-clad tomes and flicked through pages of books whose contents she could only marvel at. Even if she read a book a day – a preposterous thought given she could scarcely manage fifty pages a night by the dim candlelight – it would take her two lifetimes to peruse the hundreds upon hundreds of volumes on the store's shelves. By which time, of course, many more would have been written and printed. It was a daunting thought.

She had better get started. Now that she was wide awake, it might be possible to read for an hour or so before the burden of slumber lay heavy on her eyelids. But what to read? She eyed the offerings on a table marked "American novels", and stopped on one with a familiar name. *Uncle Tom's Cabin*, by Harriet Beecher Stowe. Mother had told her that it was the 'most important book of the century'. How could she know that when the century was not yet over? Mother had explained a little about the story, and its ramifications for the American people. It was the first time she had heard the words 'slavery' and 'controversial', but it had been Father, not Mother, who had explained their meanings.

Mother told her she would need to wait until she was much older to tackle it. Mother wasn't always right. Mother tended to underestimate her.

She studied a copy. *Uncle Tom's Cabin or, Life among the Lowly*. She flipped past the illustration on the flyleaf and determined that if she could comprehend the first chapter, she would read on.

IN WHICH THE READER IS INTRODUCED
TO A MAN OF HUMANITY.

Late in the afternoon of a chilly day in February, two gentlemen were sitting alone over their wine, in a well-furnished dining parlor, in the town of P − − , in Kentucky. There were no servants present, and the gentlemen, with chairs closely approaching, seemed to be discussing some subject with great earnestness.

With the book in her right hand and candle in her left, she read out loud as she climbed the stairs, being careful not to let wax drip onto the pages. She reached the desk and was soon lost in Beecher Stowe's words and descriptions of life in America's troubled south. She had looked for a definition of the word 'nigger' in the dictionary on the desk, since it was foreign to her, but it seemed the dictionary didn't know it either. She fathomed, however, that it applied to dark-skinned people, in a contemptuous fashion. What made these white people regard themselves as superior? What gave them the right to own other people? The whole concept was anathema to her. She wished Father were here to explain. He had a knack of imparting logic where none was evident. Had Mother ever met a black person? Would she have regarded that person – for surely they *were* people too – with disdain? Surely Mother would not be so intolerant.

But then she considered the episode with the young lad on the ship, when she had given him water, and Mother's stern admonishment.

The boy had grabbed her tin cup and sculled its contents, wiping his lips on his shirt sleeve when it was empty. He nodded to her and grinned a scungy-toothed grin.

'Fidelia Patience! Whatever are you doing?' Only her mother could speak in such a tone. She was most displeased. 'Get away from that vagabond. Remember your manners.'

Fidelia replied that she thought she *was* showing her manners, when nobody else had given thought to the boy's plight.

'That scoundrel does not deserve your manners, child. He's not worthy of your second glance. Come now.' She waved her hand frantically, as if to convey impending doom. Fidelia obliged reluctantly; glanced back to smile at the boy.

Father heard that the boy was berated at length by Captain Chapman before being put to work in the galley. He came to be named 'Stowaway Sam' during the two-month voyage. His only possession was a tin whistle, with which he entertained the crew. Father had mentioned him later. A Liverpudlian, the boy was, who thought the *SS Great Britain* was sailing to Ireland when he stole aboard, not halfway around the world to Australia.

Fidelia thought it probable she would never see the boy again. Mother would make sure of that. 'You are the lioness,' she said, 'he is the jackal.' Fidelia didn't understand what she meant. Nor could she, at the time, recall what a jackal was. She had gone below to their cabin to look it up in Father's dictionary.

Jackál. *n.s.* [*chacal*, French.] A small animal supposed to start prey for the lyon.

The Belgians tack upon our rear,
And raking chase-guns through our sterns they send:
Close by their fireships, like *jackals*, appear,
Who on their lions for the prey attend. *Dryd. Ann. Mirab.*

She still wasn't sure she understood and Mother was in no mood to explain. Did it mean that she was important and he not? That didn't seem right. Did not all people feel thirst? Hunger? What made his thirst less vital to assuage?

Jackal came right before Jackalént (*n.s. [Jack in Lent, a poor starven fellow.] A simple sheepish fellow*) which, she thought, much more aptly described the lad.

She suspected that the strange man would appear again the following night; he had, after all, the remaining alphabet to complete. But this time, she was awake and sitting cross-legged under the table; her ears pricked for the sound of footfalls on the steps.

He arrived at one o'clock and was soon musing over the letter 'O'. It was a difficult one, of course, but she like the name *Obadiah Orpheus* for his character. The rest, however, she thought mundane. If she were writing such a verse, she might have Obadiah *obequitate* or *obambulate* around.

The letter 'X' took him an eternity, and he cheated – for want of words starting with the pesky letter – by using 'E' words in which X appeared at the second letter. Had he not heard of *xenodochial* or *xanthippe*?

He took three hours to work his way to 'Z', in which *Zachariah Zany Zealously studied Zoology*, by which time she was struggling to keep her eyes open. She rested her head against the wall and was asleep before he left the room.

B

Bernadette Bacciferous Buried her Blackberries
Before Buying Balbriggan and Baize for her Balistarius Beau
And then enjoyed Beer and Banana Bread at
Billings Better Bookstore and Cafeteria
Did she Blissfully? She did indeed!

A few days later, Fidelia ambled down Bourke-street towards Swanston-street and lost herself in the crowds. She carefully skirted the piles of horse dung which festered in steaming, smelly blobs here and there. She momentarily got lost in the rustling ruffles of a red taffeta dress as a lady stopped without warning in front of her. She could have vanished in those voluminous folds and furbelows for a week – the susurration like leaves in the wind – or never found her way out. She was reminded of her favourite hiding place behind Grandmama's chintz curtains when she and her siblings played hide and go seek.

The lady never noticed her.

Where did all these people come from? Where were they going? Perhaps to the theatre or for morning tea at one of the many restaurants. Or out shopping for a new hat or gloves or gown or parasol. Perhaps they were merely there to be seen. So many people walking idly, aimlessly. Preening and promenading to show off their wealth and opulence.

In contrast, a young boy shovelled the offending horse pats into a cart, his face and hands smeared with the noxious stuff. Unlikely, she thought, that *his* mother, if he had one, would know what taffeta was, nor know how it susurrated with lyric sensibility.

She gazed into shop windows and wished she had a few pence to spend on silky gloves, a hat, a pretty token. Or a *pain à la duchesse* like Father had shared with her in Paris. Choux pastry filled with cream and topped with chocolate. She licked her lips at the memory of that wondrous week with Father. They walked the Champs Élysées, marvelled at the enormity of the Cathédral Notre-Dame de Paris, strolled idly along the Seine and feasted on the collections at the Louvre. Father had barely let go of her hand lest she venture off and become lost.

She would return to Paris one day, of that she was certain. When old enough to experience its pleasures and appreciate its history and culture. Melbourne was nothing like Paris. Melbourne had barely any history. It had been here scarcely forty years, sprung out of the ground like an apparition. But at least the people here mostly spoke English, or a recognisable form of it.

No, Bourke-street reminded her more of Oxford Street, which she had frequented with her parents before leaving London for Liverpool prior to the voyage. But it had a rawness about it. The buildings, which loomed and seemed to bow toward her as she gazed up at them, looked polished and new. But the street was filthy with dirt and equine excreta.

Oxford Street always felt stuffy and constrained. There, Fidelia had known better than to squeal with delight at the wonderful sights. A well brought-up child should not behave that way. She had tired of the conventionality of it. What was the point of being a child, if one could not exhibit an element of exuberant behaviour occasionally? Was life always to be stilted and contrived? Could she never be seen in public without rag-bound curls, pristine pinafores and a mute, painted smile? She had often wanted to let go of Mother's hand and run, run, run along the street and call out about how glad she was to be alive. She knew better than to incur Mother's stinging reprimands.

But here, in Melbourne, she felt a strange freedom. Was it because she was alone, with nobody to monitor her every breath, her every word? Here, nobody questioned her. Nobody stopped to ask where her mother was. Nobody gave her a second glance.

Perhaps she really *was* invisible. She might be able to run, run, run down the street as fast as she could, with her hands outstretched like a whale's flippers or a starling's wings.

She resisted the urge and instead, skipped further down the street, past theatres and hotels and beyond to where the dip of Bourke-street was abuzz with Cobb and Co coaches offloading and loading passengers and goods for journeys north, east and west. She wanted to journey on one, to see what lay beyond the dusty, smelly hive of Melbourne. The horses and cabs lined up along the centre of the street; their passengers crawling on and off like ants, or off imbibing some drink or other at one of the many hotels. The *Royal Mail*, the *Albion Inn*, the *Temperance Hotel*; or further down across Elizabeth-street, the *Britannia Inn*, the *Australian Hotel*, the *Plough Inn* or the *Saracen's Head*. The names sounded majestic. Manifold hotels and yet she was too young, not to mention penniless, to enter any of them. She could only speculate at the opulence inside some, the stench of beer and whiskey inside others. And she could only wonder at the meals that might be served up to the well-to-do (like she used to be). The roast mutton or tender lamb, the Yorkshire pudding, the gravy and potatoes and peas. The apple pie and strawberry tarts.

She usually loved to wander down to look in the window of Buckley and Nunn and occasionally to venture inside, to admire the ever-changing costumes of the mannequins and touch the fabrics; the brocades, velvets and laces. It always made her think of Mother and her impeccable outfits. But she didn't feel like it today. Besides, she was conscious of the fact that her own personal odour, from having not bathed for a long while, might be frowned upon by anybody at close quarters. She was not fit to enter the likes of Buckley and Nunn in her worn cover-slut and with her grimy face and mass of tangled hair. She was hardly better than those scruffy street urchins that Mother had so carefully avoided.

She crossed to the south side of the street and walked back north-east; she knew it was east because the morning sun was now firmly in her eyes. Further up the street a bootblack was hard at work; a short queue of men discussed the weather while waiting patiently for their turn, their persiflage ringing above their heads, while a spruiker near the corner of Russell-street expounded the attributes of Ford's Pectoral Balsam of Horehound as a cure for coughs, colds and influenza to passers-by. It sounded awful. Probably tasted dreadful. But then most medicines were worse than the malaise they purported to cure.

Fidelia gazed up the hill towards Parliament House. She wasn't too sure what happened there but she suspected important men gathered there to talk about important things. It was not a place for women and especially not for young girls. But one day she would go there and not just to sit on the bank. She would go inside and make it her business to find out what went on inside those imposing walls.

Bourke-street was a noisy place. The clamour of hammers and the calls of labourers working on new additions to the streetscape almost drowned out the sounds of cartwheels, horses' hooves, the chatter of people, the tintinnabulation from a distant church and the clatter of businesses going about their daily rituals, all combined into a cacophony. She liked that word; she had learned it from one of Mr Cole's dictionaries. She didn't recall it from Samuel Johnson. She pictured his listings for 'C' in her head. *Cachinnation* – loud laughter, another fine word to add to cacophony; *Cackerel* – a fish with laxative qualities; *Cackle* (noun), *Cackle* (verb), *Cackler, Cacochymical, Cacochymick, Cacochymy* – all relating to humours and unpleasant bodily functions; *Cake* (noun). No *cacophony*.

It was from the Greek, meaning "bad sound". In itself it was a bad sound, almost onomatopoeic, which was why she thought it precise for its use. Curious that Samuel Johnson did not know the word. Perhaps he wasn't *au fait* with Greek. *Caterwaul* was an excellent word too, although it did pertain more to cats than to the dissonance of humans. She didn't think Samuel Johnson knew that one either. He might not have thought much about cats.

After weeks of feasting her eyes on Mr Cole's many dictionaries by candlelight, she had added many new words to her vocabulary. She was confident she already knew many more than Samuel

Johnson ever did. But new words were being invented all the time. She was determined to learn every word that man had ever uttered or written. She also thought it likely she might invent some herself. Why, for example, was there no word meaning "to screw up one's nose at a bad smell", which was what she was doing now? Why couldn't horses wait until they were back in their stables to divest themselves of their breakfast? *Shnerkeling*, she decided, best described what she was doing. She pictured it in a dictionary…

Shnerkel. v.a. 1 To screw up one's nose in defence of an unpleasant smell. [Fidelia Knight].

The thought made her smile. She watched other people shnerkel and wanted to tell them she had invented a word for the expression. They tried to disguise their shnerkeling with hands or handkerchiefs. There should be a word for that too. *Shoap* or *sneep*?

A soignée lady on the arm of an equally elegant and well-groomed gentleman soodled past her. She immaculate in peach satin and lace and delicate lace-up boots; he sprauncy in top hat and morning coat, their demeanour affected and counterfeit. Did these people have nothing to do? Such a life of hedonism and idle pleasure. Did they not have to work for a living? It mystified her. But Melbourne seemed to be filled with those who wanted for nothing and those who wanted for everything. The contrast between them was what made it such a fascinating and vibrant place.

Fidelia grasped a veranda post and swung around it to watch the couple as they passed. She saw them dodge to avoid being bowled over by a man who was falling raucously from the door of a hotel. Goodness, it was still morning and this man already reeked of spirits. She could smell it from several yards away. Polrumptious individual. She could hear many more polrumptious individuals inside the establishment. It was not, she thought, a place that would appeal to the couple. She watched them continue down the street. Across the street, a small crowd was gathering in front of a shop. The window was screened by newspapers fastened to the glass, but the people were taking turns to peer through a small gap between the sheets of paper. What was going on? She skipped across. Her curiosity was piqued, like the others.

She waited her turn and peered through the gap. She couldn't see anything much as the gap was slightly above her eye level, even though she stood on tip toes. The space behind the window was bare, but for a wicker chair and a ladder. What was all the excitement about? She felt a hand on her shoulder, pulling her back.

'Come on lassie, let the others look.' A toothless man snarled foul breath into her face. She gladly retreated a few paces. She then noticed the hand-written sign above her head.

Billings Better Bookstore - and Cafeteria!

Opening soon!

Also stocking haberdashery, travel goods, jewellery, maps and charts, music, fresh flowers and general items. No contrivances!

Ooh, she almost squealed out loud. Another book store. Somebody was planning to compete with Mr Cole? It seemed a foolhardy notion. Certainly it was a brave move to want to emulate Mr Cole's success. And almost opposite his establishment.

'Nuffin to see here,' the smelly man grunted. The crowd soon dissipated; the people melded back into the morning haze like spectres. Fidelia decided to look again and discovered a larger gap, where a corner of the paper had peeled down further along. She peered in and flinched when a man, not too old but not so young, dressed in a shabby brown suit, appeared from behind the back wall of the display area. He scratched his head and paced the back of the window display like an expectant cat. He was quite perturbed. What troubled him?

A commotion further down the street, a man calling wildly, drew her attention from the window for just a moment. When she looked back, the perturbed man was gone.

Distractedly, she eyed the newspapers covering the window. They were recent. The front page of *The Herald*, Wednesday, March 3, 1875. Just a week ago. Something in the right column caught her eye. An advertisement running right down the page.

As she read, she could hear the voice of the bearded interloper at Cole's.

> *A* Alderman Absolute Always Adjudicated with Astonishing Ability,
> After he had read some books from Cole's Cheap Book Arcade.
> > *Ish dat so?.........Yaw.*
>
> *B* Benjamin Bouncer Banged a Brown Bear with a Blunderbuss,
> In a lane at the back of Cole's Cheap Book Arcade.
> > *Ish dat so?.........Yaw.*
>
> *C* Christopher Crabstick was Cross, Captious, Cutting and Caustic,
> Whenever he could not get a book brought from Cole's Cheap Book Arcade.
> > *Ish dat so?.........Yaw.*

Now she understood what his nightly vigils had been about. It wasn't a nursery rhyme – thank the heavens, since it didn't rhyme at all – it was an advertisement. She dearly wished he'd sought her help with this. Even at nine years old, she had a superior vocabulary to him. But she doubted most newspaper readers would understand some of Samuel Johnson's wonderful words; many of which she'd never heard spoken herself. The advertisement continued, right through the alphabet. She read all the way down to 'Z' and shrugged.

> *Z* Zachariah Zany Zealously studied Zoology,
> Out of the works which he bought at Cole's Cheap Book Arcade.
> > *Ish dat so?.........Yaw.*

Clever, but hardly brilliant. Samuel Johnson would scarcely have been impressed. Nor Father. She read another notice immediately below, at the bottom of the column.

> Every reasonable-minded person – every rationally-inclined person – every well-intentioned person – every seriously disposed person – and each and every person who is not simply a fool – a humbug – a thief – a liar – a vagabond – a sophist – a pedant – a bigot – a sneak – a burglar – a kidnapper – a bushranger – a pirate – a landabark – a drunkard – a wifebeater – a swindler – a brute – a body snatcher – an idolater – an egotist – an incendiary – an imposter – an ignoramus – in fact, any person who is not a diddler, a dullhead, a dolt, a donkey, or a duffer is invited to call and inspect the large and varied stock of Cheap Books, Cheap Stationery, Cheap Music, and particularly the large assortment of pianoforte music, including dances, songs, pieces etc., at quarter English price.
>
> *Datso?*...........

It was true, Fidelia thought, that this man had a way with words, but surely he was alienating almost the entire population of Melbourne with this advertisement. Fidelia was sure she hadn't yet met a man, except Father perhaps, who didn't fall into at least one of those undesirable categories. Mr Cole was evidently most particular about who should cross the threshold of Cole's Cheap Book Arcade.

She wondered whether the proprietor of Billings Better Bookstore and Cafeteria would be so discriminatory. Was that Mr Billings himself she had seen so anxious in the window? Did he realise what he would be up against – trying to outdo Mr Cole?

She peered through the window again.

There he was. Distracted. He looked like a kind man despite his harassed expression. She could tell from his face that he had a good heart and a sympathetic disposition. Funny how you could tell that about people just by looking at them. Their goodness or badness was always in their eyes. It could not be disguised.

Presently, another man appeared. A large, surly sod with a moustache like a besom broom. Quite the cankerdoodle. He was gesticulating wildly at the first man who, Fidelia realised, was subordinate to him. Maybe *this* was Billings. He appeared to be in none too good a mood. Why was he agitated? She put her ear to the glass to try to catch his words.

'We have to make the people want to *buy*. What have I hired you for if you can't even imagine a simple display? Now get on with it. Just fourteen days we have until the opening, mind. A fortnight.' Mr Moustache turned on his heel and disappeared into the bowels of the shop.

A fortnight.

The first man didn't respond. Instead, he stood dumbstruck. Stared at his feet. His shoulders sagged. A look of defeat like Napoleon at Waterloo. He looked up slowly and caught Fidelia's eye. She didn't flinch, but held his gaze until his brow relaxed and his face softened to a meek smile. He spread the fingers on his right hand and waved a peculiar wave, level with his face. She mirrored him and his smile widened. He raised his left hand and with both hands made a quizzical gesture – like one does when they have no notion how to answer a stupid question. She mirrored him again. She rolled her eyes in a full circle – an exaggerated question-mark-type movement – asking him what he was doing. He made another gesture to signal that he had no idea – no imagination mayhap – as to how to furnish the window display to attract the attention of future passers-by.

Fidelia didn't know why, but she felt sorry for him.

Why do you look so perplexed
My dear Mr Quandary man?
Have you no thought in your head?
Or grand word to be said?
Is your mind like a pineapple flan?

Why do you look so bewildered
My dear Mr Quandary man?
Is it not your intention
To show some invention?
You must try it, try if you can.

Why do you look so befuddled
My dear Mr Quandary man?
If you're stuck on a task
You have only to ask
And I'll do what I can, if I can.

Why do you look so confounded
My dear Mr Quandary man?
It is not becoming
To have fingers a-drumming
And a look like you haven't a plan.

Why do you look so bamboozled
My dear Mr Quandary man?
I can tell you are kind
But you must use your mind
And show me some dash and élan.

Like her father, sometimes Fidelia's mind worked in rhymes. They just popped into her head, crowding out logical thought. And like Father, she never actually wrote them down, though she was able to bring them to mind later.

She remembered many of Father's poems by heart. (Was that why the phrase was coined? Because you always remembered things that were close to your heart?)

Fidelia pursed her lips and looked down. Thinking. Scheming. Cogitating. When she lifted her eyes to the man again, they twinkled. A wry smile crinkled her mouth and dimpled her cheeks.

She had an idea.

Jasper Godwin didn't know what to make of the little girl. Something about her eyes had captivated him and he couldn't get her face out of his mind. None of the other children who scuffled around outside for a peek in the window were worth a second glance. But this girl – for all her eight or nine years – had a serenity about her. A sadness but yet a wisdom. A solitude. Her eyes had searched his soul and laid bare his deceit. Was his jiggery-pokery so transparent? His mind felt blank. Had she read his thoughts? Emptied his head of the clutter of his dishonest past? Jasper Godwin was not proud of himself, but he was trying to set his life on a more positive bearing.

The trouble was that he had told his employer of two days – the inimitable Lucas Billings – that he had a thorough knowledge of books, merchandising and shopkeeping. He had uttered this falsehood in desperation. He had little sales experience, save for a brief stint repairing shoes and selling carnauba wax and laces from a stall at the Ballarat goldfields. For the most part, he had eked a living out of cutting firewood and selling it off the back of a dray. A four-wheel dray that he had uncoupled from a horse outside a hotel in the dark of night, pushed a ways to his shanty quarters and hidden until he could repaint it and pass it off as his own.

He had never been a thief before that night. But he had a wife and baby to support – and he was desperate. Desperation did terrible things to good people. But despite his crime – the memory of which still troubled him deeply and haunted his dreams – Jasper Godwin still thought of himself as a good man.

Back in London, before he and his young bride had decided to try their luck in the new colony of Victoria, he worked as a docker along the Thames. As a fit, young man he enjoyed the physical labour, the rough and tumble lifestyle and camaraderie of his dockside colleagues. In their downtime, they all imagined a better life in that strange land called Australia, where sheep roamed the streets and those with the luck could stumble upon fistfuls of gold. As they loaded cargos of stone, timber, coal, Manchester, furniture, tableware and goodness knows what else onto many a sailing ship and newfangled steamer headed for Sydney, Melbourne, Adelaide or Hobart, they pondered what it must be like to create civilisation in such a far-off, exotic and doubtlessly Godforsaken place. And when they unloaded Australian cargo, predominantly bales of wool and wheat, along with weighty caskets of gold, they glimpsed evidence of a land of abundance, opportunity and easily-gained wealth.

That was what Jasper had thought: a few years on the goldfields of Victoria would set him and his Myrtle up for life. They would become rich beyond their wildest imagining and support a large family with countless children to inherit their wealth and status. He regaled his love with stories fictionalised from illusory truths about a future dripping with prosperity. And she believed him. So much in love with him that she would have followed him to Timbuktu or Tipperary or any place on Earth that he wanted to go. They had great expectations for their new life.

The reality was somewhat different. Life on the goldfields was austere, uncompromising and unproductive. Jasper was forced to acknowledge that that was largely due to his inability to distinguish his strengths and abandon his weaknesses. It was perennially his disposition to be the one standing *next* to the one who struck gold. Their luck never rubbed off on him.

In the seven years since leaving the goldfields and arriving in Melbourne, he had laboured at a succession of poorly paid positions, mostly in the Sandridge area. He boiled tallow and beeswax to make soap and candles until he thought his own skin would melt; he hauled grain at the rice and flour mills and at the sugar refinery until he thought his back would break. He laboured long hours, for minimal reward, at the gasworks and at a distillery. He had always worked hard, but he ached with boredom and aspired to a loftier existence. Something in which he could take pride and conceivably, one day, become his own man. The future, he was sure, was in the hustle and bustle of Bourke-street, or Swanston or Elizabeth, and he had trawled the neighbourhood for several days before coming across the advertisement in the window of number 147 Bourke-street.

Wanted: Honest, reliable and experienced salesman.
Good knowledge of books
and general merchandise essential
No time wasters. Apply within to L.H. Billings

He knew perfectly well that he didn't have those credentials, but he had an earnest desire for self-improvement and an uncanny knack for making others believe in him. And it wasn't as though he'd *never* read a book. Indeed, in the past year he had read two. Almost. The first, which had held great fascination, was Henry Gray's *Anatomy of the Human Body*, although if he were honest he might admit to having understood more from the illustrations. The other was *The Three Musketeers* by Alexandre Dumas, which he'd laboured over for months, having found the copy in the back of a cart near the candle factory. He thought it a jolly good yarn, although it was heavy going – probably due to his limited vocabulary and, he suspected, a poor translation from the French.

He decided it was worth a try, since he desperately needed the work. And so, as he extolled his virtues in the application for the situation, it was possible also that he had led Mr Billings to believe that he was a literate and articulate man, when in fact he had but a rudimentary knowledge of the English language.

Saying 'Oh yes, indeed' to Billings' many questions was a persuasive ploy. It would become plain to Billings soon enough that his skill was in trickery and cunning rather than grammar and salesmanship. Once again, he had let his tongue and his illusions get the better of him and he had hoodwinked a better man into giving him a chance.

Now it was time to prove himself. Myrtle would never forgive him if he lost another job. The Lord knew she had little enough confidence in him as a breadwinner and he was determined not to have to labour for an excuse for an empty larder again.

But what to do?

He ran his fingers through his closely cropped beard and drummed them on his cheek. Not only had Billings put him in charge of preparing the window display, which Myrtle had thought laughable, he had also assigned him the task of developing newspaper advertisements to hail the store's opening.

'Something pithy, you know, witty, clever and succinct,' were his words.

What did he, Jasper Farthing Godwin, know about advertising?

C

Claudette Callipygous Coveted a Cabochon
Curiously Carved by a Caiman,
And Capriciously Courted Coleridge at
Billings Better Bookstore and Cafeteria
Did she Categorically? She did indeed!

Fidelia dipped the brush into the bucket, shook the excess water off, and worked it across the floor. In circles, figure eights, spirals. The task was not as unpleasant here as it had been at the asylum. At least here, she could get the floor scrubbed without contending with small, bothersome feet traipsing through where she had already cleaned. At least here, she might expect more than broth, damper and turnip for dinner. At least here, she could have her chores done by five o'clock in the afternoon, partake of supper at the kitchen table and then retire unbothered to her quarters out the back.

Nobody paid her any attention. Nobody noticed whether she was there or not. Provided the floors were scrubbed, the windows cleaned, the stove lit and the dusting done – and she performed these chores with alacrity to get them over and done with – she could remain unseen, unquestioned, anonymous.

Mrs Fleet seldom spoke to her and was oblivious to her nightly escapades to Cole's Cheap Book Arcade. A certain advantage of not speaking was that most people – people who didn't matter much – thought her simple. They presumed she was deaf as well. They would never expect too much from her. Of course, they wouldn't pay her much either, but a nine-year-old didn't need much money. Not when she had a roof over her head, clothes and shoes, and almost enough food. She had an education to get and she wasn't going to get it from Mrs Fleet, nor Mr Fleet, nor Lester Fleet.

Especially not Mr Fleet. He was an ignoramus. A dolt. A gilly-gaupus. She cringed at the thought of him. The smell of him. The look in his eye. Lascivious, lecherous, licentious, libidinous, lewd, lustful, lubricious; a myriad of unseemly 'L' adjectives to describe him. Lugubrious too. Never a smile. Never a good word to say. Not to her, not to anybody. She would learn nothing from him but misery.

Lester was no better than his father. Although three or four years older than her, it was evident he paid little heed to schooling or the need for education. He was lardy, lazy, laconic and loathsome. More lovely, lively 'L' words. It seemed the Fleet family had the monopoly on 'L' words. Mrs Fleet, full of the sound of her own voice, was thereby largiloquent and loquacious while demonstrating lackadaisical and languorous traits.

It was clear to Fidelia that if she wanted an education, she would have to get it by her own guile and ingenuity. And she would do *that* with fierce alacrity too.

Provided she was out the door by quarter past five in the afternoon, she could flit from the Fleets' Russell-street house, down to Bourke-street and cover the distance to Cole's within five minutes, before the red-jacket-clad sales staff closed the imposing door. In an advertisement in the daily *Herald* some weeks ago, which Fidelia came perchance to read, the store was thus described.

> Cole's Cheap Book Arcade is 158 Bourke-street, about 12 doors below the Eastern Market, six doors below Russell-street, 100 moderate steps from Temperance Hall, 100 good lively jumps downhill from Mrs Henderson's church, and half-way between the Post Office and Parliament House.
> Ish dat so?.........Yaw

Temperance Hall was down the street from the Fleets. The day after reading the advertisement, Fidelia determined to validate the advertisement's accuracy. Immediately after supper, when the Fleets assumed that she had taken to her quarters, she crossed the road, ambled down the street a ways and stood in front of the imposing three-storey building. Sounds of conviviality spilled out and blanketed the vicinity with laughter and murmured dialogue. It sounded like a festive place to be. It was surprising that those inside, purportedly drinking 'in moderation', or more probably drinking coffee, could be so loud and animated. The Temperance Movement made no sense at all to Fidelia. Why would you run a business like the Temperance Hotel which offered people a product and then encouraged them not to buy it? Unless all the money was made in food and accommodation. Perhaps it was. Perhaps people didn't go to hotels for liquid satisfaction at all.

Mrs Fleet was an ardent member of the Temperance movement. She made it well known around the house, to whoever might be listening, that alcohol had no place in a well-mannered, Christian society.

Strange though, that Fidelia had once seen her swig brandy straight from a bottle tucked at the back of the kitchen table drawer. Mrs Fleet had seen her astonished face and scowled at her. 'For medicinal purposes, girl. *Medicinal purposes*. A sore throat. Huh! Why am I wasting me voice on you? You couldn't even 'ear the Bow Bells. I'm glad you can't tell 'is lordship, given yer dumb as well.'

It was one of the few times that Mrs Fleet had taken the time to speak to her. Fidelia shrugged a gesture of non-comprehension, which satisfied the rotund lady of the house. Given that the household was purportedly dry, it was curious that Mr Fleet could dash over the road for a rally at the Temperance Hall and come home hours later smelling of rum or whiskey. It made no sense at all.

From her starting point that day, Fidelia walked south down Russell-street, to the *Australia Felix Hotel* on the corner, counting her paces as she went, crossed Bourke-street and turned right to cross back over Russell-street. She passed several buildings. *Ninety-five, ninety-six, ninety-seven, ninety-eight, ninety-nine...one hundred!*

She looked at the building beside her. It didn't look like a book store. The advertisement was a lie. She kept walking, counting another twenty-two paces. There it was. Cole's Cheap Book Arcade. One hundred and *twenty-two* paces from Temperance Hall. As she looked in the window, a gentleman brushed past her and strode down the street. His strides covered a yard at least.

Of course! One hundred moderate man-sized steps. Not one hundred girl-sized steps. How stupid she felt. She tested it on the way back home but exaggerated her strides to emulate those of a man. It turned out to be quite accurate.

Fidelia gathered over the following days that she could sidle into the store unnoticed. She kept her eyes down to avoid the questioning gazes of browsers, pretending to be with a lingering adult making a last-minute purchase, before drifting off to one of her two hiding places, either inside the pediment of a large cabinet on the ground floor or under the cloth-covered table upstairs. She would wait patiently there until the floor-walkers had straightened books, swept floors, counted the money in the till, closed the lid on the glossy ebony pianoforte downstairs, gathered their belongings and departed.

She most enjoyed that first five minutes of silence after the door was locked. The store was vacant but for her, her captive breath and clamouring heart. Vacant but for the ticking clocks, the towering bookshelves, the curious knick-knacks and the occasional skittering mouse seeking sustenance in the dust under hard-to-sweep cabinets and tables. Their sounds always made her think of Father.

Never bother a belligerent badger
Or hobble a hirsute hare.
Don't squabble with a squeamish squirrel
Or betray a bombastic bear.

Never fetter a foolish fieldmouse
Or molest a malevolent mole.
Do not dare goad a garrulous grouse,
Or vanquish a vehement vole.

For these are creatures of the wild, my dear
Creatures of the wild.
They are creatures of the wild, my dear,
Always treasure them, my child.

She could hear him now. He had written the verse for her. It always made her laugh and clap her hands as she pictured such wayward creatures, aptly described with Father's alliterative adjectives and nouns. He would sing it to her as he tucked her into bed. She would stare into his deep brown eyes and relax to the hum of his mellifluous voice.

It might have been designed to put her to sleep. Instead she would lie awake and wonder about malevolent moles and what they got up to out on the moors or dales at night. How could they breathe underground? How could they *see* underground? She was pleased they weren't often referred to as mouldywarps – such an unpleasant name for such innocuous creatures. Granted, they weren't attractive, except possibly to each other. For them it must be true that beauty is in the eye of the beholder. It probably didn't matter much what you looked like if you led a subterranean existence. Who would see you?

And what made that squirrel squeamish? Was it the sight of a mole? Was it from eating too many acorns?

She often pondered these questions. But just when she thought she knew Father's rhyme well, he would surprise her: change an adjective here, a creature there, turn a noun into a verb. He loved to keep her guessing.

Never badger a buffle-headed bat
Or harangue a hostile hare...

How she missed him. She missed his mouth crinkling at the corner. She missed the curl of his moustache, the tick of his fob-watch, the smell of his Macassar-oiled hair – exotic coconut with tinges of ylang ylang. She missed the echo of his footfalls at night as he left her bedside after relating a story, believing her sound asleep; he would tip-toe down the hallway to the parlour, to Mother and the promise of sherry, ripened plums with custard, and evenings of shared reading by the stove.

Was it inappropriate for her to miss him more than she missed Mother? Ninian and Permelia would have missed Mother more. But they were younger; they needed Mother to spend more time tending them. She couldn't bring Mother's scent to her nostrils. Couldn't hear her voice. Could scarcely remember anything she said. Unless she was berating someone; then Mother's voice was strident and shrill. Was that how all Connecticut-born people spoke? Mother was always telling her to behave herself.

Father was always telling her to *be* herself: the best possible version of herself.

She had set about doing that. Educating herself. Entertaining herself. Enjoying herself. Alone in the wondrous Cole's Book Arcade. Where she could choose a different book every night, or continue with one of particular interest. Where nobody would interrupt her reading, her thoughts, her self-education. She may have been alone, but she seldom felt lonely; not with all the enchanting stories, written by inspired people, that emanated from the pages as she read. And every night, she added to her vocabulary. It could be time consuming, looking up an unknown word in the dictionary and risking becoming waylaid with fascination at all the words that followed it.

One night, she looked up "kelter", since a character in her book was described as being "not in kelter", which was defined as being "*not ready*". An hour later, she was reading the definition for "kyd" *to know*, her novel forgotten.

She had mused for several minutes at the fact that all those poets, from Shakespeare to Milton, seemed at loggerheads as to whether "kercheif" should be spelled thus or, as was Shakespeare's preference, 'kerchief'. If they could not decide, and a dictionary could not decide, then who was right and who was wrong? Such a mystery, the English language. Changing all the time, just to keep people thinking. An endless source of fascination.

D

Dionysus Definiens Derived Delight Devising Dastardly Designations,
Drawing him with Desiderium
to the Deltiology and Dictionary Display
at Billings Better Bookstore and Cafeteria (with postcards)!
Did he Definitely? He did indeed!

'I saw a sweet girl today,' Jasper Godwin told Myrtle as she placed a bowl of broth in front of him. 'About the age our Sarah would have been by now, bless her soul.'

'What of it? Plenty o' young girls to catch yer eye up there on Bourke-street, I imagine.'

'Quite true my dear. But this girl was wistful, such a look of longing in her face as I have never seen. And a smile to light up the universe, she had.'

'Hmph. Too many words in all them books puttin' ideas in yer soft head.' Myrtle flicked her husband on the back of the head with a tea-cloth. 'You'll want to be keepin' yer mind on the job, I say. Else yer won't 'ave it no more, like all the others.'

Jasper nodded a tacit agreement. His shoulders sagged. He tended toward silence whenever Myrtle started to harp. Much easier to agree with her than to find himself on the ineffectual side of a quarrel. He couldn't match her sharp tongue. He couldn't find the words of solace for her loss. And besides, what she said went, went.

He didn't mention the girl again. Yet he couldn't get her face out of his head. If the eyes are the windows to the soul, then he had seen the handiwork of the Lord in hers. Her soul touched his like no other had ever done – and all in a blink of her eyes. A tilt of her head. A pucker of her mouth. A moment of connection.

As he blew on his spoon to cool the greasy liquid, he wondered what the girl was eating tonight. Did she come from a good family? She was dressed respectably enough, though a tad shabby – clearly not well-to-do. Her pinafore was hardly pristine. Not likely that she was sitting at a candelabra-laden oak table, with silver cutlery and linen serviettes, to feast on a banquet. More likely she was sopping up sallow gravy with stale damper at a wobbly kitchen table with a half-dozen other youngsters. Would she be tucked under plump feather eiderdowns by an adoring mother tonight? Or struggling against hard timber and musty sackcloth in some Spartan servants' quarters? Her manner had suggested the former. Her appearance the latter.

Yes, she looked about the same age as Sarah would have been, had Sarah not succumbed to diphtheria on that fateful day in Eaglehawk. Myrtle had attributed the youngster's illness to the chill of the June weather. 'She'll be over it in no time,' she asserted. But the two-year-old's high fever and laboured breathing whispered a more terrible fate than a mere head cold. Within two days she was gone to the Lord; within two weeks many more of Eaglehawk's young 'uns had followed her blessed path.

Jasper, who had been off for two days cutting firewood, did not believe the news upon returning to their makeshift home. Never more would he see her wisps of blonde curls dance of their own accord. Now they lay flat against the pillow of her death bed. He could not abide the stillness of her. If this were God's work then God was callous and arbitrary.

At night when he closed his own eyes, his heart felt as empty as her unseeing eyes had been. Every night he thought of her. Every night he wondered what might have been. Every night she was the last thing in his mind; every morning the first. He imagined her learning to talk, to sing nursery rhymes, to read, to ride a pony. Imagine was all he could do, but it made her no more real to him. And with every day that passed, the memory of her diminished.

He had not fathered another child. For that he was heartsore. For that Myrtle was disdainful. Their marriage aimless.

Fidelia placed Samuel Johnson on the chair – a hard but utilitarian way to augment her height to desk level – plucked a sheet of parchment from the heavy desk drawer, struck a match to light the candle and loaded the pen with ink from the well. She had had the A, B, C, F and H sayings in her head most of the day and was eager to get them down on paper.

She knew how to help the flustered man in Billings Bookstore. During the afternoon, while she sat on the rise of Parliament House, she had gazed down Bourke-street. While eating an apple she had surreptitiously pilfered from the basket of a passer-by, she recalled what Mr Moustache had said to her Quandary Man. *Just fourteen days we have until the opening, mind. A fortnight.*

A fortnight.

A year has twenty-six fortnights and the alphabet has twenty-six letters. Co-incidental? Serendipitous. Propitious. One letter for each fortnight. Each letter the inspiration for a window display. A new window display every fortnight. It would become the spectacle of Bourke-street, if not of all Melbourne. That would keep Mr Cole on his toes! Show him how it should be done.

She began to write. Her childish lettering nonetheless neat and legible. Could she be Quandary Man's muse? Would he thank her for her effort? Or begrudge her presumptuousness?

A   Amelia Audacious Admonished an Amateur Abecedarian
     and Absconded with an Antediluvian Aardvark,
       After Adjourning for an Arousing Absinthe at Billings
     Better Bookstore and Cafeteria.
       Did she Absolutely? She did indeed!

B   Bernadette Bacciferous Buried her Blackberries Before
Buying Balbriggan and Baize for her Balistarius Beau,
   And then enjoyed Beer and Banana Bread at Billings
Better Bookstore and Cafeteria
   Did she Blissfully? She did indeed!

C   Claudette Callipygous Coveted a Cabochon Curiously
Carved by a Caiman,
   Then Capriciously Courted Coleridge at Billings Better
Bookstore and Cafeteria
   Did she Categorically? She did indeed!

She loved the words *callipygous* or *callipygian*. It meant having
beautiful buttocks. True, it pertained to the beauty of Aphrodite's
buttocks in particular, but surely some women of the mortal kind
could be thus described. Although she had never seen them –
naked in the flesh – Fidelia imagined that Mother's buttocks might
have been callipygous. She had a lovely figure; therefore it was
not unlikely that her buttocks were also comely. Would her own
ever be callipygous? One seldom saw women's buttocks, hidden
as they were under those preposterous crinolines and bustles.

While she pondered her entry for 'D' she cast her eye back up
the page. Something wasn't right. Something was out of place.
She tapped the nib pen on the desk to help her think. Something
was upsetting the alliterativeness of her verses.

That was it! She carefully drew a line through the word cafeteria
in the 'B' entry and wrote *Brasserie* beside it. Much better. More
fitting. She applauded her brilliance and continued to write until
she got to L. Like the man who wrote Cole's advertisement, she
could only manage half the alphabet in one sitting.

L   Lionel Lagotic Loved Listening to Lyrical Librettos and
Learning Lore,
   And Laughing Loquaciously in the Library at Billings
Better Bookstore and Brasserie (with Lending Library)
   Did he Longingly? He did indeed!

Lagotic made her think of Mr Bartholomew. His ears were ridiculously big and could be likened to those of a hare, although the rest of his body could not be described thus. His body had been more that of a bloated bovine.

Darn. She had been trying so hard not to think about Mr Bartholomew and that wretched day of her arrival in Melbourne. She hadn't understood why he had pulled her up the companionway from steerage with hands as meaty as ham hocks, while she struggled with the weight of Samuel Johnson in the pillow cover, and told her to forget about everything. Bartholomew was a bumbling fustilugs and his words were bitter and coarse.

That day, when she descended the gangway, she could barely walk. The movement of the ship had dictated her footfalls for such a long while that she found herself rocking even as she stood still. It was as though the ground moved beneath her and she had to guess at its intentions, like riding a drunken rocking horse.

Mr Bartholomew told her that was normal – that it would take a wee while to regain her land legs. She thought that rum: that one would have legs for the land and legs for the sea. They looked the same to her. It might have been different if she were a mermaid, like the ones Father told her about during the voyage. They didn't *have* legs and would have found it nigh on impossible to stand on solid ground.

'They are our shepherds under the sea,' Father had told her. 'Their beauty and strength keep us afloat. You might espy them in the glint of the moon on the water – if you watch long enough and earnestly enough and if it is their desire for you to see them.' She wanted to go up on deck during the night to try to glimpse them, but she wasn't allowed. She could only dream about their ethereal beauty that Father had described.

It had been a bleak late-winter day, the sky laden with sorrow, reflecting her own mood. Grey clouds hung like funereal shrouds and a light drizzle froze on her skin. Burdened with her case in one hand and Samuel Johnson under the arm clutched by Mr Bartholomew, she could not wipe the raindrops from her face nor brush the dripping tails of hair from her eyes. But at least the drips disguised her tears. She was miserable and cold, unable to feel her toes or fingers. She had hankered for this day; of sharing the excitement of disembarking in a strange country and embarking on a new life with Mother and Father and the new baby. 'Melbourne will be wondrously fresh and exciting,' Father had said.

Exciting was not the word that came to mind then. She felt empty. Heartbroken. Alone. What was she to do all by herself? She was not yet ten years old. That day's tears still stung her cheeks.

She had seen miserable days like that in London, but they were bearable because she was always in someone's company: Mother or Father or Grandmama. Somebody to open a gamp over her or to shepherd her to a dry haven. But Melbourne was the epitome of miserable. The man gripped her hand so tightly she feared he would squash it. He grumbled at the imposition of having to deal with her. He called out to another man, who she could not see, that they would meet later at the Menzies.

She didn't know what the Menzies was: something to do with men, she presumed. She wanted to escape from his clutch and run back up the gangplank; sail back to England, even if it meant another two months at sea. It couldn't be as bad as being here in this strange, cold, muddy, unwelcoming place, being buffeted by pushy people with combative elbows.

The dock was busy and noisy. Disembarked passengers, particularly those from steerage, stood forlornly in huddles, unsure where to go. They did not look excited or happy either. Teams of horses stood bored and idle, snorting in the freezing air as crates, barrels and sacks of goods were manhandled onto their drays. She looked back at the hulk of the *SS Great Britain,* its three masts and funnel towering above them; its black hull divesting itself of passengers and cargo like a great whale spewing its stomach contents. The huge iron vessel got *her* here safely, but it still held the secret of her parents' fate.

Were they still on board?

Mother had promised her a little brother or sister. But she hadn't seen her for a week, since the awful night with all the screaming.

Nor had she seen Father again. And he had been in such a fit. She'd seen the fear in his eyes and wanted to stay and console him. But he sent her away and she never saw him again. It wasn't possible that they were no longer aboard. Where could they have gone? There was only water all around.

Surely not into the water.

She begged Mr Bartholomew to wait for them.

'Ye might as well forget about yer folks. They cannae be wif you no more. Forget about anything you've ever seen or heard. Don't speak a word. Not a word, ye hear. Ye'll be on yer own from here on.'

He had an odd voice, Mr Bartholomew, like he was affecting an accent but not getting it right. Was he trying to disguise his tongue? Who was this strange man? Was he presuming to be her father? She hoped not. He showed nothing of Father's tenderness, or breeding for that matter. He was a bumblehead, an oaf, with a belly that betrayed him as a gormandiser. And she could sense he had not one iota of empathy.

Bartholomew instructed a cab driver to take them to Emerald Hill. She was grateful, for a while, to sit in the relative comfort of a conveyance with a cover over her head. The vegetation was strange here. The grey-green bushes looked prickly and unfriendly to the touch. Tall trees shed bark like a snake shed its skin, the remnants a blanket of brown and copper curls. A pungent smell, a little like camphor, irritated her nose. The drizzle dissipated and meek sunrays punctured the cloud, casting a pale yellow glow over the strange landscape. A glimmer of hope. A promise that all was not dark and foreboding.

'Not a word, now,' Mr Bartholomew reminded her as the carriage pulled up. The darker horse snorted as if in contempt of the weather. Bartholomew escorted her to the imposing building behind the iron fence, where he placed her hand into that of Mrs Exon, the matron.

'She dinnae speak much. I fink she's a bit simple. Not a brain in 'er wee 'ead. Knight's 'er name. Fidelia Knight. Orphaned aboard ship on the passage out. Mother in childbirth, father…ahem.'

She could barely hear his words as it was and they became entirely inaudible as he covered his mouth and whispered to the woman. She gave Fidelia a knowing look.

Bartholomew divested himself of further responsibility for her. She watched him toddle back down the path to the cab and prayed she would never see him again.

Mrs Exon was a kindly woman, not unlike Mother. She brushed Fidelia's hair from her forehead and told her she would run a bath – that she smelt like she'd been sleeping in a filthy backhouse. Which wasn't far from the truth. Indeed, after a young steward had passed her off to Mr Bartholomew, who relegated her to steerage, her quarters aboard the *SS Great Britain* in the last week were very shy of salubrious. She never understood why she was taken there. She never understood why Father and Mother didn't come to find her. Would she ever forget the stench and the accusing eyes of her fellow passengers?

In Cole's bookshop, Fidelia was growing tired. Yawning constantly. The clocks had chimed two o'clock in the morning. She would finish tomorrow night. She would spend tomorrow working out the verses in her head, as she had done today. Quandary Man would have to wait another day.

She folded the paper three times so it would fit her pocket, restored everything to its rightful place on the desk, extinguished the candle and retreated to her hiding spot under the table. She curled up on the floor and placed her head on Samuel Johnson. Did that help her to absorb his words? Possibly.

It wasn't comfortable. The floor was hard and unforgiving, but Fidelia felt more at ease here than she ever had in the Fleets' servants' quarters. It was bearable enough until the previous afternoon. She had never actually felt threatened until then.

She didn't like Mr Fleet, but before yesterday, she'd had no cause to fear him. She was preparing to set off to Cole's when he had come at her. Full of foul breath and foul mouth. And foul hands. She wasn't sure what he wanted to do to her, but she didn't like the way he touched her. On her chest and then her buttock. Callipygous or not, she knew it was not appropriate and she did not like it.

'Just pretend I'm your daddy,' he drawled with whiskey breath.

But Father would never have done *that* to her. She had escaped his clutches and run off down the back lane.

She did not return there to work in the morning.

The morning was unseasonably glum and Jasper Godwin felt as grey as the light filtering through the small bedroom window. For the past week, he had risen early, full of anticipation for what the day might bring, now that he was on the verge of a new occupation: bookseller and storeman. Certainly a position carrying greater prestige than ever before. But today, he was filled with foreboding. Today might be the day Billings would expose him as a fraud. Could he continue the pretence? He was a fish out of water. A petrified fledgling. A finger-painter passing himself off as a Gainsborough.

He sighed heavily as he sat on the edge of the bed, head in hands. How could he summon confidence when he was cloaked in despair and uncertainty? He couldn't afford to lose this position. Not with Myrtle's birthday a week away. He needed some coin in pocket to acknowledge the occasion with a trinket or keepsake. Some token to signify his enduring affection. A book would be an obvious choice, were she able to read. He might consult Billings for advice.

Myrtle stirred beside him. 'Yer up then?' she murmured. 'Give a minute and I'll fix yer tea.'

He had some time to spare. 'How about I fix you some tea instead? Rest a while longer. It's a bleak day with no need for hurry.'

His voice did not betray his anxiety. She was a good woman, his Myrtle, and he seldom waited on her. He would not allow her to be privy to his dilemma. He didn't need her to worry, and nor did he need her barbs to puncture his fragile ego. Especially not first thing in the morning. He tried to think of something positive.

Perhaps he would see the girl again today. Perhaps that was wishful thinking.

Fidelia repeated the routine that night, completing her project with a great sense of satisfaction. Like the man at Cole's, she'd had considerable trouble with the second half of the alphabet: X and Z proved quite a task. So few words started with X. But she was pleased with the result. She had outdone the man, no doubting it. Before she folded the paper and put it in her pocket, she carefully wrote on the outside.

> Ideas for window display and advertising. Remember the alphabet has twenty-six letters and a year has twenty-six fortnights. How funny is that?

In the morning, she wedged Samuel Johnson into the niche she had discovered in the sub-frame of the table – he was much too cumbersome to carry around – and waited until the first customers appeared in the store. Her stomach reminded her that it had been many hours since the stale bread and scone she had found yesterday in an alley near Mooney's *Princes Bridge Hotel*.

She had thought about taking her lucky find across Flinders-street, past the Melbourne Terminus and over the bridge spanning the railway line to the garden on the opposite side. But the shnerkel-inducing odours of the fish market had put her off that idea. Instead, she crossed Swanston-street and sat in the gardens of the Church of St Paul the Apostle. The shade offered by the church's bluestone walls on this warm day was a comfort, but her hunger had been barely satiated. Now, all she could think about was porridge and tea. She would at least have had that at the asylum, or at the Fleets. Father and Mother would have been downcast at the thought of her begging for food.

Fidelia slipped out the door of Cole's and, patting her pocket to ensure her composition was there, crossed Bourke-street and ventured up the rise to the Billings store. A man was perched precariously atop a ladder, writing on the window.

BILLINGS BETTER BOOKSTORE & Cafet

He was almost finished the sign, in green letters highlighted with gold shadowing. He was so engrossed in his labour he did not notice her.

Careful to avoid bumping the ladder, she peered through the gap in the newspapers. Several books were piled on a table, a carpet runner draped from the back wall of the window display and a theodolite stood purposelessly to the side. Mr Quandary did not have much imagination.

Then the curtain parted and through it he appeared. He scratched his head, much as he had done two days ago. He looked up and caught her eye. He smiled at her and repeated his wave from their previous encounter. She mirrored it. He looked away and while he was distracted, she slipped the paper under the door and ran away.

From her vantage point behind a horse and carriage on the opposite side of the street, she saw him open the door with the paper in his hand. He edged around the ladder and looked both ways, then inexplicably up and down like she might be flying or crawling before him. He looked again up Bourke-street toward Stephen-street and again down towards Russell-street. He spoke to the sign-writer, who shrugged and shook his head.

Quandary man shook his head in turn, as though he had imagined her. He looked at the paper in his hands and unfolded it, once again scratching his head. Did he have lice or was it a habitual gesture? Did scratching one's head help one think more clearly? He looked around again, as though willing her to appear, before he retreated inside and closed the door.

Fidelia waited until she could disguise her presence among some passers-by, then sauntered down the street. Her mission now was to forage in the waste bin behind the *Royal Mail* or the *Albion* to unearth a few morsels that might pass as breakfast.

E

Edwina Euphoria Encountered an Extraordinary Effodient Elephant,
Eliciting an Exquisite Enthusiasm to Explore at
Billings Better Bookstore and Brasserie (with travel goods)
Did she Enthusiastically? She did indeed!

'What do you have there, Godwin, that is commanding your attention?' Lucas Billings asked his employee.

Jasper started at the suddenness of Billings' address. He had been staring for five minutes at the pages he'd found on the floor by the front door. They hadn't been there ten minutes ago. He had to think quickly. Billings would never believe that these writings might be the work of a child. He couldn't believe it either. Surely another had slipped it under the door, not her at all. He knew not from whence they had come, but he was already entranced by their implications. It was a masterful idea – he wished he'd thought of it himself.

'Just some ideas I've jotted down sir,' he lied. 'I believe we need a theme of sorts for our window. A display that changes regularly.'

'Let me see that.' Billings snatched the paper from Jasper's hand. 'Goodness me, you have been busy.' He scanned the page. 'This is impressive, good man.' He eyed Jasper. 'No. Wait. I've seen something like this before, have I not? But where?'

Jasper didn't know how to answer. He certainly couldn't claim penmanship of the words now, lest he be called a plagiarist.

'Now I recall. It was in *The Herald* two or three weeks ago. An advertisement for Cole's. Right down the side of the front page, it was. I remember thinking the man was either a foolish egoist or plain demented. I could find it if I tried. Are you trying to copy his idea?'

'I just thought…'

Billings nodded knowingly. 'I see what you're up to. Clever. Very clever. Let me look at this good and proper now. *Amelia Audacious Admonished an Amateur Abecedarian and Absconded with an Antediluvian Aardvark, After Adjourning for an Arousing Absinthe at Billings Better Bookstore and Brasserie. Did she Absolutely? She did indeed!* This is marvellous stuff.'

He read the entire two pages out loud. Nodded all the time. 'This might be a stroke of genius, Godwin. Beat the man at his own game. That's what we'll do. And to think I was underestimating your value. Good man.' Billings patted Jasper on the shoulder.

Nobody had ever done that to him. It felt good. No harm in taking a tad of credit. He could only imagine that this was the girl's intention – if it had, indeed, been her and not an emissary of Cole's out to swindle.

Before Jasper could respond, Billings had tugged the carpet from the window display. 'This will never do. Now let's see what we can't do with a modicum of imagination. We need to find an aardvark – or at least a picture of one. We might find one at the Industrial and Technological museum up there at the library in Swanston-street. Or at the exhibition at the University. We might be able to borrow it, or find an artist to draw it. What a display we could make. Brilliant man. Masterly. There'll be no trouble in raising a bottle of Absinthe for show, despite the taradiddle espoused by those temperance sorts around the corner. We could make the window a diorama, I believe it's called. That would be a drawcard the likes of which Melbourne has not seen before.'

Billings slapped his hands together like he had struck gold or solved the riddle of longitude. 'Well, get *to it* Godwin. Why not trot up to the library and see how you get along? It's a brisk five minutes. If you uncover nothing there, catch a carriage up to the University. But don't be gone all day. I, in the meantime, might dash off to *The Argus* with this and see what I can organise in terms of an advertisement.'

Jasper merely nodded. Easier to acquiesce to Billings' command. After all, he was the owner and what he said went, went.

Jasper walked briskly north along Swanston-street until the imposing façade of the public library loomed on the right. Such a fancy building for the mere pastime of reading. He had never felt the need to visit it before. People might think he wanted to peruse the contents of this formidable institution. Not likely. He didn't have that many lifetimes, nor much inclination for reading. He climbed the steps and craned his neck at the Corinthian columns as he passed underneath them toward the entry. Once inside, he marvelled at the marble and stone floor, walls and staircases. Cold and forbidding, yet grand. Grand indeed.

Not knowing where to look, he recalled his mother's advice. 'Never be in a quagmire if ye can find some'un to pull ye out.' He strode purposefully towards a gentleman standing by the inner vestibule door.

'Morning to ye,' Jasper addressed the man. 'Can you tell me where I might find an aardvark?'

'An aardvark? Well, that's a first. What do you want with an aardvark?'

'Oh, yes I can see that it's a queer thing to ask. It's for a window display at Billings' new bookstore in Bourke-street.'

'Ah.' The man nodded as though he fully understood. 'I know that we don't have one on display here. You might have more luck up at the museum at the University; they have a menagerie of unusual species there.'

Jasper had no idea what a menagerie was, but responded as though he did. 'What about a picture in a book though? I profess to not having the vaguest notion of what an aardvark looks like.'

'Possible. Possible. I suggest you try the biology section. Zoology to be specific. Try titles by Charles Darwin or the Encyclopaedia Brittanica.'

It was fortunate that aardvark, being spelled thus, was the first word in alphabetical listings. Jasper was able to read a description of the creature, but he found no pictures. He spent an hour browsing through several leather-bound tomes until he finally chanced upon an engraving. A curious creature: ears like a hare, snout like the nozzle on a fire hose, short legs, long body and long tail. But this picture would never do. It was a mere two inches square. Hardly likely to be seen by passers-by. A visit to the museum was warranted.

After a short carriage ride up Swanston-street, Jasper arrived at the University of Melbourne, whereupon the cab driver gave him directions to the museum. As he approached the building he rubbed his eyes in disbelief. Stretching the length of eight of the museum's twelve windows was a behemoth. And not some man-made folly, but the skeleton of a huge whale. It must have been, Jasper reckoned, ninety feet long, give or take. Jasper read the plate beneath the whale with interest. *Physalus*. Such a sight he had never seen.

'It's a marvel isn't it?' a gentleman beside him commented. 'Mr McCoy calls it a whalebone whale, but I know it to be a blue whale. Largest creature on earth, it is.'

'Most impressive,' Jasper replied.

'I suspect that this is your first time at the museum.'

'Indeed it is.'

'Not for me. I'm a regular visitor. Fascinating, it is.'

'Perhaps you could be of assistance to me. I'm looking for an aardvark.'

The man laughed. 'What would you be wanting with an aardvark when there's dinosaurs to be seen? And gorillas and wonderful birds with plumage like an artist could never imagine. The insect display is particularly grand. You could spend a whole day admiring the pretty wee things.'

Jasper had no interest in insects. He certainly did not admire them. More of nuisance value, they were. But he did not want to appear unappreciative of the man's enthusiasm. It would be ungracious. 'I have only a little time, and an aardvark is my priority today.'

'You might need to speak to Mr McCoy. He's the curator. Wonderful man. If there's an aardvark to be had, he'll know where you can find it.'

Fidelia wondered where Mr Quandary had got to. She had kept pace with him to the library, trailing him by twenty or thirty feet to conceal her pursuit. She had marvelled at the wrought iron gates of the forecourt and marvelled some more at the wondrous bronze lions which heralded her arrival at the top of the steps, and at the elegant Corinthian columns which supported the library's octastyle portico. Now, in the foyer, he had vanished.

She peered around a group of people in front of her and saw him approach an employee by an internal door. She hid behind a column and watched him, careful in case he suddenly turned. She heard part of his conversation with the employee and was sure he had uttered the word 'aardvark'. She had hoped he might see the wisdom in her words, but she had not expected him to act on it with such fervour. A mere hour had passed since she'd slipped the paper under the door. And the other man, the gruff looking one she presumed to be Billings, had strode off in the other direction at the same time.

She did not want Mr Quandary to see her yet. She was not ready to claim ownership of the words. She was, nonetheless, pleased with herself. She remained outside the door as he entered the library proper. His demeanour reminded her of Father. Yet he was not like him at all. Father was tall and slim as a maypole and always impeccable in grooming and attire. Mr Quandary was frowsy. Unkempt. Yet his face spoke of longing. Melancholy even. A yearning for something more. Something unobtainable. Fidelia hankered to know what made him so wistful.

Consumed in his quest at this moment, he pored over one book after another, so focused that a dragon might have breathed fire beside him and he would not have flinched.

Father was like that. When researching or reading, he went

quite deaf and was oblivious to the mundanity of life going on around him. Mother could stand beside him and tell him it was time for tea and he would not hear her, his stone countenance a veil to what went on inside his head.

Fidelia was sure it wasn't deliberate, merely that he had transcended the ordinariness of everyday existence to peel back the wisdom and etymology of the words before him. She could do it too. Memorising the dictionary and picturing the words in her head had transported her through the many nights aboard ship. It had been her salvation during her months at the asylum. She could shut out the world and be alone with her thoughts. She could muse about the many uses for certain words, put them into context, ponder how the addition of an adverb or adjective might entirely alter the tone of a sentence. She didn't need to speak to anybody and they had nothing of interest to say to her, so they presumed she was both mute and stupid.

She looked again at Mr Quandary and wondered what he thought about. Was his mind filled with the wonders of the world or was it taken up with petty concerns, like whether his shoes were dusty or whether he should have one slice of bread or two? Did he have a wife? Children? Where did he come from? Did he too come from England?

He was off again. After hammering his hand on the table in delight, he leapt to his feet and made for the door, striding past her as she pressed herself against the wall, out of sight. By the time she descended the steps to Swanston-street, he had hailed a carriage and was gone in a clatter of hooves and dust. She had no hope of following him, as she had no money for a cab fare. Besides, she had no idea where he was going.

She returned to the library. So many books to captivate her. Filled with foreign – and familiar – fanciful facts. She looked around. People sat at tables and desks, heads down, buried in the words. Studious faces. A girl not much older than herself, with dark hair tied in blue ribbons, thumbed through a huge volume – a cyclopaedia? – turning the pages with effort. Could she do this too? Without having to hide?

She sauntered towards the bookcase from which Mr Quandary had selected books and studied the volumes thereon. The bookcase was devoted entirely to cyclopaedias and dictionaries. She brushed her fingers along the spines. Smelled the leather. Where would she start?

She glanced back to where he had sat. A book still lay open on the table. There on the page was an engraving, barely the size of a calling card. *That* was what an aardvark looked like. She hadn't imagined such a long snout, nor such silly ears. Almost lagotic.

She sat at the table, wishing she had Samuel Johnson beneath her for height, and flipped through the book about zoology. All manner of strange creatures emerged from the pages. An adder here. An armadillo – another curious creature – a bison, an absurd giraffe. A toucan with a comical beak. All manner of animals she had never seen. Father had promised her a trip to the museum in London. Surely she would have seen some of these creatures. But Permelia had become ill and all talk of excursions was hushed. Would she have to travel to Africa or to South America to see them?

The blue-ribboned girl, a heavy book in one arm, brushed past her table, trailing her fingers across the surface. She smiled at Fidelia and in almost the same instant sneezed. Her mother called out, 'Come along Beatrice. Time to go'. Fidelia smiled back and wiped the page of the book now dotted with moisture from the girl's sternutation.

She flipped back to the start of the book. She wanted to memorise the aardvark.

'It seems, miss, that aardvarks are inordinately popular today.' The gentleman startled her. 'I suggested to a man earlier that he might find a specimen of one at the university museum.'

Fidelia smiled at the man. Gestured for directions.

'You could walk there, dear. It's quite a way, but the day is still young.'

Her smile widened. Her lips pursed. She said nothing.

'Whatever is the matter? Cat got your tongue?' the man asked.

She didn't understand his question. She wanted to tell him that she didn't suffer from galeanthropy – the belief that one is a cat – but that might necessitate an explanation. She shook her head. She closed the book and hugged it to her chest.

'Leave it girl. I can restore it to its rightful place for you.'

F

*Felicity Flexánimous Flaunted Feathered Fascinators and
Found Facetiae, Fabric and Fervent Fandangles at
Billings Better Bookstore and Brasserie (with millinery)!
Did she Freely? She did indeed!*

Jasper's head was spinning with recollections of the wondrous things he had seen. He felt deeply honoured to have had a personal guided tour with Mr Frederick McCoy, professor of natural history and director of the national museum himself. An important man; no doubt busy. Nonetheless, he had perceived Jasper's fascination with the place and had proudly led him through the many glass display cabinets in the building, their contents illuminated by the sunlight streaming through the clerestory windows in the museum's vaulted ceiling.

Most animate he was of his display of lowland gorillas. Jasper was near struck dumb at the immensity of the creatures. McCoy was particularly proud of the specimens of Victorian native animals and took pleasure in showing Jasper a few of the intricate illustrations of various fauna by Ludwig Becker.

Becker, McCoy explained in his Irish brogue, had met an untimely demise fourteen years earlier, dying of scurvy during the ill-fated Burke and Wills expedition. Such a shame, Jasper thought, that his talent had been lost to the world. Sad, too, that such a fuss had been made of the deaths of the expedition's leaders and not of the other five who had also succumbed.

Jasper had never seen such exquisitely detailed works,

particularly those by another artist, whose name Jasper didn't catch, of several species of frog. Never had he thought that such tiny creatures could be endlessly fascinating.

He was determined to revisit the museum regularly. What a place to explore. He would take Myrtle too, to broaden her knowledge. She would be so taken with the pretty butterflies. He'd enjoy regaling her tonight with descriptions of the mighty whale and the other extraordinary things he had seen.

But alas, McCoy was not able to show him an aardvark in the flesh. He did, however, find a larger engraving of one and had allowed Jasper to roughly trace its outline onto a thin sheet of near-transparent paper.

'Perhaps sir, you could model one from clay. A stylised version at least.'

Jasper had laughed at the suggestion.

He had reluctantly taken leave from McCoy's erudite and fascinating company, explaining that he was on borrowed time from his employer. McCoy had bade him farewell and promised to visit the bookstore in the coming weeks.

McCoy's words rang in Jasper's ears as he mounted a carriage to return to Bourke-street. 'Model one from clay…'

Huh. What did he know about modelling with clay? But then…why not try? He could fashion one larger than actual size to be a certain eye-stopper for passers-by. If *he* had toiled in finding even a picture of one, who could say that his rendition was not accurate?

'I say,' he called to the carriage driver as they neared Queensbury-street, 'do you happen to know where I could buy clay? For sculpting?'

'Ya might try Hoffman's or Cornwell's brickworks up there in Brunswick, I dare say,' the driver said.

Jasper looked at his fob watch. It was already one o'clock. Billings might be wondering where the devil he had got to. No matter. 'Could you turn about and take me there?'

'Aye. I'll take ya ta Sydney if ya pay me proper.'

It was late afternoon by the time Fidelia returned to Bourke-street. She lingered outside Cole's, awaiting the appropriate opportunity to enter. She glanced over at Billings. That man was taking forever up the ladder. He was still working above the door, his body and the ladder blocking her view. Had he been up there all day? He had almost finished the sign-writing when she'd left this morning. She wandered up the street, staying on the south side. She looked again, just as the man descended the ladder, and could scarcely believe her eyes. The sign now advertised...

BILLINGS BETTER BOOKSTORE & Brasserie

She clapped her hands in delight. Mr Billings himself must have seen her alphabetic verses and liked them. *Brasserie* sounded much more exotic and fascinating than *cafeteria*. Her mother, being American, would have called it a cafeteria: the word, derived from Latin American and Spanish, was an interesting one in itself. But *brasserie* was sweet and shiny, and deliciously French. Admittedly, it originally pertained to a brewery, but she and Father had dined in fine style in one on the Champs Élysées. All of Melbourne would now be running for their dictionaries to decipher what *brasserie* meant. Was it even *in* an English dictionary?

Well, they would all have to go inside to find out.

Jasper hurled the hunk of clay onto the kitchen table, which shuddered under the weight. Lugging it first from the carriage into the shop and then out again for the walk home had taken great effort. Billings had not been impressed. 'I send you for an aardvark and you come back with a pile of mud.' But Jasper was not put off, despite Billings and now Myrtle's protests.

'What in bleedin' 'ell is that? Yer not makin' mud pies like a child in the street are ye? Not on the bleedin' table, yer not.'

'I am sculpting an aardvark.'

'Oh, course y'are. What in bleedin' 'ell is an aardvark?'

'Goodness, Myrtle. Must you preface every sentence with "bleeding"?'

'What of it? Never complained before, ye never.'

'Here, stop bleating and find me a knife, will you? A bluntish one, not too big, now.'

Jasper laid his tracing on the table. The illustration was not life-size. An adult aardvark, McCoy had told him, could weigh up to 180 pounds and measure up to seven feet long, from tip of nose to tip of tail. He clearly didn't have enough clay to make one that big; barely enough for one a third of that size. So he would make a baby aardvark. For practice.

The clay, he soon discovered, was tough to work with the hands. He kneaded the slab into a more workable form, adding a little water now and then from a basin he had Myrtle fetch for him. This made it slippery and easier to work. After moulding the clay to a rough form, he decided it might be easier to wrap the creature's tail alongside its torso, like a cat's, rather than stretch lengthways. Jasper then removed sections of clay to give more detail. The helpful fellow at the brickworks had suggested that appendages might be prone to breaking off and Jasper could understand the inevitability of such a mishap.

It had not occurred to Jasper that the finished work would need firing until the fellow mentioned it. 'He'd be a slippery customer without a firin',' he'd said. Jasper was grateful for the man's offer to place the completed sculpture in the brickworks' kiln atop the next batch of bricks.

He worked for several hours, taking clay from here and working it in there. Myrtle beside him tut-tutted and commented now and then. 'Looks more like a weasel t' me.' 'You're telling me this beggar eats only ants?' 'Whatever gave you this queer notion?'

Jasper explained about the note under the door. It was, he told her, heaven sent. He told her of Billings' reaction to it, and about his day at the library and museum.

She shook her head for the most part, incredulous and sceptical. 'So you don't know where it came from?' she asked.

'I have my suspicions.' He wasn't sure she'd believe him. He realised how foolish it would sound, that a nine-or-so-year-old girl could have come up with this. He remained dubious himself. There were words on those pages that he had never heard of.

He had looked at them again when he returned to the store and, while Billings was otherwise occupied, searched for *antediluvian* in one of Billings' copies of Noah Webster's American Dictionary of the English Language on the 'Dictionary and Cyclopaedia' shelf. *Antediluvian*, he read, referred to someone or something that lived before the great flood of Noah's time. Who would have known? Certainly not he. How could a child so young know this?

'As I said. Heaven sent, I believe.'

Fidelia couldn't sleep. She folded her coat and placed it on Samuel Johnson for comfort, but it didn't help. Such a wondrous day she'd had. It was all whirling around in her head, making sleep impossible. Entirely new horizons had unveiled themselves. Mysteries had been solved and more emerged in their place. She felt small and alone, yet excited at being on the cusp of new discoveries. She had baulked at the impressiveness of the whale skeleton outside the museum. Unbelievably gigantic. Surely it was a fiction. A fabrication of human whimsy. How could a creature grow to such bulk and yet be graceful as a sylph in the water? It had stretched almost the length of the building itself, which was a mighty way.

She recalled the suggestion of a whale that a deckhand had drawn her attention to during the passage from England. A vapourous spout of water and a grey, mottled arch breaking the surface. No telling how big it might have been.

Fidelia had thought about it for days, looked for it each time she went on deck. Perhaps it was Moby Dick come from an ocean away to accompany the *SS Great Britain*. She didn't see it again, although she revelled many times at the sight of dolphins frolicking in the bow waves.

The sea was such a vast empty space, and in it, a multitude of creatures never seen by man, save for those intent on killing and harvesting them for their own selfish purposes.

Never frustrate a floundering flathead
Or scuttle a serpentine snail
Do not torment a treacherous turtle
Or waylay a wallowing whale

For they are creatures of the deep, my child
Creatures of the deep,
They are creatures of the deep, my child
And they'll swimmingly send you to sleep

How could Father have thought such a verse would send her to sleep? Seeing a real whale – well, the bones of one – had made her mind all the more animated.

And yet the delicate insects, bedded in their glass display cases for eternity, had held her equally in awe. Beetles and spiders and grasshoppers competing in beauty and ugliness. Butterflies of iridescent, blinding blues and every other imaginable hue. She had wanted to touch them, to feel their velvet wings, but they were safely locked away from dirty fingers and careless browsers who might squash them in curiosity. Her eyes had fixed into a permanent state of dilation at the remarkable collections of fauna. Twice she had been told to not press her nose against the glass cabinets. It left smudge marks necessitating additional cleaning.

Most of all, she had been astonished at the kangaroo. Such a peculiar animal. Not right at all. And it appeared to perambulate by hopping only on its huge hind legs. It made an aardvark look ordinary, though the two creatures bore some similarities, particularly in their long tails. Did an aardvark, like a kangaroo, use its tail for propulsion and balance? She promised herself to see a kangaroo in the flesh and marvel at its awkward movement.

She wished Permelia and Ninian could have seen them. To be dead and gone and never have seen a whale, a kangaroo or the unfathomable blueness of a *Morpho rhetenor* was so wretched it didn't bear thinking about. They would have been just tall enough now to peer into the display cases, especially with the aid of a step-stool. She could have read the labels on the cases to them and heard them laugh at her dubious Latin pronunciations. Maybe, when she grew up and if she studied hard enough, she could become an entomologist or a lepidopterist. A mammologist or an ichthyologist. Or she could be like Father; a master of words. A lexicographer. Whatever she became, it must be a vocation with a grand and impressive name, of that she was certain.

Father had told her that they were headed to Melbourne for his new position, but he had never elaborated. Fidelia had never questioned his reason for not telling her. He wanted to maintain the mystery. But she knew it was an important position; one that held prestige. She now wished she'd probed him more thoroughly. Presumably it was an engagement pertaining to writing, etymology, language, words; something that would have given the family an identity in the City of Melbourne in the Colony of Victoria.

Now here she was, with no identity to speak of. No voice to speak with. No father or mother, or brother or sister, to succour her. Yet she was no longer daunted or depressed by this actuality. As of today, she knew she would find a future. No. She would *make* a future. She could spend her days at the library, her nights in the bookstore, and learn everything there was to know about – everything.

It would be a fabulous, fantastic, fruitful and fortunate future. And she was convinced that Mr Quandary would play a role in that future. She had seen him and heard him discussing his quest with the man at the museum. She knew he was on her case. The mere fact that he had taken her gift seriously meant he must be a gentleman of good taste and sensitivity. Though perhaps a little sly.

G

Gertrude Gallivanter Gathered Geraniums and Gypsophila in a Gabion,
And Garnered Gaudy Gardening Gloves at
Billings Better Bookstore and Brasserie
Did she Gladly? She did indeed!

Jasper could not stop thinking about the girl. Here he was, sitting at the table in the wee small hours doing something he'd never done before. After a whole day of doing things he'd never done before. He had learned more today than he had in twenty years. For the want of it. And the joy of it. Had it been at her instigation? Or was he just hoping it to be so?

Even while he worked the clay into a vague semblance of an African ant-eater, he saw her face. The smile that warmed his heart and in an instant made him believe that life was still worth living. He did not know her name or from whence she came, but he had an affinity for her like he'd never felt for another living being. He wanted to at once absorb her wisdom and protect her innocence. To nurture her enthusiasm and share her memories. But maybe she had her own father to do that. And maybe he was just imagining her. Perhaps she was a reincarnation of Sarah, or a manifestation of his longing for her. Either way, his thoughts were tormenting him.

He worked on the creature until he could no longer keep his eyes open. He was satisfied that his first ever effort looked not unlike the aardvark of his sketch. He had relished the exercise. Never had he thought of the possibility of sculpture as a pastime. Now he didn't want to stop.

Finally, at near two o'clock, he extinguished the lamp in the kitchen and made his way to lie beside Myrtle. The rhythmic ebb and flow of her breathing did not soothe him to sleep as it usually did. Despite his tiredness, his mind would not stop conjuring and creating and *cogitating*. Were the girl's verses rubbing off on him? He lay awake for a long time thinking about how Billings Better Bookstore's window display would become the talk of Melbourne. He would make it happen.

Tomorrow, he would use his modicum of artistic talent to create a backdrop for the window display. All things starting with 'A'. He would dress a mannequin as Amelia Audacious, in colours of amethyst and aubergine, and furnish the window with all manner of eye-catching objects. An abacus, an atlas, an admiral in uniform. Perhaps he could get Billings' sign-writer to copy the words in a calligraphic hand for a banner to complete the picture. Yes, that would do nicely.

The following day was overcast and not at all warm for March. Fidelia was mystified that here in this strange country, it could be baking hot one day and glacial the next. She was grateful she had wrapped her coat around her for the walk to the library, rather than stuffing it back in its hiding place with Samuel Johnson.

Her gait quickened to a run as a light shower created a pattern like a leopard's coat on the pavement before her. She dodged around a couple sauntering up Swanston-street in idle chatter, oblivious to the raindrops. She didn't veer from her quest to get back to the library. Back to the books. Back to her self-styled education. She wondered what it would be like to go to school. Did they even have schools here in Melbourne? Surely, she chided herself, if they had an orphan asylum and a university, they must have a school. What would it be like to go to school?

Father had always intended that Ninian would go to school. But for her and Permelia, apart from a brief period in which Father afforded a governess – a seedy, stringy young woman named Miss

Henderson who was prone to laziness and apathy – Mother and Father had been their teachers. Father particularly.

Mother had taught them the basic rules of etiquette of course, and had been an able, though not terribly patient, tutor in cookery and embroidery. She had told them stories about her home in New Haven; about the times before she had met Father. Her own parents, who Fidelia had never met, were haberdashers, selling the finest of men's clothing in their own store. Haberdashers in America, she had explained, sold clothing, whereas haberdashers in England sold the bits and bobs used for dressmaking and embroidery.

Fidelia had thought it strange that the same word might have different meanings in different countries. Americans, her mother had said, did a lot of things differently from their English ancestors. Mother had promised that, one day, she would take Fidelia to New Haven and show her what it was like to live in a burgeoning foreign city.

Fidelia was experiencing that for herself now, although she suspected Melbourne did not compare to New Haven in history and grandeur. One day, when she became a woman of the world, she would travel to New Haven by herself and learn about her mother's birthplace and about Father's visit to Yale College to meet Noah Porter, the lexicographer and editor of Webster's dictionary.

Father had often told her about how this visit had inspired his work in lexicography. He confessed to also having been inspired by the sight of one Miss Jessamine Hart, a beautiful young woman who had served him in a haberdasher's in the city and who would become his wife and Fidelia's mother. Fidelia especially loved Father's story about becoming entranced by the young woman's accent; a peculiar variant of English.

Fidelia could only imagine what it might be like to visit such a prestigious college and work, for a time, in the company of such an esteemed gentleman as Mr Porter. She recalled her father's excitement at the news, four years ago now, that Mr Porter had become president of Yale College. That, Father had said, made him an important man indeed.

Fidelia could only dream of ever going to a college or university. She had no hope even of going to school now. But that was no matter. Not when she could learn everything from books. Now all she had to do was decide what she wanted to learn first. Biology or history? Languages or literature? Shakespeare or Austen?

A novel was what she had a mind to read now. She browsed through the fiction section and found a fine-looking volume of *Wuthering Heights*. She had oft times heard her mother speak of Emily Brontë's brooding and enigmatic Heathcliff and scheming Cathy.

She took up her seat in the same place as the previous day. The heavy oak furniture was timeless and reassuring. It reminded her of her home in London. The smell of furniture wax and of leather-bound books. Of afternoons spent reading, sewing or learning French. Mother playing the piano and Grandmama Knight reciting poetry or working her tapestry.

Fidelia turned to chapter one.

1801. – I have just returned from a visit to my landlord – the solitary neighbour that I shall be troubled with.

Brontë's words painted fine descriptions of daily life at Thrushcross Grange and Wuthering Heights and Fidelia was immediately transported to a time long before Father and Mother, or even her grandparents, were born. A time and a place of coldness and isolation, of need and want and solitude. Of lonely, windswept moors and treeless dales. She imagined that she, herself, was Lockwood and that she was meeting the dark skinned gypsy, Heathcliff, *slovenly yet with the manners of a gentleman*. She read on avidly. She became so lost in the words that before long she was up to chapter nine and several hours had passed. Were it not for the infernal rumbling of her stomach, which she became sure those around her could hear, she would have continued unabated.

This business of trying to fill her stomach with cast-offs from hotels or restaurant refuse bins was clearly inadequate. It was a laboursome task to find such scraps and their sustenance never lasted long. She was beginning to feel feeble. It was difficult to concentrate.

It was time, she acknowledged reluctantly, to seek another position as a house servant. She might at least get fed and have a bed in which to sleep. She grudgingly replaced the book on the shelf after memorising the page number. As she had done before, she would look in the newspaper. How convenient to be in a library where she could see others in lounge chairs with *The Age* or *The Herald* or *The Argus* held in outstretched arms, rather than hoping to chance upon one discarded in the street.

She wandered to a newspaper-laden shelf and retrieved that day's copy of *The Age*. March 23. Goodness, it had been her tenth birthday on Sunday. And she had never given it a thought. Had Mother and Father been here, they would have made such a fuss of her. Reaching ten was a milestone: one that Ninian and Permelia would never attain.

On the front page she quickly found two possible positions. The first said:

Wanted, a GIRL to make herself generally useful.
Apply 121 King-street.

The second:

Wanted, a young girl to assist in housework,
2 Carolina-terrace, Drummond-street, Carlton.

King-street was closer. She found a piece of paper and a pencil on the counter and noted the details. She turned to page three and scanned it for anything of interest. A sub-heading caught her eye.

POLICE INTELLIGENCE

CITY COURT. – MONDAY, 22ND MARCH

VAGRANTS. –Six ill-clad men severally named Richard Smith, Wm. Connelly, Thomas Fanning, Robt. Wilson, Robt. Miles, and Edward Wilson were

> charged with having no lawful visible means of
> support. Sergeant Mooney stated that in
> consequence of complaints he had received from
> come residents of South Yarra, who, on their way in
> and out of town through the Government Domain,
> have had their sense of decency shocked by men and
> women of the vagrant class sleeping under the trees,
> and behaving disgracefully, he went to the place on
> Saturday last, and found the prisoners sleeping as
> described by those who had complained. Several of
> the prisoners had been before the court on previous
> occasions, and now they were sentenced to six
> months' imprisonment each, with hard labour.

Fidelia was dismayed that six men might be sent to jail for such a time, and with hard labour, simply for having nowhere to live. Was she too a vagrant? Yes, it was true. She had no abode and no lawful visible means of support. Could she too be sent to prison if she were detained by the police? What might happen to a young girl in prison? God forbid that she might end up in the female penitentiary behind the Eastern Market in Stephen-street. She had passed it one evening when exploring the streets and had shuddered at the wailing and shrewish banter she could hear within. Was this like purgatory? Only for the Catholics she supposed. No, it was imperative she should not be sent there. More likely, she would be sent back to the asylum.

This revelation gave her added impetus to seek work and lodgings, and quickly. Imagine if the police were to discover she'd been hiding in Cole's at night for weeks. But there was the downside. If she were to be employed by another family, she would no longer be able to visit the library, or the bookstore, or the museum. Her time would be theirs. And what manner of laborious chores might be in store for her? What if the new master of the house were like Mr Fleet – he of the stinking breath, warty nose and ugly, menacing hands? Fidelia flinched at the thought of him.

Surely it was not right for a man to behave in such a way, especially with a child.

Of course, she had remained silent. She had never let on that she could speak. Mr Fleet belonged in prison, she was sure. Imagine if he were sent to the women's penitentiary. Think what those wailing women might do to a man who thought it meet to molest a child.

H

Helvetia Harebrain Hamshackled her Hunger
and Hankering for Haddock,
But Had the Hardihood to Hide it in Her Habiliment at
Billings Better Bookstore and Brasserie
Did she Honestly? She did indeed!

Jasper Godwin handled the sculpture with the utmost care. It would not do to drop the creature now and break off an ear or a leg. William, his new-found friend at the brickworks, had been supremely impressed by the sculpture and, although confessing illiteracy, had promised to come for the opening of the bookstore. Jasper had promised a cup of brasserie coffee in return.

He sat the clay beast on his lap for the ride to Bourke-street, much to the humour of the cab driver. Jasper was pleased that he'd accepted William's help to glaze the sculpture. It gave the aardvark a wonderful lustre. Almost ten days had gone by and Jasper suspected that Billings was losing patience.

'I will believe it when I see it with my own eyes and lay my hands on it,' he'd told Jasper more than once.

Jasper hoped Billings would be pleased. The rest of the window display was complete. Blackshaw the sign-writer had made an impressive banner, shaped like a long scroll, to explain the diorama. He was already commissioned to work on the banners for B, C and D.

When Jasper arrived at the store, Billings stood waiting, hands on hips, a grin on his face like a Cheshire cat replete with a full bowl of milk.

'You've missed quite a scene,' he reported.

Jasper was taken aback. 'A scene?'

'Indeed. Mr Cole himself has been here to take me to task.'

'Yes?'

'Accused me, in no uncertain terms, of copying his ideas with our advertisement.'

'I guess it was bound to come. I'm surprised that it's taken him three days.'

'That was because he's been out of town and hadn't seen it, nor heard of it. Nor does he usually read *The Argus*, but our advertisement was shown to him by an indignant loyal customer. He questioned me at length about the meaning of some of the words. How foolish did I feel that I could not explain to him the meaning of abecedarian and antediluvian? Called me an impostor, he did.'

'What did you say to him?'

'Why, I said that it weren't me who had copied the idea. That it was my esteemed and literate employee, Mr Jasper Godwin.'

'Aha.' Jasper nodded this time.

'Hence I might ask you – for an explanation, that is.'

Jasper felt ill. Sagged under the weight of the aardvark. Of course he could not tell Billings what abecedarian meant. It could have been made up, for all he knew. And try as he might, he could not bring to mind the definition of antediluvian. Was it something to do with Noah, or some other biblical person? Would his deception be discovered now?

'Might I put Mr Ant-eater down first? He's heavy.'

'And impressive, I must say. I confess that, until this point, I doubted his existence.'

'Yes, it took much longer than anticipated.' Jasper carefully placed the sculpture on the table in the window. Turned it this way and that. Stood back and admired it, as did Billings. Jasper hoped the diversion might cause Billings to forget his earlier question. It did not.

'So tell me Godwin, what does "lagotic" mean?'

Jasper contemplated making something up. If Billings didn't

know, then hopefully he would accept any explanation. But what if Billings were to look it up in the dictionary, as *he* had done with *antediluvian?* The lie would be revealed. He would be uncloaked as a fraud. Besides, he didn't have the imagination to guess at a meaning.

Should he confess to Billings that the verses were not of his pen? Again, he might be called a fraud. Could he just shrug in smug contempt and suggest that Billings look it up for himself? What to do? A dilemma. A predicament indeed. Or was there another solution?

'I confess, sir, to not being able to recall at this moment. Which isn't to say that I never knew. I spent a little time poring over your dictionaries and cannot remember the meaning of all the words used.' It was a lie, true, but a small one of no consequence.

Surprisingly, Billings was satisfied with his response. 'Perhaps I should do as you did and spend time in perusal of the dictionary.' He smacked his hands together. 'Now, Godwin, we have two days left to get set for the opening. I will need your assistance later to unpack the shipment lately arrived from the United States of America.'

Jasper nodded. He was excited to see what was in the boxes. No doubt books the likes of which he had never seen before. He was excited also about the opening of the bookshop. He looked through the gap in the newspapers in the window. Tomorrow they would be removed to give passers-by a preview of what was in store for them.

Bourke-street was busy this morning. The sky was overcast but showing promise that the cloud might clear and unveil a brilliant blue.

The street was still muddy from yesterday's rain. People milled about. Women with parasols lifted skirts out of the mud as they crossed the street and men slowed their pace to check fob watches, adjust collars or run their fingers through their hair. All tried to avoid the sludge of mud and horse excrement, noses covered with handkerchiefs to mask the smell. All were screened, now and then, by passing blurs of horse flesh and cart wheels. Three or four stopped to peer through the gap in the paper and reeled backwards when they came eye to eye with Jasper.

He hoped to see the girl. She wasn't there. Ten days had gone by and he had not seen her at all. Perhaps she was, after all, a figment of his imagination. Each day he had willed her to appear. She would have loved the museum, a wondrous place for a child. Of course, it was likely she had been there already, with her family.

It was well Fidelia knew that life held more promise than days spent scrubbing floors and polishing furniture. It demanded effort to clean the flagstones of the humble premises at 121 King-street. Moreso in the past two days, for her energy was flagging; she was as flat as these flagstones. She felt hot and tired, her thirst unquenchable and her throat painful and constricted. Especially hard to swallow was the dry toast Florence, the housekeeper, had given to her as breakfast. But she had forced it down. Better than to be hungry.

Mr Darling's name did not reflect his temperament, but he had not raised his voice to her, despite understanding that she might be deaf as well as mute. He seemed more genteel than Mr Fleet; and he had not had that look in his eye, which was a comfort.

She hadn't been allowed off the property since being accepted for the position, which chafed at her. Having gone straight there from the library, she had foolishly left Samuel Johnson under the table at Cole's. What if someone found him? He might be lost to her forever. When might she have the opportunity to fetch him?

Playing on her mind more than that, and more than feeling unwell, was Billings. Today was opening day and she wasn't there to see it. Was there a pretext by which she could take leave of the Darling house for the afternoon? Without being able to speak her mind?

Just as she was thinking that hope was lost, the opportunity presented itself.

'Do ye know where the eastern market is, lass? Up in Bourke-street? On the corner of Stephen-street,' Florence enquired in an unseemly, loud voice.

Fidelia nodded animatedly. The market stood a few doors up from Billings on the other side.

'I usually go on a Thursday, but with my gammie leg, I dinnae think I can walk so far. Can I trust ye with a penny to fetch tatties, leeks, cabbage, and carrots or parsnips? Go to the fellow with the cart nearest the entry on the right. You know left from right, hen?'

Fidelia nodded again and held out her hand. She loved the Eastern Market. She had spent many a morning there scavenging for food. The atmosphere was dynamic, bustling. It reminded her of Covent Garden Market, though decidedly less grand. People spruiking all manner of wares under the high vaulted roof. Ducks, chickens and geese crammed into tiny cages, drowning each other out in a chorus of clucking and cackling along the street front. Haywains and vegetable carts lining Stephen-street, horses tethered and glum – inured to the boredom of the day.

She might get to see Mr Lin, the Chinese man, who had kindly offered her a wee cup of his delicious noodles once. If she smiled at him enough, he might reprise his generosity. Or if she mustered her pleading, half-starved face, she might beguile a Cornish pasty from the jovial red-bearded man. It was a wondrous, noisy, stinky place – stalls selling foul-smelling cheeses, bottles of pickles and jams with dubious contents, salted fish as tough as weathered leather, dried fruits which stuck to the roof of the mouth with their sickly sweetness. The smell of hay, horse manure, the unwashed bodies of traders who had come straight from their market gardens with produce, dirt trapped permanently under their nails. It was, indeed, a place for shnerkeling.

'Well go along wi' ye, and don't be all day,' Florence instructed.

Despite her lethargy, Fidelia donned her coat and almost skipped out of the double-storey dwelling. Darling was a tea merchant; his warehouse alongside his home. The best thing about working for him was the assurance of a good cup of tea in the morning.

But Fidelia missed the independence of life on the street, the freedom to go to the library or to Cole's. She had read nothing for several days, save for the label on the tin of carnauba wax. Florence had shown her how to mix the carnauba with beeswax and turpentine to make a malleable paste for the furniture and floors. It was sticky and not at all pleasant. Working it took effort.

She walked briskly to Bourke-street and turned right. It was past 11 o'clock and the sun caught her in the eyes each time it emerged from a cloud, but it was by no means warm. It was six blocks to Stephen-street and the Eastern Market. King, William, Queen, Elizabeth, Swanston, Russell, Stephen. She recited the streets in her head, though she could see all the way up to Parliament House in Spring-street. Of course, she passed many smaller laneways too. Past banks, cobblers, jewellers, tobacconists, hotels, tailors.

By the time she reached Swanston-street, she was fatigued. Hot and thirsty. Her throat like the boiler aboard the *SS Great Britain*. Her skin was prickling and sore to the touch.

She continued to Russell-street and noted the bustling crowd. As she neared it, she found herself at the end of a queue. People ahead of her craned their necks to see into the new shop on the left. The crowd was eighteen or twenty people deep outside the store. Everyone was trying to view the diorama. By contrast, all looked quiet at Cole's across the street. Usually the place was abuzz with browsers, readers, those wanting to be seen. Like bees in a hive. But not today. The only buzzing today was at Billings Better Bookstore and Brasserie.

A tout held the crowd spellbound and expectant.

'Come one, come all and feast your eyes. For no better sight will you behold in Melbourne today. Come and meet Amelia Audacious and cast your eyes upon the strangest sight. An aardvark, would you believe? An aardvark cast in stone.'

Fidelia thought she would explode with pride, if she didn't

feel so fevered and ill. She looked for gaps in the crowd and fought her way through to the front row of the spectators. Her mouth widened to a grin as her words – *her very words* – came to life before her. Painted on a banner spanning the back wall of the window display.

Amelia Abstainer Admonished an Amateur Abecedarian and Absconded with an Antediluvian Aardvark, After Adjourning for an Arousing Absinthe at Billings Better Bookstore and Brasserie. Did she Absolutely? She did indeed!

And then she saw an amazing thing – an aardvark, for sure.

And then she saw *him*.

And he saw *her*.

Quandary Man pushed his way past the patrons cramming the door and held his hand out to her.

'A sneak peek for the little girl,' he said calmly to those protesting. She took his hand without pause. He led her through the door.

It was standing room only. Browsers crammed elbow to elbow. The air was stiflingly redolent of perfume. Not like the calm of the library or even the sedateness of Cole's. The earthy, pungent smell of coffee filled her nostrils and she thought she might vomit. She had never felt like this before. Was it the excitement of the occasion? Was it the claustrophobic atmosphere? So hot and close. Too many people breathing too much hot air.

She remembered nothing after that.

Somehow, in the longing recesses of his mind, Jasper had known she would come. And here she was, smiling, and allowing him to guide her through the store. And then he felt her hand go limp and before he could react, the girl had slumped to the floor.

'Stand back everyone. Stand back I say.' His voice barely audible over the hubbub of patrons. A woman, seeing his plight, bade customers to make room.

'Oh gosh,' the woman exclaimed. 'She must have the scarlet fever. Look at her arms, the poor wee thing.' The woman felt Fidelia's forehead. 'And she's burning up. Like a furnace.'

Jasper scooped the girl into his arms. He pressed his way through the crowd to the back of the store. He sat her in a chair and fetched a cup of water from the basin out the back. He pulled his handkerchief from his pocket, dampened it and patted her brow as she rallied a little. The woman stood by him, motherly concern on her face.

'Is she your child?' Jasper asked her.

'No.'

'Would you mind seeing if you can find her mother or father?'

'She's shaking her head at you sir. I believe she must be here alone. Is that right, dear?'

Fidelia nodded and motioned for the cup of water.

'Where are your parents? Or guardian?' Jasper asked.

She shook her head.

'You need someone to take care of you, that's for certain.' He looked at the woman. 'You perhaps?'

'No, goodness no. Not me. I've enough problems of my own.' The woman made for the door.

'What's going on here, Godwin?' Billings stood, arms crossed, not at all pleased at the sideshow going on around the girl.

'She's ill and needs somebody to tend to her. My Myrtle could, but I'd have to get her home.'

Billings swore under his breath. 'We're far too busy, Godwin, for you to be taking off home now. What say I send young Billy around to fetch your wife?'

'Yes, that would be agreeable.' Jasper waited until the small crowd around them dispersed. Off to browse the shelves, sample the coffee, marvel at the merchandise. He leant across and brushed the wisps of fair hair from her forehead. 'Goodness me, girl, but you are hot. Do you feel unwell?'

Fidelia pointed to her throat.

'Your throat. Is it sore? Or can you not speak?'

Fidelia nodded again. Looked about the shop, wide-eyed. She tried to take in every detail. Every book.

Ain't nothing so wondrous as a child in awe, Jasper thought. 'Yes, it's a marvellous place. Wait until it's quieter and you're feeling better. I'll show you around properly if you like.'

She smiled wanly, too weak to show her excitement. But his words calmed her. She almost felt like she was with Father. She knew she could be at ease with this man. She had seen it in his eyes when first she'd seen him.

'Tell me,' Jasper whispered, 'do I have *you* to thank? For the inspiration, I mean?'

Fidelia stared into his watery green eyes. Said nothing. Tried to stem a crinkle at the edge of her mouth.

He understood her perfectly. 'Did you like my aardvark? I made it with my own hands, I did. Quite pleased, I am,' he whispered.

She could not stop the smile, no matter how hard she tried.

'Do you think it will help us sell books?'

She pointed to the pile of dictionaries on a table nearby.

He followed her finger with his eyes. 'Yes, I see, it will help us sell dictionaries. Good, very good. I'll suggest to Mr Billings that we stock up on dictionaries. Clever girl.'

Father had been the last person to say that to her. He had tested her vocabulary, comprehension and spelling almost every day. He'd made it fun. Never laborious. Never boring. Always engaging. She'd been a willing pupil. A voracious learner. Forever trying to impress or surprise Father with her wisdom. Always cramming. Always searching for new words, new definitions, new contexts. And she revelled in his praise of her.

'Never be afraid to show your intellect, my darling. It is a blessing to be fervent in your quest for knowledge. Those who have no passion to learn have no passion to live and they are not of your ilk. They will try only to shrink you to their base level. Never be a wiseacre, mind. Nobody likes a wiseacre.'

But it was fun being clever and knowing words other people didn't know. Some she liked to keep to herself; her secret. She was never sure when she might have cause to utter the words: *helminthick* – relating to worms; or *féuillemort* – French for the colour of a faded leaf; but she was glad she knew them. When Catherine, her friend in England, had told her of her pet sheep delivering twins, Fidelia had proudly described the animal as gemélliparous. Catherine had looked perplexed; Fidelia, smug.

She felt smug now. But not so smug as to be thought a wiseacre by her new friend. And then she felt faint. A buzz, louder than a hive of bumble bees, reverberated around her head.

I

Isabella Insouciant Iterated Infandous and Incendiary Insults in Iambic Illustrations, Inveigled from Intelligentsia and Illuminati at Billings Better Bookstore and Brasserie Did she Indisputably? She did indeed!

It had been a long while since Myrtle Godwin had had to tip-toe about the place for fear of waking a child. But the girl clearly needed sleep. And cool cloths applied to forehead and chest, back and arms, to get her fever down. And probably a good square meal. But that could wait until she felt a little stronger. A red rash covered the girl's arms, throat, chest and abdomen and, Myrtle suspected, lower down her body as well. Her cheeks were flushed red; nobbly as a thimble and burning hot.

Myrtle recalled having had scarlet fever when she was a girl. A most unpleasant time it had been. Her younger brother had succumbed to it, just as her daughter had later succumbed to the diphtheria. Sometimes there was no salvation for wee children. It was as if God had looked down upon them and considered them unworthy. Unworthy to love until they reached double figures in years, with childhood maladies behind them. Chances were He would do it to this one as well.

She had been irked when young Billy had knocked on her door and told her that she was required at the store. She had been in the throes of baking bread for supper and was reluctant to leave, lest it burn. And she had been none too pleased when she came upon the reason for her summons. What business was this child of Jasper's and hers? To add insult to injury, the little miss had spoken nary a word to her. Nor to anybody, it seemed. It wouldn't do. It simply wouldn't do. And she would tell Jasper in no uncertain terms when he arrived home.

In the meantime, she would do her duty – as a good Christian should – and provide comfort for the child. She'd obviously had none too much of that for a while. Matted hair, dirty fingernails and smelling of a farmyard dog. Fixing for a bath, she were. Her coat, once peacock blue – Myrtle could tell that from the inside of the cuffs and collar which weren't usually exposed to the light – now faded and stained with grime and goodness knew what else. She'd hung the coat on the hook by the door. As she did, she noticed, written in ink inside the collar, but partially rubbed away, *F… ight*. Maybe the tailor's name. Maybe the girl's.

Maybe, if she felt inclined tomorrow, she'd give it a launder. Or maybe not. 'Twasn't her responsibility to do such. 'Twas 'er mother's. It wasn't like she didn't have enough to do without having to worry about other people's laundry. If the girl wanted the coat laundered, she could take it to the Chinese chappy in Lonsdale-street and pay for it to be done. And that would be an end of it.

Myrtle brushed her hands together. That was enough thinking about that.

It was bad enough that Jasper had taken over the kitchen table with his blooming clay. Now it was a blessed reptile he was sculpting. Where in the name of Queen Victoria did this notion come from? Suddenly out of nowhere he considered himself a sculptor. A caiman or some such thing, he said it was, not unlike a wee crocodile, he said. She'd never seen one of *them* neither. Back up to that museum he'd gone day before yesterday and returned with another drawing. What was it going to be next? An elephant? A bleedin' hippopotamus? One o' them kangaroo things he'd been going on about? And here was she, trying to prepare supper in all this mess.

'Now, wha'ever's 'appened to that blessed 'usband o' mine?'

The woman's words, spoken audibly, stole Fidelia from her sleep. Where was she? This was not her quarters at the Darlings. And that woman sounded not at all like Florence. She rubbed her eyes and tried to focus on her surroundings.

A small, high window revealed nought but the proximity of a neighbouring building and violet evening sky beyond. How, for the love of Aphrodite, did she get here? Her memory was blank as a newly-dusted chalkboard.

She had been inside the store. Quandary Man was tending to her. She remembered nothing after that. Had she gone to sleep?

Her fingers tightened on something in her hand. Something round and flat. Of course. A penny. She was on her way to the market and she'd stopped at Billings.

Oh no! Florence would think she had absconded with the money like a common thief.

She must go. She tried to lift the coverlet but it was tucked in tightly. Wrapped snugly like Mother had swaddled Permelia when she was tiny. She grunted with the effort. Her throat was still dry and her skin was a thousand needles pricking. Presently, a strange woman drew back the curtain and stared at her, a basin under one arm, wooden spoon in her other hand. Flour all over. A large woman, forbidding. A glower like a long-eared owl.

'Mrs Godwin's the name. Now, I'll get ye a cup of water. And then I'll set to drawin' ye a bath. See if we can't get that sting out of ye skin. Eh?'

Fidelia nodded. She still didn't know how she'd come here, though she'd a vague recollection of being carried. Her mind was like pea soup.

'And then a peck of supper. I'm guessin' ye could be doin' with some supper. My Jasper, that's me 'usband, 'e'll be arriving shortly and we'll sit at table and eat together. Eh?'

Fidelia was a little taken aback. This was not a servant attending to her. This was a woman with a husband and this was, presumably, their home. Then she heard the creak of a door and heavy footsteps.

'Ah. And 'ere 'e is now, speak of the devil.'

'How's the wee girl? Are you taking care of her?'

It was Quandary Man. Fidelia recognised his voice instantly.

'Of course I am. Did ye think otherwise?' He didn't reply. 'She's just awake. Don't ye go peekin' in there in case she's not decent.'

Quandary Man poked his head through the curtain anyway. He smiled and performed his customary wave. Fidelia reciprocated.

He stepped towards her and held out his hand. 'Allow me to introduce myself. Mr Jasper Farthing Godwin at your service.' He bowed.

Fidelia pulled her hand from under the cover and placed it in his. She didn't have to think of him as Quandary Man any more. He had a name now. *Jasper. Farthing. Godwin.* Jasper, she recalled from Samuel Johnson, was:

Jásper. *n.s.* [*jaspe*, Fr. *iaspis*, Lat.] A hard stone of a bright beautiful green colour, sometimes clouded with white, found in masses of various sizes and shapes. It is capable of a very elegant polish, and is found in many parts of the East Indies, and in Egypt, Africa, Tartary, and China. *Hill's Mat. Med.*

He was a precious stone. Jasper. The colour of his eyes matched his name. A farthing held little value; a mere quarter of a penny, but Mr Jasper's smile was worth at least a pound sterling. His face showed no malice, no nefarious intent. Nothing lustful and degenerate like Mr Fleet's. Merely empathy and benevolence. His eyes suggested humour. In an instant, she felt like she belonged here and that all her hardship might be cast asunder at this propitious point in time.

'May we have the pleasure of your name? Now that you have mine?'

Fidelia wanted to tell him, but Mr Bartholomew's words rang in her ears. *Forget about anything you've ever seen or heard. Don't speak a word. Not a word.* She put her fingers to her lips and looked away.

Jasper told her not to be shy. There was no harm at all in her speaking her name. But she remained silent.

He pulled up a stool. Told her about the splendid day. The grand opening of Billings Better Bookstore...*and Brasserie* had eclipsed his and Mr Billings' wildest imaginings. Never had he seen such an array of people with fascinated, awe-filled faces. It had been almost entirely down to the captivating window display, and, of course, the advertisement in *The Argus* the previous week.

The opening had been the talk of the afternoon. People had come from Hawthorn and Elsternwick, Williamstown and Camberwell, and a queer place out east called Nunawading – a long trip by coach. They had sold out of dictionaries by two o'clock!

'I'm embarrassed to say that Mr Billings gave me credit for the display, which should be due to you, if I'm not wrong. I hope you don't mind me assuming the praise. Presuming, that is, that it was from your hand.'

Fidelia's smile crinkled her eyes. She didn't mind at all. It was a gift she had been willing to give. Now this man had only smiles for her – and smiles *only* for her. He had made her feel that life was worth living. What price a few carefully chosen words? His voice, despite its tendency towards excited crescendo, was soothing. She forgot, for a time, about her scratchy throat and her itching skin. She forgot, for a time, about her aborted errand for Florence and about Samuel Johnson languishing, forgotten, at Cole's. She forgot about Heathcliff and Cathy and the goings on at Wuthering Heights. She listened like she had when Father had told her stories. Each word like a ribbon pulled to unveil the mystery of a wrapped present. She could easily have slept more – her body was direly in need of it – but she was spellbound by this man. *Jasper Farthing Godwin.*

'A caiman – not unlike an aardvark', Jasper explained, 'has a long tail. Difficult to create in clay, lest it break off during firing or transport. Too fragile'.

Fidelia pulled the picture towards her and cocked her head to the side, thinking. She picked up her fork and stuck it into the hind-quarters of the partly-formed reptile. Gestured that inserting such an object might strengthen the clay, enabling a long tail.

'Bravo girl.' Jasper nodded. 'I have just the thing.' He disappeared briefly out the back door and returned with a length of stiff wire. 'From a hairpin fence, dear, fallen on the path, up in Stephen-street. Never know when you might have a use for such a thing.'

'I carn't believe that yer sittin' there with a mute child creatin' a queer creature from mud 'n' wire,' Myrtle harped.

'An excellent way to spend an evening, I say. Don't you think, girl?'

Fidelia couldn't think of a better way. Except to be with Father and Mother, reading by the fireside. She grinned.

Mrs Godwin's bread and broth, pork and peas, and jam tart to follow, had been a veritable banquet. She was full for the first time in months. It had been an age, too, since she had savoured the heavenly taste of milk, which had soothed her burning throat.

'It's mighty slippery stuff, this clay,' Jasper observed, as he slid his fingers down the caiman's back.

Oleaginous, Fidelia thought, better described the greasy clay.

'I wish you would tell us your name,' Jasper said.

'Might be in 'er coat. 'Ere, look at this.' Myrtle pulled the coat from the hook and showed the label to Jasper.

'*F* something *ight*. Hmm. Fright!' he exclaimed.

Fidelia put her hand to her mouth and shook her head wildly.

'Fanlight maybe?'

More head shaking.

'Fortnight? Forthright?'

Fidelia was enjoying the game. Her head shook more exaggeratedly each time. A giggle threatened to emerge from her mouth.

'Footlight? Fanlight?'

'Frostbite?' Myrtle suggested, not aware of its different spelling. 'Or perhaps it's her initial and part of her surname'.

'Ah.' Jasper nodded. 'You could be right dear.' A flicker of Fidelia's eyes suggested they were on the right track.

'Now, what would one call a girl so pretty?' he said teasingly. 'Frances? No? Flora? Fanny? Florence?' Jasper shook his head, exasperated. 'I can think of no more.'

'She might be Scottish or Irish,' Myrtle suggested. 'Could be one o' them peculiar names like Fionnuala, Fiona, Finella.'

Fidelia kept shaking her head. Would they ever guess it? This was more fun than making up her verses had been. That had been a lonely affair; this, engaging. She felt like Rumpelstiltskin.

'Felicity. No? Aha,' Jasper said. 'I have it. 'Freya!' His shoulders sank in defeat as Fidelia again shook her head. 'All right girl. If your name starts with 'F', we'll call you Effie'.

Fidelia tipped her head back and shook it vehemently. That had been the name of her uncle's maidservant. A nasty, corrugated, fascinous woman. A witch. Always spitting and cussing. No way would she be relegated to sharing such an unpleasant name.

'I have to admit defeat, girl. I suspect you're playing a game with us.'

Fidelia gestured for an implement to write with. Jasper armed her with a pencil and pointed to the paper on which the caiman was sketched. *Fidelia,* she wrote.

'Aha,' Jasper exclaimed. 'I might have known it would be a lovely name. An extra-ordinary name. A positively superlative name. And your family name?'

Knight. Fidelia Patience Knight.

Jasper repeated her name out loud. 'A name fit for a princess.' He had a thought. 'Perhaps now, since you're in a mood to write, you might tell me what *callipygous* means, if I pronounce it correctly. I confess to be at a loss with that one.'

Her face, already red with spots, flushed redder. She stifled a giggle. *Having beautiful buttocks,* she wrote.

'Good lord. Such a word for a child to know.'

'What is it?' Myrtle asked.

Jasper turned to Fidelia, put his finger to his lips conspiratorially. 'Beautiful, Myrtle. Just means beautiful.'

J

Josephine Jiggumbob Juggled Jasmine and Jonquils into a Jardiniere,
And Joined a Jongleur buying Jewellery at
Billings Better Bookstore and Brasserie (with flowers and jewellery)
Did she Joyously? She did indeed!

After a week of bed rest, Fidelia was much stronger. Her rash
had dissolved away, leaving her skin fair and untroubled again.
Mrs Godwin had fed her well, three times a day, and she felt almost
as strong as before she'd left England. Such a lifetime ago and yet
but a year. Today, she would go for a walk. Jasper had left for
work and had suggested she might care to visit him there later.
He had given her directions, not that she needed them.

At the door, she donned her coat, now almost blue again
thanks to a dunking in the tub. The moment she stepped onto
the footpath, she knew where she was. A few doors up from the
Fleets' lodgings in Russell-street. She would have to take care to
avoid being seen by any member of the Fleet family on her way
past. Fortunately, Mrs Godwin had fashioned her a bonnet,
adjusting the crown of one of her own to size. An aqua bow
fastened at her left cheek might provide adequate disguise.

Fidelia was looking forward to seeing Billings Bookstore
properly; not in a fever-induced haze as a week ago. But she had
another mission this morning. To retrieve Samuel Johnson from
Cole's bookstore. She prayed that he hadn't been found by
somebody else. She'd missed his familiarity, his smell. It was as
though he beckoned to her from another place in time, when she
was part of a family with parents who cherished her.

She kept to the east-side footpath as she approached Temperance Hall. She lowered her head, concentrated on her footfalls. Safely past, she set her sights towards Bourke-street, the buildings now old friends. She stopped as two carriages passed, and crossed the street. She loitered, nonchalant, transparent, until a woman and boy approached. She watched them enter Cole's and trailed behind her casually-adopted sibling; lingered with them as they browsed. The woman's bustle was awkward among the cabinets. Bustles were such stupid contrivances. Imagine what you could hide under there.

What's hiding under your bustle?
Maybe something you'd ne'er think to find
Is it a small man bent double?
Seeking refuge from trouble?
And tailing you closely behind?

What's hiding under your bustle
In that empty, voluminous space?
There's room enough there
For a small pied-a-terre,
With terrace and spiral staircase

What's hiding under your bustle,
Under all of that satin and lace?
'Tis a whale out of water
Or somebody's daughter
Trying to keep up the pace

She devised a few more verses in her head as she bided her time. She watched her spurious brother with distaste. The boy's hands were on everything. Grasping, pawing. No delicacy of touch. Like a grey seal wallowing onto a beach in Cornwall. She drifted away, disowning his company. Nobody paid her any heed. When she was certain nobody was watching her, she crept upstairs, crawled into her erstwhile hiding place and pulled Samuel Johnson from beneath the table-top. It was good to feel the weight of him in her arms again – to feel the worn texture of his skin. To admire the gilt-edged shine of his pages. Re-united with a dear friend.

She stuffed him under her coat, hugged him to her chest like a long-lost doll and made her way downstairs again. She resisted the temptation to see what was new in store since her last visit almost three weeks ago, and headed towards the daylight. She crossed the threshold and stepped onto the footpath, the sun bright in her eyes.

'Stop! Thief!'

A woman's voice echoed, shrill in Fidelia's ears. She stopped and looked each way. She could see no suspicious felon. She turned around. The woman with the bustle was pointing at her accusingly. A small group gathered around the woman. Fidelia stood still as a leafless tree. She didn't know what to do.

'Show us what you have under your coat there, girl,' a man demanded. A big man, with dark hair and beard. His voice was familiar. *Christopher Crabstick was Cross, Captious, Cutting and Caustic...* His piercing eyes made her quiver in fear.

'I'm sure she has something, a book most likely, under her coat, Mr Cole.'

This man was Mr Cole? Mr Cole himself? Not an employee? This man who had insinuated himself into his very own building in the middle of the night to create those verses that she had emulated, transcended even? And she had thought that man a buffoon. Not the man held in highest esteem by his many patrons.

'Come on, girl. Give it up now and I'll see that the magistrate goes easy on you.'

Fidelia could not believe his words. She was no criminal. No thief. She wanted to cry out and deny the biting accusation. But she couldn't. She especially feared the thought of court after what happened to those vagrants. She might end up in prison – with the wailing women. Just when she had found solace from her lonely existence.

Before long, people had gathered from all directions. She was surrounded. She felt like Stowaway Sam. She recalled the scent of his fear. No chance of slipping away. No longer invisible. A canary cornered by a cat.

She pulled Samuel Johnson from her coat.

'See I told you,' the woman shouted.

Fidelia looked up at the accusing faces. Every one a blur. She shook her head. How could she explain? She tried to back away, but the bodies closed in around her. *A lamb to the slaughter.* Then, as though her situation was not already dire, another voice, again familiar. Another shrill accusation.

'You'd better check her pockets. I gave her a penny a week ago to buy vegetables and she never come back. I shouldae known she couldnae be trusted. Left me to explain it to the master, she did. I'm lucky I didnae lose ma position.'

Florence.

'Is this true?' Edward Cole asked. His voice was accusatory but not aggressive as his piercing eyes drilled into her.

Fidelia nodded. Hung her head. Pulled the penny from her pocket and held it in her open palm for all to see.

'You should call the police. There's a constable down at the corner of Swanston-street,' a different woman said.

'Yes,' Cole said. 'Jones, do what the lady suggested and scoot down and summon the constable.' He was addressing a red-jacketed man, a Cole's employee Fidelia had seen on many occasions. 'We'll let *him* deal with the little cutpurse.'

'Wait!' A voice called from the back of the crowd. Another familiar voice. *Jasper Farthing Godwin.* He parted the crowd and stepped forward.

'I will vouch for the girl. She is under my guardianship. I think you will find, madam,' he addressed Florence formally, despite her evidently lowly attire, 'that the girl will be more than willing to return your penny. She has been ill for a week with the scarlet fever. I would suggest that you might have known that, since she was covered in a violent rash when I encountered her last Thursday. She was too ill, I should think, to complete your errand and she has been under the care of my wife since. You should be ashamed to have sent a child in her condition on such an errand.'

'But what of the book? Stolen from Mr Cole here,' the bustle-woman spat.

Fidelia started to open the book. It was awkward with nothing to rest it upon. She gestured to Jasper for help. Jasper took it. 'It's an old book. Not one I imagine *you* to be selling,' he said to Cole.

Cole looked at Jasper with contempt. 'And who might you be? I take it you must be a regular customer, to know what books I might or might not be inclined to stock in my emporium.'

'Jasper Godwin sir. An employee of Mr Lucas Billings.' He proffered his hand, but Cole ignored the gesture.

'Aha. The man of words who copied my advertisements. I finally get to meet you. The walking dictionary. And I might have known that scoundrel Billings would be behind this. Sending spies and thieves into my store now, is he? Is that his latest work of subterfuge?'

Fidelia shook her head wildly and gestured to Jasper to open the book. He turned to the flyleaf and read out loud:

This book remains the property of
Pleasant Fidelius Knight Esq.

Jasper looked down at Fidelia. 'Is this your father? Is it your father's book?'

Fidelia nodded.

'Show it to me,' Cole said. He pushed Jones forward. Jones grasped the book from Jasper and pulled, tearing the endpaper from its hinge. The cover flopped limply from the spine.

Fidelia was distressed. Father's dictionary. Samuel Johnson. Her only possession. Her only reminder of Father. Broken. She burst into tears.

Jasper put his hand on her shoulder in comfort. 'Never mind. We can get it repaired. The girl's name is Fidelia Knight. I think that should be proof enough that the book belongs to her. Or, at least, to her family.'

'Aye. That's the name she gie us. She wrote it down,' Florence agreed.

'Why could she not tell us that herself?' Cole asked.

'She's mute. Doesn't speak,' Jasper replied.

'Dumb as a stump,' Florence agreed.

'What would a stupid girl want with a book like that? Surely she cannot read it,' bustle-woman said.

'I said she was mute, madam. I did not say she was stupid,' Jasper retorted. 'On the contrary, I suspect that this child knows every word in that book. And I suspect she knows words that you, *madam*, have never even heard of.'

The woman clenched her hands and thrust them onto her hips. 'Well, I never.'

Jasper stepped towards Jones, who placed the book into his hands. He slipped it under his left arm and took Fidelia's hand in his right hand. 'Come child. What say we bounce away from this kangaroo court and see what's to be done with your book?'

They took a few paces across the street. Fidelia stopped. She ran back to Florence and placed the penny in her hand.

'Hmm, it's right damaged. It'll take a bit more than hide glue to restore it,' Lucas Billings observed. 'It's a mighty book.' He nodded to Fidelia who nodded back.

She had presumed, from her first sight of the bearded man and how he had admonished Jasper, that he was a bad-tempered buffoon. But she now saw him in a kindlier light. He had smiled genuinely at her and made her feel at ease.

'More than 100 years old, I see,' he said. 'See Jasper, it says right here, MDCCLV. 1755, no less. Do you have the other half, sweetie? Volume two?'

Fidelia shook her head and pouted. Tears welled and she blinked to stem their travel. The last time she had seen Volume Two had been in the modest cabin aboard the *SS Great Britain,* on that awful night with all the screaming. Father had been studying it while he kept vigil by Mother's bed. Mother had been in fits of panting and wailing and Father had beckoned a steward to take Fidelia up on deck. He had put the first volume into a cloth pillow cover and instructed Fidelia to use it for comfort. She could see his face now. He had put his finger to his lips and touched her on the cheek with it. Though he had been agitated earlier, he was calm now, but with fear in his eyes that she had never seen before. She'd gone up on deck with the steward, the dictionary clutched tightly, heavy in her arms.

She never saw Father or Mother again.

Billings ran his hands lightly over the cover. 'This was, I believe, the first ever true dictionary of the English language to be printed. Certainly the first of any note. A few trifles, long out of print, came before. But Mr Johnson's work, what can I say? Such a revelation. I have not had the pleasure of seeing one, in the flesh so to speak, before. Those of Mr Webster's 1864 unabridged editions, which we sold out of on opening day, were not nearly so splendid as this.' Billings opened the book and read the title page out loud.

A

DICTIONARY

OF THE

ENGLISH LANGUAGE

IN WHICH

THE WORDS ARE DEDUCED FROM THEIR ORIGINALS,

AND

ILLUSTRATED IN THEIR DIFFERENT SIGNIFICATIONS

BY

EXAMPLES FROM THE BEST WRITERS.

TO WHICH ARE PREFIXED,

A HISTORY OF THE LANGUAGE,

AND AN ENGLISH GRAMMAR.

BY SAMUEL JOHNSON, A.M.

IN TWO VOLUMES

VOL 1

'I see that the words English Language and Samuel Johnson's name, are printed in red,' Billings said.

Jasper noted that Fidelia had been mouthing the words as Billings spoke them. She knew them by heart. The men eyed each other; a tacit acknowledgement that they were in the presence of a clever child.

Jasper suspected in that instant, that his game was up. His suspicion was confirmed when Billings commented, 'I wonder if Miss Fidelia might know what *lagotic* means. Or *quagswag*.' He winked at Jasper.

Fidelia grinned. Said nothing. But her silence said it all.

'I suspected as much, Godwin. It would seem that you work as a team.'

Jasper's eyes widened. He braced for the backlash, the admonition he deserved from Billings. He half expected to be shown the door in no polite terms and he would have understood entirely.

It didn't happen. Instead, Billings was looking at the child with the same expression of awe and fatherly admiration that *he* had felt on first sight.

'Yes, I guess you could say that, sir.'

Billings massaged his chin. Ran his fingers through his beard. Squinted his left eye in thoughtfulness. 'Your father. Where is he?'

Fidelia pouted. Shook her head.

'And your mother?'

She looked at the floor.

'Do you have any siblings, family?' Billings asked.

Again, she shook her head dejectedly.

Billings whispered to Jasper, 'Such a shame she can't speak. I could use a girl like this. She could be most helpful.' He winked again.

Jasper understood his intimation. 'Yes, such a shame. Imagine having such knowledge and not being able to share it readily, to speak of it. What a shame.'

Fidelia thought she might burst. Would it hurt if she spoke out loud? Who was Mr Bartholomew to tell her never to speak? He was not her kin. She had seen neither hide nor hair of him all these months. Perhaps it was all right to speak provided she didn't disclose anything about the voyage. Was that what Bartholomew meant? Not that she shouldn't speak at all. Besides, these men, she felt, were *worth* speaking to. It appeared they had her interests at heart. They were the first people in Melbourne who might be worth speaking to. And Mrs Godwin. Yes, she might speak to Mrs Godwin too. She had warmed to Mrs Godwin in the past few days. That disgruntlement had left her voice, replaced by a more motherly and tender resonance.

'You know, Godwin,' Billings said, 'I would think a girl like this might be able to earn board and lodging if she were to make herself useful. That is unless she is already gainfully accommodated.'

'Hmm. I see what you're getting at, sir.'

Fidelia imagined more blistering floor scrubbing, clothes washing, insufferable kitchen chores. She wasn't born for that. Servants were born for that. Servants like Florence and Effie.

She was born to be educated, erudite. Mistress of her own destiny. Woman of the world. A teacher maybe, an author, an academic. A *toutfleur* – French for "all flower" – her own word for a girl who blossomed in all possible ways and for whom nothing was beyond her grasp.

No. Fidelia Patience Knight would be nobody's servant. Pleasant Fidelius Knight would never have let that happen. Jessamine Mary Knight would not have countenanced such shame for her only surviving daughter. And until now, Fidelia had been certain that Jasper Godwin would not let that happen. Would he?

On the other hand, being a servant might be preferable to going to prison. An hour ago she was sure that that was where she was headed. To prison with the vagrants, vagabonds and villains. She had not been born to such ignominy. But was being a servant any less ignoble? Perhaps not *as* shameful, as one could be lowly without having criminal intent.

'Tell me Godwin, your wife. Does she read?'

'No, sir. She cannot.'

'Nor mine. She's always asking me to teach her, but I haven't the time. Nor do I countenance the likelihood that I have the patience. My thought was that if such a girl, who could evidently read well, were able to speak, she might be of a mind to teach other, clearly less well-educated people to read.'

'Hmm,' Jasper replied. 'A sterling idea, sir. But alas, it would be troublesome, I feel.'

'Yes, yes. Troublesome, as you say.'

The two men stared at Fidelia. Waited. Raised their eyebrows. Shrugged at each other.

K

Katarina Kleptomaniac Keenly Kept Kickshaws
for her Knick-Knackertory,
To the Kippage and Ken of Keepers at
Billings Better Bookstore and Brasserie (with collectibles)
Did she Knowingly? She did indeed!

Fidelia could contain herself no longer. She cleared her throat.

'My name is Fidelia Patience Knight. I am ten years old. I came here from London with my parents, Pleasant Fidelius Knight and Jessamine Mary Knight aboard the *SS Great Britain* last August. When we arrived here my parents were gone. I have not seen them since. My father was to take up a position here in Melbourne. My mother was with child. I had a brother, Ninian, and sister, Permelia. They're dead. They died from the consumption back in England. I think Father and Mother must be dead too. Else why would I be alone? I was at the orphan asylum until I ran away. I should never have been there. I worked for a family around the corner for a time but they were horrible so I ran away again and then I stayed at night in Cole's bookstore and then I discovered the library and the museum and then I worked for Mr Darling in King Street and then I got ill and then I met you, Mr Godwin, and Mrs Godwin and…quagswag means to shake to and fro, lagotic is to have ears like a hare. Mr Bartholomew had lagotic ears.' She hardly drew breath.

She had the voice of an angel. Jasper's eyes widened in wonderment as he stared at her then softened to a smile before his mouth followed suit. He felt a lump in his throat – a sensation he had never experienced before. He couldn't find the words to speak, nor the voice to do so. He put out his hands to her. As she placed her delicate hand into his, he knew that this was the start of something significant. Something that would change his life.

'Goodness girl. I knew you had it in you to speak. And once you've started, well...yet you have been silent as a mouse this past week.'

Fidelia daren't tell him that mice weren't in fact silent. 'It was Mr Bartholomew from the ship who told me not to speak.'

Jasper and Billings looked at each other. 'Why would he say that to you?' Jasper said.

'He told me to forget about Mother and Father. That I would never see them again. That I shouldn't say a word.'

'And you took him literally?' Billings said.

'Have you not said a word since?' Jasper asked.

She shook her head. 'Nobody worth talking to and I didn't want to speak of such awful things.' She hesitated. 'Until now.'

Billings crouched, hands on knees, hazel eyes glistening, and whispered, 'How would you like to work for me? If your friend Godwin here, and his good wife, are willing to house you, I would have you teach my wife to read. And possibly help around the store here, if you like. You could read anything you want.'

Fidelia could not believe her ears. 'Yes, sir, I...' She was lost for words. She had often thought she would become a teacher. She didn't know she would do it when she was ten.

'Just found your voice and now you can't speak again?' Billings cajoled. 'Perhaps you might teach Mrs Godwin also. If she were of a mind to learn. Everybody should be able to read, else I'd have no customers.'

'I know she could teach me a thing or two,' Jasper confessed.

'I suspect me also. You like to read?'

'I do. That is why I spent my nights at Cole's. I have read many of his books; and dictionaries.'

'But how did that come about? Surely Mr Cole was not privy to this.'

Fidelia explained about the nights that Cole – although she didn't know it was him at the time – entertained her while he was compiling his advertisement and how she was convinced she could do better.

'And indeed you did,' Billings said.

Jasper furrowed his brow. 'Why then, did you not make yourself known to Mr Cole? Why to me?'

'Because you appeared in such a quandary. And because of your eyes. And because I thought…' Fidelia bit her tongue.

'And, you thought?' Billings said.

'Because, pardon me for saying so, but because I thought you were being mean to Jasper, ah, Mr Godwin.'

'Ah. You thought so, did you?

Fidelia wished she could take back her words, now that she could see Billings was not the ogre she had initially surmised.

Billings brushed off the remark. 'You like to read then. What do you like to read? We have plenty of children's books here. Fairy stories and such.'

Fidelia screwed up her nose. 'Do you have *Wuthering Heights*? I was reading it at the library but I have not finished it.'

'Why my dear, I believe we do,' Billings said, 'and many more great works besides. We have Austen, Dickens, Charlotte Brontë, Swift, Disraeli…'

'Disraeli? You mean Prime Minister Disraeli?'

'Yes, dear. One and the same. Also a prolific author, although possibly not to your taste. And Shakespeare; we have most of Shakespeare's works. Now *they* would be requisite reading for a word-hungry girl.'

'Yes, Shakespeare.' Mother loved Shakespeare. She had been particularly taken with *King Lear*. She had, one night in the depths of winter, recounted the fateful story of the waning king and his three daughters, Goneril, Regan and Cordelia. Permelia was mortally ill and fell asleep to the lulling timbre of Mother's voice. Father sat, engaged at Mother's re-creation of the story, a look of veneration about him.

Fidelia couldn't remember too much of the story, except for

the lingering impression that Goneril and Regan should not have been trusted. But she remembered her mother's words.

'Be true to yourself and to others always, Fidelia. *Be Cordelia.*'

It might be nice to read the story for herself, in Shakespeare's *own* words. *Macbeth* and *Hamlet* and *Romeo and Juliet* and *Othello* would be nice too. Mother had spoken of them also. All tragedies. Was Shakespeare such a sad soul?

The walk to Gisborne-street wasn't long, but progress was slow. Carrying Samuel Johnson for any distance was, as always, a laborious affair. Jasper had directed her to go the top of Bourke-street and cross over Spring-street to the Parliament House side. She could cut across the garden beside the government building and she wouldn't be able to miss the Government Printer's office, right there opposite, across Gisborne-street.

John Ferres's name would be there, perhaps on a brass plate, on the building's façade. Billings had kindly offered to pay whatever the book-binders' cost might be to restore Samuel Johnson to his original state.

Fidelia had no trouble finding the building. Its three storeys loomed above her. She pushed open the heavy door and entered a vestibule, not nearly as impressive as that of Parliament House from what she had seen when she had peeked in the door one day. It looked like an important place.

She explained to a gentleman at a desk in the foyer what she wanted and showed Samuel Johnson to him. He took her through to a large room. She could barely hear him speak over the clatter and thumping of printing presses. To one side lay a pile of two-inch thick books, all with red covers.

'That's *Hansard,*' he shouted as he pointed to them. Fidelia didn't understand him. She presumed *Hansard* to be an author, perhaps a novelist or poet. Beyond them on another table, a pile of thinner books with green bindings. They passed a printing machine at which a lad of twelve or thirteen was gathering small tickets and forming them into a pile to wrap in brown paper, his fingertips black with ink.

'Train tickets,' the man explained.

It was a fascinating place. Fidelia was entranced by the rhythm of the machines, though they drowned out all thought. She almost wanted to dance. A highland fling or a sailors' jig.

They passed through the printing room into a smaller room where several people, mostly young boys, were busy at tables. Deeply engrossed in their work, nobody looked up.

'The bindery. I'll see if anyone is free to help you.'

'Thank you, sir.' What a place this was. Earthy smells of leather and hide glue. Racks of paper, odd-looking tools, presses and guillotines. She wished she could stay all day to watch how these people turned sheafs of paper into proper bound books. She cast her eye over the top page of a stack on the table before her. At the top of the page numbered 1826, the heading said *Floating of the new loan* with the word ASSEMBLY in brackets in the middle. This must indeed be a large book, to have that many pages. In the right column she read...

NUISANCE IN FAWKNER PARK.

Mr. DIXON asked the Attorney-General if he would carry out the promise which he made last week, and take immediate steps to secure the abatement of the nuisance in Fawkner-park? He had been informed that the City Corporation continued to deposit night-soil at that place, to the great annoyance of the inhabitants in the neighbourhood.

Mr. KERFERD observed that, immediately after the honourable member for St. Kilda (Mr. Smith) called his attention to

She didn't know where Fawkner-park was, nor what an Attorney-General was, though it sounded prestigious, but she did know what night-soil was and how noxious it could be. A nuisance indeed. Enough to make one shnerkel. This, she concluded, must be a book of newspaper stories, but the date at the top of the page was October 27. Old news. Hopefully the smell in Fawknerpark was abated by now.

Something in this room was almost as smelly. Was it the hide glue? Its pungency filled her nostrils and made her feel nauseated. The sensation was not unlike that she had experienced in Billings on opening day. She hoped she wasn't going to vomit. Not here. She felt flushed and hot, like she had with the fever. Then she felt faint, a buzzing sound again welling up her neck into her ears. She could see the man walking towards her but he looked fuzzy. He was speaking but his words were garbled and she began to droop at the knees. He caught her as she swooned.

'Are you all right dear? You look pale as Banquo's ghost.'

'Some water?'

'Yes, of course,' the man said, 'Joshua, fetch a cup of water. There's a good lad.'

The faint feeling passed quickly. She now felt flushed with embarrassment, rather than fever. She lay against the man's knee, his hands supporting her back. She looked up as two boys approached, one with a cup in his hand. He offered it to her. The second lad looked strangely familiar. She sipped the water and was almost immediately restored.

'I've had the scarlet fever. I thought I was better.'

'Are you right to get back to your feet?' the man asked.

She nodded and stood slowly. Why was that boy staring at her? Where had she seen him before? On the street, or in the library? He stared at her incessantly.

'I know you,' he said, in what Fidelia thought a strange accent, 'you were on the *Great Britain*. You gave me water. When I heard you say "some water" now, I 'membered your voice.'

The boy with the sheep dags hair. The stowaway. *Stowaway Sam*. Mother had berated her for giving him water. A jackal, she had said. He did not look like such a lowly, devious creature now that he was groomed and neatly attired.

'Stowaway Sam! I never thought to ever see you again.'

'Nor I you. But I've never forgot your kindness when I was

thirsty and hungry.' He smiled. Dimples puckered his cheeks. His eyes laughed.

She held out her hand and he shook it. 'I am Fidelia Knight. Pleased to meet you.'

'And you. My name isn't Sam, though they called me that aboard the ship. It's Secret.'

'Why is it secret? Do you not want anybody to know?'

'No, it's *Secret*. My name is Secret Livingston Jenkins. And I come from Lilliput.'

Fidelia thought Secret a silly name but she was too polite to say it. Perhaps his parents named him that because they wanted nobody to know about him. But it should be expected that a Lilliputian would have a funny name. She had never before met a person from Lilliput. It was somewhere far across the sea from England. Further than Australia. Mother had told her a story, long ago, about a chap named Gulliver who had spent time there. And she had thought the place a fantasy. She was a little surprised that Secret was so tall.

'I wonder,' the man said, 'since you already know the girl, you might help repair her book. The jacket has come loose, torn here at the end paper. You will need to create a new hinge by adhering some webbing.'

Secret nodded. 'Yes sir. I will.'

'And I think you will find, young man,' the man whispered, 'that you come from Liverpool.'

Fidelia laughed and then laughed louder and more heartily when Secret protested and vehemently maintained that he did indeed 'come from Lilliput'.

Fidelia enjoyed watching Secret work. He had become proficient at his assigned tasks in a very short time. His job, he explained, was to glue the endpapers of the books and ensure that they were uniformly affixed. He showed her how the roller worked to evenly coat the glue. He could not wait until the day he might learn stitching, tipping in, casing and case-binding.

She wanted to know where he had been and what he had been

doing since arriving in Melbourne last August. She was astonished to learn that, like her, he had been at the asylum. They had been there at the same time, for three or four months, and had never seen each other. He had become ill with consumption shortly before disembarking the *Great Britain*. He had spent time in hospital upon arrival in Melbourne and had been bedridden at the asylum much of the time, seldom allowed to leave his dormitory. But three months ago, he, and Joshua had been taken up as apprentices with Mr Ferres. They were now allowed to go to work each day and return to Emerald Hill for dinner, bed and breakfast. It was not too unpleasant there.

He and Joshua slept side by side in the dormitory now and sat shoulder to shoulder at mealtime. They talked about their day at work.

Their work was much more engrossing than that done by the boys going to Stewart's jam factory in West Melbourne or at the meat market or coach builders. Both were now twelve, although, he confided, they had lied and told Mr Exon that they were fourteen, so that they might be chosen for a position sooner than otherwise. They were well aware that in another three years, when they turned seventeen (fifteen really) they would have to find their own lodgings. Pay their way. Become, to all intents and purposes, young men.

Secret told her also that her disappearance had been the talk of the asylum for the past months. Some speculated that she had been stolen by men who had evil intent in store for little girls; others presumed she had run away and got lost; others still hinted that she might have met foul play and been disposed of in some gruesome way.

Fidelia laughed at the presumptions and recounted to Secret some of her experiences at the orphanage. Though not an entirely unpleasant place, she said, the other children were horrid to her. More than once they tried to rob her of Samuel Johnson – her only possession by which to remember Father and Mother. Her only possession at all. Her treasure. The children had taunted her so. Called her a snob for reading beyond her tender age. Such an awful, unimaginative word, snob. And all the worse when spat with venom. Why not *parvenu*? They were all buffleheads.

Had she been of a mind to speak, she would have found it quite impossible to converse with those her age or younger in their simple childspeak, as she called it; that senseless jibber-jabber. So she didn't speak at all. Besides, she had been instructed not to.

'I didn't belong there and I slipped silent as a stalking cat through the fence a few weeks ago. I don't know why it was so easy for me to escape, or why nobody seemed to have missed me.'

She told Secret that she refused to believe she was an orphan; that perhaps the word had another meaning. Samuel Johnson was no help: his listings in her volume finished at 'K'.

Marcus, one of the boys at the asylum, had told her it mightn't mean that her parents were dead. Some of the children's parents, he'd said, weren't *actually* dead. Some were too poor to care for them. Some just didn't care *about* them. And some of the children were bastards.

She was not sure which category she fitted into, though she knew it was not the last. He was talking blather, blobberlip that he was.

Fidelia promised to tell Secret more about her adventures since leaving the asylum some other time. For now, she wanted him to concentrate on her repair and not risk being reprimanded for absconding from his work through idle chatter.

'What is this book?' Fidelia pointed to the volume beside them.

'Oh that. That's Hansard.' Secret, like the older man, said it as though it should be abundantly obvious. She looked at him querulously. 'It's the parelmenty dates. You know, all that stuff they talk about next door. Them guvment types. I do the covers on them.'

'It's a big book. All those pages. Is this a whole year?'

'Nup, just about three months. See here?' He turned to the front page. 'Think it says the date there.'

Fidelia read the title page out loud.

'**Parliamentary Debates, Session 1874. Legislative Council** and Legislative Assembly. Volume twenty. Comprising the period from October 27 to December 24.'

''S'at what it says?'

'Yes. You can't read it?'

'Nup. Some. Only a bit.'

'You want to be a book-binder and you cannot read?'

'Don't need to read to…'

'But wouldn't you *like* to be able to read them? Or any book, for that matter?'

'Course. But I dun never learned.'

'Would you like to? I can teach you.'

'But you're just a little girl.'

'Yes. But I am a little girl who can read.'

L

Lionel Lagotic Loved Listening to Lyrical Librettos and Learning Lore,
And Laughing Loquaciously in the Library at
Billings Better Bookstore and Brasserie (with Lending Library)
Did he Longingly? He did indeed!

This fine Saturday, puffy clouds dotted the sky like sheep scattered in a blue field. But Secret and Joshua were not interested in clouds today. Nor were they interested in the goings on as they walked apace east along Dorcas-street to St. Kilda Road. They could barely control their excitement at what the day might bring as they then walked towards town, passing the army barracks and crossing the Yarra River over Princes Bridge. The walk was so familiar now that they could almost pace the route blindfolded.

The only difference today was that they were not headed to the government printer, but to Billings Better Bookstore and Brasserie for their first lesson with the strange and captivating girl they had met two days ago. Mr Exon had given them leave from the asylum for the reading class, on the understanding that it was Mr Billings himself who would be teaching them. Fidelia had given them strict instructions not to mention her name, nor her whereabouts to Mr or Mrs Exon, or anybody else at the asylum.

Myrtle wiped her hands on her apron, took it off and hung it on the hook on the back of the kitchen door. She wanted to be neat and tidy for her first day of school.

It was a big day for her. Her first ever reading lesson. Fancy that such a young child could teach her to read. She was dubious, but her dear Jasper had insisted that Fidelia was a progedy – that was what he'd called her – a progedy, and that if she, at ten years of age could read, then anybody could learn to read. The very thought of it had Myrtle all a-flutter. Imagine how different her life might be if she could entertain herself, once in a while, by reading – a book perhaps. And there was talk that writing might be in the offing too.

'Goodness me,' she said out loud, 'I'm in peril of gettin' educated. Who'd ever 'ave thought?'

She glanced at the mantle clock. It was, fortunately, the one thing she had learned to read, thanks to her dear Jasper. Ten minutes to nine. She ran her hands down her dress to smooth the folds, tucked some errant curls behind her ears and secured her favourite straw hat with a butterfly-shaped hat pin. She was ready to take on the world.

Jasper appeared through the back door with a scuttle of coal. 'Are you ready then, my dear? It is indeed a lucky day.' He set the scuttle beside the stove, wiped his hands on a cloth and crooked his arm. 'Shall I escort you to school?'

Madeleine stood poised and graceful in front of the mirror. She too felt a ripple of excitement at the prospect of a new beginning. A first step towards erudition. She was no less excited than a five-year-old preparing for her first day of school. She did not, however, know what to make of having a ten-year-old teacher. How could a child of such tender years know enough about anything to presume to teach those three or four times her age? But Madeleine was open-minded about most things. Did open-mindedness come from a lack of knowledge or a breadth of knowledge? She didn't know.

But if her Lucas thought that she could learn from a ten-year-old, who was she to argue the point? Besides, arguing with Lucas was a mere matter of beguiling him with her smile and agreeing, in the knowledge that to disagree was futile. Lucas always knew what was best for her and there had never been an occasion when she thought him wrong or felt the need to protest.

But if she were better educated, and if she simply *knew* more about the things a woman should know about, she might find cause to voice her opinion once in a while. Now *that* was an exciting prospect!

She did, however, feel a flutter in her stomach; not unlike that of her first outing with the handsome young man, Lucas Billings, some nineteen years ago. She had no notion of what to expect, though he had promptly calmed her timidity with his temperate style and impeccable manners. In half an hour she knew she wanted to be his for life. She was seldom wrong and not prone to rash judgement. And he had proved himself a paragon of decency – a model husband. She was overcome with joy at Lucas's suggestion that she learn to read and wondered therefore, why she should now feel so apprehensive .

'What is to fear? Nothing comes from not trying,' she said to herself out loud. She nodded at herself in the mirror. She too was ready to take on the world.

Billings had provided a space in the back room of the store and set up a table and chairs. He had even rustled up a blackboard and chalk to complete the makeshift classroom. Fidelia had claimed some of the paper used by the sign-writer for the window-display banner and some crayons provided by Billings to create her own banner of the alphabet, which she had pegged to a string fastened across the wall.

Here they sat: two women in their thirties and two boys of twelve, equally expectant. Equally nervous. Equally attentive. And before them, dressed in a new pinafore Myrtle had sewn for her from a yard of rose cotton, stood Fidelia – the teacher.

Myrtle Godwin and Madeleine Billings had but a rudimentary knowledge of the alphabet. To Secret and Joshua, it might well have been hieroglyphics. Though they had had the opportunity to learn at the asylum, they had never applied themselves to the classroom environment, each thinking he was too old to learn with the youngsters.

Fidelia quickly saw that it would take more than a few Saturdays to teach these boys and women to read. It would depend on how avidly they applied themselves to the task. The fact that they were here at all, however, made manifest their passion. One had to *want* to learn, to learn. Just as one had to want to live, to live. But passion and aptitude were two different things. Some people couldn't be taught, no matter how persistent the teacher. And really, what did she know about teaching? Yes, she knew how to read and write, but that did not necessarily give her the skills to share this knowledge with others. How to approach this?

The answer was clear. The same way that Father had taught *her*. A rhythm and a rhyme always helped the memory. Samuel Johnson supplied the words, Fidelia Knight supplied the rhyme.

Abacke is to go backwards,
an Abactor steals flocks of cows,
an Abacus counts to a thousand and more,
Abaft is opposed to bows,
Abaisance is to take a bow,
Abalienate by law to give,
Abandon to alas forsake,
Abannition to banish though let live.

But these words were much too difficult for beginners. She would have to start with simple words that her students could identify with and understand. Bat, cat, rat, mat, pat, scat. After all, one could scat a rat or bat, or pat a cat on a mat. How simple was that?

It was evident that one could not learn to read in the absence of learning to write. The latter naturally following the former. The two went hand in hand. Like scones and jam. Like autumn and falling leaves. Billings had placed the emphasis on reading, but before the first hour was past, Fidelia had begged him to furnish her students with paper, ink and writing implements.

Her pupils needed to learn the alphabet and what better way than to have them form the letters themselves. It would aid in the memory.

Myrtle and Madeleine proved to be neat of hand, forming almost perfect calligraphic alphabets in short order. A product of their meticulous eyes for detail. Dexterity of fingers and keenness of eyes, garnered from years of plying embroidery and tapestry needles, lent the formation of letters on paper a *petit-point* uniformity. For the boys, learning how to hold the steel-nibbed pens and load the correct amount of ink was a messy and torturous affair. Their hands were all thumbs; their pages smudged by forearms and elbows. Their fingers were stained black. Secret's right cheek was smeared with ink.

He reminded Fidelia of her brother. Ninian had been no less clumsy when Father had tried to teach him to write. He could not master holding the nib pen; his movement across the page clumsy and laboured. Fidelia had watched the awkwardness of it for days before coming up with a preposterous solution. She had placed the pen in his left hand. Father had not thought of that. Mother was mortified. Unnatural, she said. Unacceptable. The work of the devil. Ninian had cried in frustration more than once. Yet in Mother's absence, when Fidelia helped Permelia and Ninian with their writing, he penned beautifully; his letters rounded and consistent – with his left hand.

Fidelia watched how the boys looked up at her letters and down at their pages to copy. The eagerness in their eyes reflected her own hunger for knowledge. She bade them echo her pronunciations of the letters as they went. She showed them how to put the letters together to spell their own names.

She soon realised the root of their awkwardness. They were sitting too close; as though they were joined at the hip.

'Move apart, lads,' she instructed. 'You need elbow room to write.'

The boys reluctantly shuffled their seats further apart.

Secret wrote "Secret Livingston Jenkins" so large it took up three and a half lines. Fidelia showed him how to place a hyphen at the end of 'Living' to indicate the word was not complete and was to be continued on the next line. Secret thought that extraordinary.

Joshua Benedict Wright followed suit, inserting a hyphen after 'Bene'. He was insistent, however, that as far as he knew, Wright did *not* begin with 'W'. Fidelia explained to him where the name originated – that probably in his ancestry was a man who made windmills or water wheels or ships. Joshua shrugged. He knew barely anything about his parents, he told her, and nothing at all about his grandparents or their forebears, other than the likelihood that they came from England.

Nevertheless, Fidelia said, it was appropriate that their names should be the first words they learned to write. 'It doesn't matter so much who you are, it matters more that you know what your name looks like. It is your identity after all. Being able to write your name precludes you from being anonymous.'

Madeleine had seen her name written, but only by another hand. To write it for herself was a joyous achievement.

'It is astonishing, Miss Knight,' Secret commented, 'that so many words can be made with just twenty-six letters. That isn't even three times the number of my fingers.'

'Indeed Secret. And I'm pleased that you can count. You might be interested to know that prior to Samuel Johnson's time, 'I' was considered as both vowel and consonant but since the two differed in form as well as sound, 'J' became the consonant form. Samuel Johnson deemed that they should be more properly accounted as two letters, yet they appear in his dictionary under the same entry. The same applied to 'U' and 'V'.

'Therefore, some 200 years ago, our alphabet had only twenty-four letters. And not long before that, W was not to be found in the alphabets of the learned languages. And even though we now know many 'W' words, Samuel Johnson ascribed a definition to fewer than one hundred.'

Secret shook his head in disbelief. 'It is confoundering – is that the right word? It will take so long to learn all them words, when even now I carn't read.'

'Confounding is the word. Do not be daunted by the task, Secret. I thought I had learned all the words ever coined, at least all those from A to K, from Samuel Johnson. But new ones are being invented all the time and we borrow words from other languages; from French, German, Italian – even Chinese. Every new thing created must have a noun to name it and an adjective to describe it, else nobody would know what was what. And so our language can be infinite. You will never stop learning new words. And neither, I hope, will I. And if no word exists where one should be, I will coin my own.' Fidelia nodded her particular satisfied nod.

Now Joshua was apprehensive. 'More words will be made?'

'Yes. Our language is evolving – growing and changing all the time. Dare I say my dear Samuel Johnson is already well out of date?' She tapped her fingers on Samuel Johnson's cover and picked up the volume beside it.

'We now have Mr Webster's unabridged edition, which is much more expansive. But many words are already missing from this. My father told me, before we left London, that the Oxford University is planning a comprehensive lexicon of the English language.'

'But who makes up all these new words and 'ow can we ever 'ope to keep up with 'em all?' Myrtle asked. She was astonished that this slip of a girl, who a month ago had been silent and ailing, seemed infinitely clever and fascinating. A child genius. Her own life might have been different had she learned to read. She might have thought to be a teacher, a secretary, a poet, or at least gainfully employed in her own right and not totally reliant on her husband. It was not too late, but it was a formidable prospect. What joy it might bring to *read* books – not merely dust them. To open the pages and gorge oneself on their words. Take oneself to times and places unknown, unseen. Real and fantastic.

'Almost anyone can make up new words. Writers, politicians, industrialists, inventors. Often the thing comes before the word for it. Even I have made up my own words, where none exists to suit my purpose, although Mr Johnson, Mr Webster and those men at Oxford may never hear of them. You just have to keep learning, Mrs Godwin. Keep learning.'

'No, girl, I have to *start* learning. I should never expect to know as much as you, despite having twenty-five years on top of your ten. That's some catchin' up to do.'

If Myrtle were daunted, Madeleine looked blank as the fresh sheet of paper before her. As though her brain would never absorb a thing. A marble statue. Lapidescent, Fidelia mused. Petrified by a Medusan stare.

'Oh Mrs Billings, you look ever so pale. Are you ill? Should I fetch your husband?' Fidelia asked.

'No, dear. On the contrary. I'm all right. Quite all right.' Madeleine's face lit up. 'In fact, as of this instant, I feel there is a purpose to life. I must seek out every opportunity to learn. Like you, I want to learn all there is to know about *everything*. I want to read every book on the shelves out there.'

'You've had an epiphany, I would say – a moment of sudden and great realisation. Then first you must learn to read and write. We should get on with this, lickety-split.'

'Lickety-split?' Madeleine's laugh was echoed by Secret and Joshua. 'I would come every day, dear, if I could.'

'Yes, lickety-split. It's a phrase my mother used to hurry my siblings and me if we were tardy. And why could you not come every day Mrs Billings? If Mr Billings were to permit it.'

'I too, would come every day. Every day but Sunday,' Myrtle said.

'And I, if I had not to work. And you, Joshua,' Secret said.

'Why not after work, in the evening, boys?' Fidelia asked.

'But Mrs Exon wouldn't let us. We must be back at Emerald Hill by five-thirty lest we miss supper. And lamps out is at seven o'clock.' Joshua shook his head dejectedly.

Madeleine tousled Joshua's head with her gloved hand. 'Perhaps child, we might do something about that. And perhaps, at your tender age, you might not have to work for a living.'

Joshua looked at her quizzically and then at Secret, who donned an impish expression and shrugged.

M

Minerva Meretricious Mafficked Merrily and Magniloquently
with a Mannequin, While Manipulating Magnificent Manchester at
Billings Better Bookstore and Brasserie (with Manchester)
Did she Meaningfully? She did indeed!

Lucas Billings drummed his fingers on his knee as he waited in the anteroom off the foyer of the Melbourne Orphan Asylum. A young girl named Lucy had instructed him to sit while she trundled off to find Mr Edwin Exon, the superintendent.

'Might take a while, given I do not know where he is, could be upstairs or down, or over at the wards, and you have come with no appointment,' she had said.

Billings crinkled his nose at the smell of turpentine. Two girls of eleven or twelve were scrubbing the floor in the hallway. The orphanage was an industrious place. He could tell from the clangs of hammering, alternating between metal on wood from the carpentry shop and metal on tacks from the shoe-making room. The echoes of children fulfilling their everyday duties permeated the building as if coming from the walls themselves. The children sounded happy, cheerful even, as they learned the trades to become useful members of society.

Billings cringed at the recollection of his own childhood. A Spartan, cold, unfriendly existence in an austere orphanage in London, where a ladle of gruel or oily soup and, if luck had it, a stale hunk of bread, was all one could look forward to. Mostly eaten in silence for fear of a beating. Laughter frowned upon by the administrators. Hope stripped away with each passing day.

Not unlike the orphanage depicted by Dickens in *Oliver Twist*; or *The Parish Boy's Progress*. It was no surprise that he now enjoyed his suppers so much. His waistline was testament to that.

He wondered whether mealtime here at Emerald Hill was the highlight of the day for these lean, stringy children; the only thing that drove their aspirations from one laborious day to the next. But this place, at least, seemed positive. Lucy's smile had been genuine, not fabricated to please. It was not such a bad place for Secret and Joshua to be.

Yet it could not be deemed a home with all that that entailed. Billings had not hesitated at Madeleine's suggestion to offer a home to the boys, in whatever capacity was deemed appropriate by the orphanage. Despite their rudimentary schooling here, it was evident their potential to learn was hindered by the sheer number of children in the class. Perhaps they had started too late. Too much catching up to do, when younger children were already outdoing them at mathematics and literacy. They needed a tutor who could give them one-on-one attention.

In short, they needed Fidelia.

Such a child Billings had never seen. The change he had seen in Madeleine after one afternoon under the girl's tutelage was a transformation of spirit. A rosebud unfolding or a week-old kitten opening its eyes. Jasper had made a similar observation about his Myrtle. Billings hoped the two women might become friends, as Madeleine was prone to shyness. A companion of similar age and near-equal standing would do her the world of good, and give her a reason to leave the house for occasions other than church on Sundays. He had hoped that opening the bookstore might draw her from her seclusion, but she had deemed it inappropriate to bide time in a bookstore when she couldn't read.

Billings was quietly pleased at the opening month's trade of his store. He had aspired to emulate or outdo Cole. If the press of daily customers was a criterion on which to judge success then that alone, if not the copious takings of the till, surpassed his wildest imaginings. But if he were honest with himself, he would have to admit that much of that success had been due to the girl and to her special relationship with Godwin. Even Godwin appeared to have found his mettle since the arrival of this mysterious girl, who came from nowhere but was surely going somewhere.

Though he had met Myrtle but twice, he had likewise noticed the change in her demeanour after her first session with Fidelia. The girl had turned on lamps in Myrtle's eyes and her look of wonderment had not escaped Billings' notice.

'Edwin Exon at your service sir.' The pleasant-faced man with cropped beard and round glasses held out his hand in greeting. 'How might I be of assistance?'

Billings exchanged pleasantries and commented on the orderliness of the establishment.

'Ah yes, we run a tight ship here sir,' Exon said jovially, 'which isn't to say that we do not have our share of rapscallions and ne'er-do-wells. The laws of probability would suggest that, among the more than 300 children here, a small percentage might fall into the scoundrel category, despite our best efforts. But on the whole, these are God's good children and our aim is to maintain their virtue. In fact, shortly we will be relocating our whole institution. Those councilmen have their eyes on this site for the purposes of a new town hall.'

'Goodness. And yet this building looks like it would serve the purpose well for many years to come.'

'Why yes, that is true. The administrators are looking at land in Brighton. More befitting the purpose they say. But, you did not, I'm sure, come here to listen to my discourse on the vagaries of those in power. I could have your ear all afternoon if you were to indulge me.'

'You have two young boys resident here, Secret Jenkins and Joshua—'

'Yes, Joshua Wright. I know the lads. They spend a lot of time together; they have a brotherly bond. Good boys, they are. What of them?'

'I enquire as to whether they might be fostered to us, perhaps with a view to adoption.'

Exon raised his eyebrows. 'You are married sir, I take it? And of means?'

'I am a shopkeeper. I have not long ago opened my own establishment specialising in books and general merchandise in Bourke-street. You must come and visit.'

'Indeed I will. I am a poet, with a minor following, I might say, with several volumes now published. If you would allow, I should take the opportunity to visit and show them to you.'

'I would be delighted.'

Exon nodded. 'You say that you and your wife would take on the boys; provide lodgings and victuals?'

'Indeed. We have no children of our own, much to my wife's chagrin. We did have a son, dear Wallace, but alas he succumbed to the typhoid some years back.'

'I too, and my dear wife Frances, have borne the bereavement of a child. Two in fact. Both girls. Fifteen years ago now, bless their souls. An epidemic, not long after we took the helm here,' Exon said. 'Thus I am father, and she mother, to all these young souls. They are our commitment and our salvation. Blessed by God, we are.'

'It is a sterling thing you do. But if I could relieve your establishment of these two boys, it would allow for another needy child to receive your grace. They can maintain their positions at the Government Printer and continue with private tutoring at my premises.'

'Very good. It shall be done,' Exon said.

Billings, however, was not finished. 'There is another matter, good man, of a young girl. Miss Fidelia Knight...'

Exon furrowed his brow in thought. 'Ah. Yes, the mute child. Always carried a large book. We searched for her, day after day. You know of her?' Exon gave Billings no chance to respond. 'Whatever happened to her? It was as though she vanished into the morning mist.'

'She is well, sir. In the care of my employee and his wife. And neither mute, nor dumb, if you understand my meaning. In fact, she will be the boys' tutor in reading and writing.'

'Goodness. But she is only, what, nine years old?'

'Ten now, and a very clever ten. But I wanted to know what you knew of her history – before she arrived here.'

'For that, I might have to trouble my wife Frances for an answer. She was the one who took the girl when she first arrived.'

Madeleine was dressing for a special occasion. She had instructed Cynthia, the cook, to prepare the finest meal possible. She would be entertaining tonight: welcoming two children into her permanent embrace and a third for the evening repast. Fancy having children at the dining table. It would be a first. Young Wallace had never arrived at an age at which he could share meals at the table.

For this dinner, she would don her favourite turquoise chintz dress. The one she kept for special occasions and in which she never failed to garner unbridled flattery from her husband.

She was happy beyond words. In two or three days, all her desires had come to fruition. She was on the brink of a new life. Fulfilling and meaningful. Exciting and inspiring. And with the addition of children.

She wished Penelope was here to cajole her hair into order, but her maid had pleaded for the night off to attend a pantomime at the *Theatre Royal*. It had been planned long before Madeleine's last-minute dinner.

Madeleine could not wait for the boys to arrive. They were to walk from Gisborne-street after work. How was she to regard them? As a mother? As mistress of the house? As a fellow pupil? Her nerves jangled almost audibly. It was one thing to be learning alongside them, but it was another thing entirely to have them under her care. She barely knew the boys, but her instinct told her they would add a missing dimension to her life. Now that she would be, to all intents and purposes, their mother.

What did she know about being a mother? What did she *need* to know? At least the boys were no longer babies. No need to deal with flannels, no need for a wet nurse. They could speak their mind and follow directives. But she would give them all the love, the understanding, the support they needed. She would be their guiding light, their beacon of solace, their human hearth. That was what a mother should be. And she would endow them with the love that they so sorely lacked. Every child needed a mother.

The dinnertime discussion was animated. At Billings' bidding, Jasper regaled the diners with a discourse about his new-found talent for sculpting. He gesticulated as though a lump of clay was before him on the table and he was bending it to his will.

Billings was intrigued by the fact that, prior to the creation of the aardvark, Godwin had never sculpted before. Now he was embarking on an Aphrodite-esque statue of *Claudia Callipygous* – or at least the suggestion of her from a rear view – to complement his caiman for the next window display. He did not elaborate on the meaning of callipygous in front of the women. The boys were fascinated.

Fidelia occasionally interrupted to fill in some detail of the procedure that Jasper had overlooked or to describe his creative method. 'He sits like a sculpture himself a-pondering and then assails the clay with a gusto befitting a conductor leading a Beethoven symphony.'

Jasper recounted his latest visit to the library with Fidelia to scrutinise books on sculpture so that he might learn more about techniques. 'I aspire to have the talent and following of a John Bacon, or his son John Bacon Junior, whose sculptures grace St Paul's Cathedral and Westminster Abbey. Of course, their works are carved from stone or marble, while mine are made from scratch out of clay. I dream that one day, I should be so famous.'

'Oh, don't be daft.' Myrtle slapped him lightly on the leg. 'They're whales in Windermere and you're a mackerel in the Atlantic'.

'No harm in having aspirations, Myrtle,' Billings said. 'Our world is created on aspirations. Do you not agree?' Billings had raised the subject of discussion for good reason. 'I have some news for you, Godwin.'

Jasper presumed the news was about Fidelia, something gleaned from his visit to the asylum that day. He was not sure this was the appropriate time to raise such a matter, in the girl's presence. 'Yes, Mr Billings?'

'While you were away at the post office today, a gentleman of some means came by to ask what had happened to the aardvark.'

'Yes?' Jasper was intrigued.

'He would, as it happens, like to buy it for his wife. She was quite taken by it on our opening day.'

'Are you serious, sir?' Myrtle asked.

'I am. In fact the gentleman offered me fifty shillings for it.' Billings waited until the collective gasping of his dinner guests had subsided before continuing. Jasper still looked like a worm about to be snatched by a sparrow to feed its nestlings.

'I told him, of course, that I would have to consult the master artisan whose hands had modelled such a fine specimen, as to whether that was acceptable remuneration for such a unique work of art.'

Jasper could not believe his ears. Somebody wanted to buy his jolly aardvark. Who would have thought? He was still unconvinced that Billings wasn't having a lend of him.

'Not only that, Godwin, he wanted to know what else you'd made. That is, whether other pieces were available. I did, by the way, intimate that sixty shillings might be a more appropriate offer.'

Sixty shillings? Jasper was dumbstruck. 'Why, that's three pounds. I cannot believe it. I have never seen three pounds in my hand. But I'm a novice, as you know, sir. And the Lord knows that my dear Myrtle is not at all happy with my using the kitchen table for my sculpting. She-'

'You can be sure about that,' Myrtle interrupted. 'Such a messy business it is.'

'To this point, sir, I have the caiman and my lady away being fired for our display of next fortnight. Beyond that...it is, of course, quite hard to find the time to work, given that I have just the evenings, and that by lamplight.'

'Hmm.' Billings ran his fingers through his beard and narrowed his eyes in thought. All eyes were on him, spellbound.

'I have a proposition for you then, Godwin. What say we set up a space in the back of the store and I supply you with clay? You can work on your sculptures at any time that you're not needed on the floor, and we can offer your works for sale. That may also appease Myrtle.'

Fidelia clapped her hands in glee. Jasper covered his gaping mouth with his hand.

Billings continued. 'We can come to some mutual agreement about the proceeds of any sales.' He nodded in satisfaction at his own wisdom and generosity. 'What do you say?'

Jasper put one hand to his chest and touched Myrtle's hand with the other. 'I think I would say absolutely, and whole-heartedly and resoundingly, yes. And thank you, of course. Thank you.'

'I'll arrange it.' Billings waved his hand dismissively; his means of ending the discussion. 'Now come on boys, eat up your peas. And you, Miss Fidelia. Do not let those sprouts perturb you so.'

Jasper was still reeling from the evening as he pulled the covers up to his chin. It had been a wonderful meal and the children had tucked in with great relish. Myrtle was asleep already. More wine than she had ever drunk at one time had guaranteed her drowsiness. Fidelia had bedded down in the adjoining alcove and quickly fallen asleep; a copy of *Pride and Prejudice* steepled on her chest. Jasper had carefully earmarked the open page, placed the book on the upturned bread tin which served as a side table and extinguished her lamp before retiring himself.

But sleep was not forthcoming for Jasper. Billings' offer to furnish him with the wherewithal to create his sculptures heralded another new opportunity for him. He visualised all manner of creatures that he might bring to life in clay. He had given much thought to how to tackle an elephant for the 'E' display. Should it be standing? Sitting perhaps? Trunk up or down? He could not recall where he had heard that it was more auspicious, at least to the observer, for an elephant's trunk to be up. It would need to be quite large – for impact. Much larger, of course, than an aardvark or caiman.

And Fidelia had suggested, to a resounding response, that a giraffe was an essential addition for the following month's display. It would necessitate another visit to the museum for reference material. Billings' suggestion that he might take the children with him had been met with much hand-clapping, smiles and chatter at the dinner table.

While his mind's eye captured images of wet clay, elephant trunks and beautiful bottoms, other thoughts hovered at the periphery of his consciousness.

Fidelia.

How would he - how *could* he – *should* he even – tell her about her parents?

He and Billings had adjourned to the smoking room after dinner, where Billings related his discussion with the woman from the orphan asylum. Fidelia evidently suspected her parents were dead. But did she know of the circumstances, other than her probable awareness that her mother had died in childbirth aboard the ship?

According to Billings, the woman had not been able to tell him anything about the man who delivered Fidelia to the asylum. Nor did she know what had happened to Pleasant Knight. Had that man known the true fate of Fidelia's father? Was that why he had silenced her? What was the chap's name? Fidelia *had* mentioned it at some time. He revisited the girl's first words in his head. *Mr Bartholomew had lagotic ears.* Bartholomew. Who was he? A crew member of the *SS Great Britain*? A passenger? Was his identity of any import?

Jasper dozed off with the questions in his head.

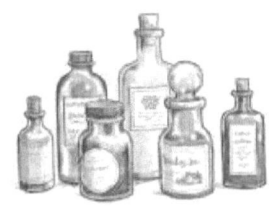

N

Nathaniel Ninnyhammer Naughtily Needed a Nostrum or Nepenthe,
And got it, with a Noggin of Nectar at
Billings Better Bookstore and Brasserie (plus drugs)
Did he Necessarily? He did indeed!

As Melbourne slipped further into autumn and the days grew cooler and yellower, the sun less intense, Fidelia and the pupils of her makeshift school fell into a routine. Now that the boys were attending each afternoon, after a shortened workday at the printer's, their studies progressed apace. Madeleine's and Myrtle's presence was a calming influence on the boys' often rowdy behaviour. Fidelia could see the women's pleasure in their sparkling eyes. Not just the pleasure from their learning, but from their interaction with each other. They soon became firm friends; a joy that neither had experienced before.

Madeleine grew in confidence each day, discovering that the world outside her modest abode was worth the engagement, while Myrtle lost the scowl which had heretofore set her face to perpetual disgruntlement. Both women had learned to smile more each day. Their pleasure did not appear rehearsed; rather, it was unaffected.

Fidelia's days, aside from the time taken up with her teaching, were filled with a mix of chores about the shop – dusting, unpacking stock and alphabetising the books on the shelves – and reading of her own. She had long since finished *Wuthering Heights*, Dickens' *A Tale of Two Cities*, Austen's *Sense and Sensibility* and Jules Verne's *Around the World in Eighty Days*.

Verne's novel had taken her imagination to places never before visualised or contemplated. The world was a mighty big place and she was determined to see much more of it than Phileas Fogg ever did on his headlong adventure.

The long voyage to Melbourne had given but a glimpse of the vastness of the world. One day, she would see Paris again. She would visit Italy, Africa, China, India and the United States. Mother always promised that one day she would take Fidelia to her home. Father had told many stories of his adventures there. She might meet a cowboy or, more interestingly, a Red Indian.

She felt guilty at times that she didn't think of Mother more often. She simply didn't have the time. Occasionally, words spoken by others engendered recollections of Mother. But they were as fleeting as a butterfly glimpsed on a breeze. At night, when she retired to her litter behind the kitchen curtain, she always thought of Father, but even he was becoming vague. Indistinct. Metamorphosing at times into Jasper Farthing Godwin.

She visited the library regularly, finding volumes that Mr Billings did not have on his shelves. She had also discovered the Athenaeum Library in Collins-street. Awe inspiring. She had to crane her neck to see to the top shelves, which reached to the ceiling. More than 40,000 books. How to choose? Given she was only four feet four inches tall with a reach of about five feet four, that exiled the three top shelves from the equation.

The reading room was most comfortable and afforded opportunity to snuggle in with a novel or history or geography text. Stuffy though; the heat from the gas-lights melded with the pungency of cigar smoke rising in plumes from the many sedentary gentlemen, yellowing the volumes on the shelves and irritating readers' eyes and noses. Some men, by their demeanour, made it patent that they saw no place in their establishment for females, let alone children. And worse still, *a female child*. Fidelia ignored their disdain and had, on more than one occasion, deliberately sat next to the most contemptuous of them to read audibly from a historic treatise or scientific journal until silenced by furrowed eyebrows and index fingers put to lips.

Secret had gone with her a few times but had found it too stuffy. His lungs, he complained, were still delicate from the consumption. He and Joshua much preferred the museum. Less time spent sitting with eyes on pages. Rather, they could wander and feast their senses on all things three-dimensional. Fabulous, impossible creatures. Many new-found Australian creatures took the beholder by surprise, as though a fabrication of God's perverse imagination. A strange flat, furry thing looking like a slipper, but with webbed feet and a flat nose like a duck. *Ornithorhynchus anatinus.*

Fidelia and the boys skipped back to Billings after that visit – each trying in turn to recall and pronounce the peculiar biological name of the duck-billed platypus.

Jasper refused to believe that such a creature existed. Fidelia tried to draw a picture for him, but in her untrained hand it did, sadly, look like a squashed slipper. A return visit to the museum was quickly arranged. Jasper had to see it for himself.

He suggested that Madeleine and Myrtle accompany them for a Sunday outing as they, too, were sceptical. Equally perplexing and with an equally unpronounceable name, thought the women, was the emu, *Dromaius novaehollandiae.* Deemed the second largest bird in the world, the specimen on display peered over their heads in an arrogant, forthright manner. Madeleine quickly announced that if this were the *second* largest bird, she would not be comfortable in such close proximity to an ostrich. Myrtle had been more intrigued by the *Chlamydosaurus kingii* – 'why must they have such complicated names?' – a positively prehistoric-looking lizard with a frilled neck. Fidelia threatened to test all her pupils on their pronunciation at the next class.

Jasper was determined to sculpt all three in clay. He had re-acquainted himself with Frederick McCoy, who was generous with time and knowledge. McCoy had promised to visit Billings to see Jasper's sculptures for himself. He had heard talk about town that a benefactor of the museum had been the mystery admirer of Jasper's aardvark and that the figurine now held pride of place in the foyer of the gentleman's East Melbourne residence. Jasper had swelled with pride on hearing this news and inflated more still when McCoy intimated that he, himself, might become a future customer. It was merely a matter of deciding which of the good Lord's wondrous creatures he found worthy of forming in clay for eternity.

Jasper was brimful of enthusiasm, like a foxhound preparing for the chase. For the first time in his life, people had praised him, and it was a mighty feeling. Like floating on air, the passenger of angels. With some of the money from his aardvark sale, he treated himself to a new suit and a barbershop haircut, which had transformed him into a debonair man-about-town. He also treated Myrtle to a new outfit, complete with matching hat and shoes, from none other than *Buckley and Nunn*. Maybe his life had some worth after all. If the curator of a museum deigned to engage him in conversation and afterwards take leave with an encouraging pat on the back, he had surely become *somebody*.

His world had, quite suddenly, metamorphosed into an exciting and ever-expanding horizon of new possibilities and he had the girl to thank for that. Were it not for her, Billings might have long since tired of him; recognised him as a fraud. How proud of her, her parents must have been. That such a young, sweet thing could have the capacity to enable others to see the world through her awe-filled eyes. Had they seen that goodness in her soul; that wisdom in her heart? So much was there to be learned and embraced and she was the muse brought from the heavens to show others how to open their eyes.

How could he tell her about her father? Or should he not? Might it destroy her innocence; shatter her illusions about the man she had loved so dearly?

He thought about what his next project might be. Should he sculpt some of these bizarre Australian creatures? Wombats and wallabies, kangaroos and koalas, platypus and possums. It was likely that those who had never ventured beyond the fringes of Melbourne or frequented the museum, might never otherwise see these peculiarities of God's creation. Of course, most would never have seen an elephant, aardvark or caiman in the flesh either. So many wonderful animals. He could sculpt a new one every week and still never recreate them all. Besides, explorers, here and in Africa, South America and Asia, were discovering new ones all the time.

What a lot of clay it would take. What a lot of time and effort. And glaze. Would Billings stretch to covering the costs of some glazes? It simply wasn't practical to glaze his sculptures up at the brickworks. William had been most obliging at first, but Jasper sensed he was exploiting the man's generosity. He did not want to overdo his welcome.

Then the idea came to him of sculpting more of Fidelia's characters. Amelia Abstainer, Philomena Phrontistes, Helvetia Harebrained. That would put the pipe up E.W. Cole's nose. Not that Jasper had anything at all against E.W. Cole. In fact, he found him intriguing. He believed the rivalry between Cole and Billings could only be good for business, though it was whispered about town that Cole was still fuming at Billings' audacity in copying the idea of his advertising campaign. But he could not accuse Billings – or for that matter, Fidelia – of plagiarism, since Fidelia's words were as original as his own.

But giving these characters 'life' in three dimensions was a triumphant idea. Before long, Fidelia's characters, like Jasper's sculpted animals, would become collectors' items. A set of twenty-six.

Jasper was confident of it.

Fidelia was optimistic about it.

Billings was certain of it.

While the ad-hoc Billings classroom was in session in one back room of the store, the other was occupied by Jasper and his mushrooming sculpture hobby. Billings had, in the meantime, employed another chap to man the register and help with book enquiries, to deal with the burgeoning trade. This allowed Jasper to spend more time on his craft and less time making the transition from clay-covered artisan to polished floor-walker. Billings had acknowledged where Godwin's expertise lay and that was proving to be a more profitable adjunct to his business than having Godwin deal directly with customers. He suggested to Godwin that, in changing the window display each fortnight in unison with Fidelia's advertising tracts, he might attempt miniature replicas of each work to add to the store's stock of collectibles. It proved a winning idea.

Before long, the anticipation of customers to see each new window unveiled – every other Monday morning – was the best possible form of advertising. Billings would place the next instalment of Fidelia's alliterative verses in the Saturday *Age* once a fortnight, his staff (and newly-extended family) would spend Sunday afternoon setting up the new window display under Godwin's guidance, and at nine o'clock on the Monday morning, the crowd would be six deep outside the store, waiting for the curtain to rise. All vied to be the first to claim one of Jasper's limited-edition replica sculptures.

Cole's might have *more* books and more attractions, but *Billings Better Bookstore* was fast gaining ground as a major stakeholder in Melbourne's book trade, and as a centre for those who appreciated artistic talent. On the few occasions that they came face to face, Cole and Billings greeted each other with perfunctory nods, neither giving ground.

O

Ophelia Obstreperous Ominously Ordered Ostrich Oatcakes,
When she Ought to have Opined over
Offenbach in the music department of
Billings Better Bookstore and Brasserie (with music)
Did she Openly? She did indeed!

Jasper loved to watch how Fidelia dealt with the peas on her plate.
They were evidently distasteful to her, but Myrtle insisted that
she could not leave the table until she had eaten every single one
of them.

Fidelia would pop one, and only one, in her mouth and wash it
down with a slug of milk; or she'd line three or four peas along
the inside of her bottom lip, taking care not to squash them, so
that she could spit them out later. It was a long process, which
often occasioned a second helping of milk. It never ceased to
amaze him how this child was at once sophisticated and naïve. By
day, citing Shakespeare and Austen and Webster, by night
scrimmaging with peas and Brussels sprouts. At times he had to
remind himself that she was, indeed, a child.

In moments like this, her innocence brought a tear to his eye.
She had no idea how much warmth she had brought to the Godwin
household. She had made Myrtle happy beyond his hopes. She
had brought his wife back to him and unearthed the latent mother
so many years forlorn.

It was time to tell her about her father.

He waited until Myrtle had finished with the dinner dishes and retired. He had rehearsed this in his head many times, but it still was not an easy matter to broach.

'Fidelia dear, I have some news about your father.'

Her eyes lit up. 'Father?'

'Yes. Mr Billings took it upon himself, when he went to see Mr Exon at the asylum, to ask what was known of the fate of your parents. I think you know already that your mother did not survive childbirth.'

Fidelia nodded, a tear welling in her eye.

'According to the story told by the man who took you to the orphanage, your father was so gripped with grief at the loss of his dear wife – your mother – that he…he cast himself overboard. Mr Bartholomew told Mrs Exon that he saw the event unfold and had, in the dark, been unable to prevent it.'

She shook her head wildly. 'No, that cannot be right. The man must have lied. Father would not have done that. Not when he was looking forward to reaching Melbourne. And he would not have left me all alone.'

'I'm afraid it is the only possible answer, Fidelia. I'm sorry that this happened.'

'You have no cause to be sorry, Jasper. It wasn't your fault.' Fidelia wiped her eyes with her sleeve. 'I think I'll go to bed now'.

Sleep would not come.

He deliberately abandoned me. How could he do such a thing? He was supposed to love me and nurture me.

Fidelia was back aboard the *SS Great Britain* looking into Father's face as he told her to leave the cabin. Grief was in his eyes, but not resignation. Not abject despair. Did he really jump? What were his last words to her? She could not recall. Instead, she saw him gulping the seawater. Arms flailing, eyes desperate. Lost on the great rolling waves of the Indian Ocean.

Were the mermaids carrying him, as he said they would? Supporting him? Were they floating him to safety or escorting him to the deep? She could see him trailing off behind the ship to the unknown clutches of King Neptune. Would he be reunited with Mother there?

Would they be together for all eternity at the bottom of the sea? Would they find solace there among those swimming creatures?

For they are creatures of the deep, my child
Creatures of the deep,
They are creatures of the deep, my child
And they'll swimmingly send you to sleep

Thirty weeks had passed since the grand opening of *Billings Better Bookstore and Brasserie* which meant that fifteen fortnights had also been relegated to history. Accordingly, fifteen window displays had been created and the Billings crew was now working on the letter 'P'.

Jasper had worked tirelessly creating a new sculpture each fortnight, a process much aided by the construction of a small brick kiln in the back yard of his domicile. It obviated the necessity of visiting the brickworks, and gave him much more flexibility in his firing.

Aside from bringing various animals to life in clay, Jasper's repertoire of alliterative characters was gathering an enthusiastic following. As each fortnight passed, his technique improved. The visages of his pint-sized clay mannequins featured more and more detail and collectors revelled in the distinct expressions of each character's adjectival aftername. Gertrude Gallivanter, Isabella Insouciant and Minerva Meretricious had been the most popular.

Jasper was most perplexed that he could have arrived at the age of thirty-nine without knowing that he possessed such artistic talent. He would never have thought his hands might be of use for anything more than menial labour. He would look at his hands, front and back, then at Fidelia, and wonder how all this had come to pass. Was she responsible? Was she a muse of sculpture? Did such a muse exist? Whatever it was, he was certain he would not have made this discovery without her.

Fidelia's students were progressing at a cracking pace and she was deriving great pleasure from teaching them. Madeleine, in particular, had taken to her studies with fervour and, in her own time, was engrossed in reading simple stories aimed at a much younger readership. She could not wait to tackle works by Austen and the Brontë sisters, and the Frenchman, Alexandre Dumas. Fidelia was forever regaling her charges with excerpts from these illustrious writers and often intimated that she might one day write novels of her own.

'These stories are all about emotion, discovery, enlightenment and, most of all, conflict. All stories of worth must have conflict, else there's no nemesis to overcome. No point in the telling. To capture the essence of human frailty and redemption in such a way is to conquer all knowledge.'

Secret regarded her with unbridled admiration when she made such comments. How could a girl know so much? He would almost burst at the unfairness of it. If he read as widely, could he ever hope to know as much as she did? She'd never even been to school.

'Did you make that up yourself Miss Fidelia, or did you read it somewhere?'

'Straight from my lips, Secret,' she replied, 'and if you concentrate hard on your studies, you also will learn to speak learnedly and in so doing, lose your Liverpudlian – or is that Lilliputian – accent. You will *sound* more learned if you speak the Queen's English.' She winked at him teasingly.

'Maybe one day you will aspire to write well, too. As Samuel Johnson said, "Words are the daughters of earth and things are the sons of heaven".'

Joshua, on the other hand, was not so taken with his English studies. Instead, he filled his notebook with drawings of the classroom and his fellow occupants. Madeleine, he depicted with ample bosoms peeping from a lace-edged neckline, a beaky nose and closely-set eyes, and always in tailored and highly ornate attire, complete with exaggerated hat. Myrtle was craggier. Stringy and careworn, with bun pulled so tightly it drew her eyes up at the corners, giving her the look of a long-eared owl. Secret's face always sported more freckles than in life, fringed by an impossible cowlick and a ludicrously cheeky expression.

Miss Fidelia was the only one whose depiction was not exaggerated. In fact the likeness was uncannily realistic. It would not do to make fun of the teacher. The only exceptions were the instances when he added a mortar board to her image in deference to her wisdom. But those were drawings best kept to himself and which he later stashed under his mattress in the bedroom he shared with Secret at the Billings' house. Besides, he was more engaged by the tilt of her head and the set of her mouth than what came out of them. If she approached him while he doodled, he would quickly turn a page and write furiously to dispel any notion that he was not concentrating on the task at hand.

But Fidelia was wise to him. She had noted early on in their acquaintance that Joshua was not much into literature. He was a simpler soul than Secret, not prone to self-acclamation and lacking Secret's innate curiosity about language. Perhaps his talents lay elsewhere. Every soul on earth had a talent, she was sure, but for some it might take a lifetime to unearth. Jasper, for example had only recently discovered his talent for sculpture and now, for him, it was all-consuming. He was still relatively young and could look forward to many, many years of perfecting his skills.

Fidelia, having observed Joshua's penchant for idle drawing, set about to catch him unawares.

She assigned her students an essay about their recent visit to the museum and feigned having to leave the room for a call of nature. Instead, she tiptoed up behind Joshua and watched the unmistakable outline of a platypus emerging from his pencil. Certainly, it looked more platypus and less slipper-like. She put her finger to her lips to discourage the others from giving her presence away, as she watched him begin to shade the drawing.

Before long, the creature appeared to lift from the page as if attaining a third dimension. Fidelia pursed her lips to stifle a grin. She was witnessing the genesis of a gifted artist – one who could bring the world to life in pictures rather than words. Indeed he was a prodigy. She now knew somebody deserving of the noun.

As expected, he jumped out of his skin with fright when she placed her hand on his shoulder and whispered, 'If you can write the botanic name of this creature underneath, I will assign to you full marks for today's exercise. And then I want you to show this picture to Mr Billings. I suspect he can make better use of your talents, when he knows where your talent lies.'

Joshua's smile almost reached his ears, until Fidelia added, 'And then I would have you show the rest of us – but perhaps not Mr Billings – those other pictures in your book. The ones which, I suspect, show all of us in not such a pleasant guise.'

His secret was out. 'But…how?'

'I have eyes in the back of my head.'

Joshua's eyes widened. 'But that is not possible. Is it?' He looked to the others for confirmation.

'I see many things that you don't see because I look to find the truth and reason in things. I look for what is hiding in the shadows.'

'Isn't that like seeing pigments of your imagination?'

Fidelia pressed her hand to her mouth, suppressing laughter. She did not want to ridicule the boy. Nobody ever thrived on ridicule and it always said more about the perpetrator than the victim.

'A *pigment* is something you have in your skin, or an artist might have on his palette, Joshua. A *figment,* however, is something that exists only in your imagination.'

'Like a ghost or a fairy?' Secret said.

'Exactly. And you know, Joshua, if you were to *really* use your imagination with your drawings, I think you might have a big future as an artist, illustrator, cartoonist–'

'Do you think so? Honestly?'

Fidelia motioned for him to show her his book. He gave it up reluctantly. She was a little taken aback by the caricatures. 'Joshua, these are not flattering pictures. I hope you drew them in playful humour.'

'Oh, of course Miss Fidelia. I wouldn't mean to offend anyone.'

'On the contrary,' Fidelia said, 'I think we should all be impressed that you have produced such insightful likenesses.'

Fidelia passed the book to Madeleine who at once sucked in a deep breath as though set to complain. But she looked more carefully at the drawing, appreciating both the realism and the humour of it.

'I too think my nose is a touch bird-like and my eyes too closely set,' she commented in good humour, 'but there is no doubt that it is me. I'm not so sure about that hat though. It appears to be full of wildlife.'

'Artistic licence, I believe that is called,' Fidelia said.

'Show me,' Myrtle said impatiently. 'Well goodness me, goodness me, goodness me. Am I really so wrinkled?'

'Sorry ma'am,' Joshua said. 'Only in poor light I think. Please forgive me.'

'Don't apologise, dear boy. I should wish to be so clever with pencil and paper. And this picture *is* like what I see in my mirror each morning. You shouldn't be hiding such talent.'

'That is what I keep telling him,' Secret said. 'Every night, when there is enough light, he sits on his bed and draws, draws, draws. Mostly he draws things from memory. He can see something one day and draw it the next. He did that with the whale and the emu at the museum, and that platypus. I can't remember what they look like the minute I stop looking at them.'

'It is indeed a gift,' Madeleine observed, 'and one to which I think Mr Billings should be privy. Who knows, there might be a market for your drawings, as there is with Mr Jasper's sculptures. Of course they would need to be framed,' she paused for thought, 'and better still if they could be replicated.'

'Hmm,' Fidelia drummed her fingers on her chin. 'Have you ever heard of lithography, Joshua?'

'Thilography?'

'Lith-og-raphy,' Fidelia enunciated.

'Nope.'

Fidelia was right, as usual. The lad showed great talent. In a few short days, Lucas Billings had set up a studio for his young charge, alongside Jasper's sculpting benches. He could rely on Godwin to keep an eye on the boy and ensure he made productive use of his time, for a boy's mind easily wandered towards idleness or mischief. Godwin was happy with the arrangement. Joshua's occasional presence was a comfort.

After some venturing around town, Billings procured a lithography stone, ink, sponges, rollers and paper for Joshua.

'I can give you the wherewithal,' he told the boy, 'but I can't give you the know-how. For that, son, you might have to read up on it or find an artist who can show you the process. But if you can readily reproduce your drawings, I can readily sell them. I'm sure of it. In time, if the arrangement is successful, you might forgo your position at the printers and earn your keep as an artist.'

Joshua was delirious with joy, not only because Billings had acknowledged his talent and was actively promoting its progress, but because he had referred to him as "son".

Joshua could not remember ever having been called "son" and it gave him a sense of belonging. He had no recollection of his parents. When he was six, Mr Exon told him that they had died when he was not yet two years old, when their Cobb and Co stagecoach hit a kangaroo, overturned and crashed down an embankment on the road from Bendigo to Melbourne. Joshua had been protected by the enveloping arms of his mother as they were flung from the coach. She had broken her neck. His father had died slowly by the side of the road after crawling up the slope on his stomach. Joshua was the only survivor, along with one of the four horses. Following that unfortunate day in the autumn of 1864, his home had been the Melbourne Orphan Asylum.

His recollections of his early years there were hazy and not altogether happy, but since the arrival of Mr and Mrs Exon in 1869, his life improved. Mrs Exon was a kindly woman, able to share a piece of her heart with every one of the hundreds of individuals in her charge. She wasn't quite a mother, but Joshua had no notion of what a mother was. Nor a father. If a father laid down the rules and taught a boy what it was to *be* a boy and instilled in him the virtues of empathy, civility, industriousness and humility, he guessed Mr Exon was as close to a father as a child could ever want. He always wished to have more of him. More than a fleeting smile, an occasional hand on the shoulder or an even rarer word of praise. Those occasions were few and precious. At least now, he only had to share Mr Billings with Secret, and not 300 other children.

Despite sharing quarters with dozens of other children, life at the asylum had been lonely for Joshua. That was until Secret Jenkins arrived. He was ill with consumption for a time, but since he had emerged from isolation, he had occupied the bed next to Joshua's. Being the same age, the two boys had formed a special bond.

Secret was the only other person in the world who had seen his drawings. He knew that Secret was impressed by his creations. 'I don't know how you can do that', Secret would say, and Joshua would reply that he didn't know either. It just came naturally, like a pencil was an extension of his hand and the paper a mirror of his eyes. He didn't know how he could capture the detail of a person or creature so realistically. But it was more fun to depict them with theatrical, exaggerated visages – to portray them in a humorous, satirical way.

Billings had been considering adding artists' supplies to his ever-growing range of merchandise and the discovery of Joshua's talent gave him the impetus to do so. His store was becoming known around Melbourne as much for its fostering of artistic talent, as for its growing stock of books.

He might re-assess the merchandise on the first floor of the store and create more space for art supplies – easels, paints, lithography tools, papers, pastels, brushes. He would create a gallery space to exhibit Joshua's and Godwin's works and a studio area where he could charge customers for Joshua to sketch their portraits. He would have to see about picture framing!

Godwin's experiments of late with slip-casting were enabling him to create a master mould of each of his small sculptures and replicate them. They were almost literally walking out the door in the hands of admiring customers.

His decision to concentrate, for the time being, on Australian fauna had been a masterstroke. Billings was certain that Godwin's followers would feel compelled to collect a full set – however many that be – of his creatures.

Oh, he would need more staff. He could see it now. Yes, Lucas Billings would give E.W. Cole a run for his money. Cole thought himself a lone talent in the bookselling game, but *Billings Better Bookstore and Brasserie* would be renowned throughout Australia, the world even, before long. It would be a one-stop shop for all things literary, cultural, artistic and educational.

Billings never stopped thinking about the betterment of his business and the betterment of others. It filled his days with joy. In many ways, Billings was like his nemesis, Mr Cole. They were both driven by a desire for personal achievement, the getting of knowledge and the advancement of Melbourne. Both had arrived in Melbourne after plying tough and dubious trades on the Victorian goldfields.

Billings recalled the first time they had crossed paths, though he'd not realised the significance at the time. Billings had found himself in Castlemaine on a hot day, making an arduous overnight delivery for a Creswick merchant. He had sampled some fine lemon cordial at a market stall and asked the stall-holder whether he would share the recipe. He was somewhat taken aback at the bearded man's response.

'I'd sooner read you a book than divulge such a trade secret.'

Billings found the man fascinating and presumed him to be of similar age. He engaged the man in light banter. They compared tales of the rigorous life of scratching out a living among the desperate and mostly penniless fortune seekers.

'No, books are my interest,' the man had said. 'In fact I plan to make my mark in Melbourne. My health is not up to this itinerant and uncertain trade. One day, you'll see, I will have the biggest bookstore you can imagine.'

Billings had admired the man's vision and wished him luck in his ambitious venture.

He had never consciously acknowledged that his brief encounter with Edward Cole might have provided the spark for his own bookshop venture. And despite his efforts over the past few years, he had never tasted a better lemon cordial.

A new word had been coined this century for men like them. *Entrepreneur*. Billings loved to assign it to himself, if only in secret. It sat very well with him. Cole may have had a head start with his business, opening his shop a year earlier, after running a successful fledgling business within the Eastern Market – which everyone knew that he now owned – but Billings had the same passion for business and for giving people what they needed. Even if they didn't *know* what they needed. *Especially* if they didn't know what they needed.

Billings enjoyed watching customers as they entered the store. He made particular note of what most attracted their attention. The window display always diverted their eyes and prompted them to cross the threshold. Almost without fail, their expressions showed wonderment, awe, fascination. He derived great pleasure from approaching them and enquiring as to which department he could direct them. He strutted, peacock-like, hands behind his back, upon a compliment.

His policy was that all customers be made to feel welcome – like they were the only person in the store. Undivided attention, without pushiness, he instructed his staff.

Lila, the dark-haired girl who enticed customers to the brasserie with the luscious aromas of her brewed coffee and cinnamon-infused cakes, enticed also with her unaffected smile. She was blessed with near perfect teeth and she loved to show them off.

She was as much a drawcard as the refreshments she served. Billings was glad he had found her by means of a simple newspaper advertisement. She loved her work and the independence it gave her, and it showed in her demeanour.

Since opening, Billings had already added to the seating, placing more tables toward the front of the store so that patrons might view the passing tide of human traffic along Bourke-street.

So popular had his establishment become, he began to wonder whether he shouldn't replicate it at another location – perhaps Toorak or Brighton or St. Kilda. Not everyone could come to the heart of the city to shop and besides, his enterprise was more about leisure and lifestyle, smiles on faces, than purchases and pennies. Although the pennies were adding up most nicely.

P

Philomena Phrontistes Penned a Pandect on Palaeography,
Prior to Plagiarising Plato, Pliny and Pope on Paper Purchased at
Billings Better Bookstore and Brasserie (with stationery)
Did she Positively? She did indeed!

Summer had returned and Fidelia and the boys could barely contain their excitement at the prospect of a carriage ride to the beach at St. Kilda. Billings took charge of the excursion and ensured the children had suitable attire for swimming. He had business to attend to: commercial premises to inspect with a view to taking up a lease. He had in mind something a little different from his Bourke-street store. Something more reflective of the seaside location. More coffee and cool refreshments and a more selective range of books, with a now-mandatory gallery space. He would wait and see whether the locality would sustain further expansion of merchandise.

Melbourne was growing fast and, for the children, it was fascinating to see so much building work going on as they wheeled through Emerald Hill, Middle Park and Albert Park.

The trip took them past the brackish, mosquito-plagued Albert Park lagoons. Billings explained to the children that the public works department was in the process of excavating the lagoons to create a larger lake which might, one day soon, become a venue for fresh-water boating pursuits. He painted a picture in words of rowers and yacht regattas, family picnics and cooling dips on hot summer days. Fidelia suggested the boys might like to write about their excursion in class the next day.

Fidelia's eyes lit up at her first glimpse of Port Phillip Bay. It was the first time she had seen it since she'd arrived in Melbourne aboard the *SS Great Britain*. That had been a tumultuous day for her, full of emotion. She'd had to leave the ship which had been her home for two longs months. At the time, she had missed the comforting thrum of the engines but she would never miss the smell of it.

And she had left it without Mother and Father. What should have been a happy and festive arrival, full of promise and excitement was, instead, a harrowing ordeal. She had thought her life over when she had arrived at the asylum, its towering austerity filling her with the dread of what would become of her.

Now, she knew. In only eighteen months, she had found her feet and her purpose in life. Not bad for a ten-year-old. But where would she have been if Mother and Father had arrived with her? Where would she have lived? Would she have been attending school now, instead of running one? She missed her parents terribly. She missed the promise of a young sibling with whom to share her experiences of the new country.

But life was not so bad. Life was what you made of it. And Fidelia Knight was determined to make the most of hers.

So too, was Lucas Billings. As the carriage approached St. Kilda junction and the gravel surface blended into the cobblestone gutters, Billings directed the driver to stop in front of *Sparrow's Hotel*. He was thirsting for a pint of ale. He gave Secret sixpence to buy the children a lemonade or dry ginger ale each and instructed him to escort Joshua and Fidelia to the sea baths.

'I shall be an hour or two. Mind you don't make a nuisance of yourselves. I shall fetch you at four o'clock, so be sure to be waiting out front.'

After finishing their drinks, the children wandered down Fitzroy-street. It was steamy hot and they were eager to get to the

baths to cool their feet and paddle around. Fidelia skipped ahead
and sang:

> *We'll all go a bathing*
> *Yes we'll all have a swim,*
> *We'll paddle about*
> *And holler and shout*
> *And not be boringly prim.*
>
> *We'll all go a swimming,*
> *Yes we'll cool off in the sea,*
> *We'll have lots of fun,*
> *In the midday sun*
> *And be home in time for tea.*

'What's that song?' Joshua asked.

'I don't know,' Fidelia said. 'I made it up'.

'Made it up? Just now?'

'Yes Joshua. Well, the tune's a tune I already knew, but I just
made up the words to go with it. Why don't you try it?'

'I can't.'

'I'm sure you can, if you try.'

Joshua cleared his throat and sang.

> *We'll all go a barthing*
> *And it won't cost a farthing,*
> *Um, da da da da da*
> *And we'll get ourselves wet*
> *Um, oh I don't know, that's silly.*

'Hmm, needs some work, Joshua, but a good try.'

'I know,' Secret interjected.

> *We'll all go a paddling*
> *Yes, we'll all play in the water*
> *We'll all have a dip*
> *And take care not to slip*
> *And behave like Papa said we oughtta*

145

Fidelia clapped her hands. 'Well done, Secret. It even rhymed. But you have me curious now. Do you call Mr Billings "Papa"?'

'Oh. No. Leastways, not to his face.'

'Did he ask you to?'

'No. No, he never. But, you know, he's the closest thing to a father that I've had since I left Liverpool.'

Fidelia was the more curious. She had never actually asked him how he had come to be alone aboard the *SS Great Britain*. Nor had she given much thought to any family he'd left behind. Was it true, as Father had said, that he thought he was going to Ireland? 'Why was it that you stowed away? Where were your parents?'

Secret looked at his feet. Fidelia's question had stung him like a cat o' nine tails. 'I don't know. No, that's not really true. I know where my mother was, the stinkin' whore–'

'Secret!'

'Well, she was – a whore. A strumpet. All of Liverpool knew that. And my six brothers and sisters knew that. Didn't everyone constantly remind us of it?'

'You have six brothers and sisters? My goodness.' Secret merely nodded. 'Yet you've never mentioned them. What about your father?'

'Fathers,' he corrected.

'Oh.'

'Yes, oh. None of us knew who our fathers were. All different, probably. Don't think Mama knew either. Leastways, they never came a calling with gifts. I was the first, er, the eldest. Then there was Charity, Hunter, Factor, Mercer, Sailor and Velvet.'

'Goodness, what unusual names. And I had thought Secret odd.'

'I think I got Secret 'cos she didn't know who *my* father was. The rest, we all thought, she named after their fathers' callings; meaning p'raps she did, in fact, know who they were, though she told us otherwise.'

'Which of these are girls and which are boys?'

'Hunter, Factor and Sailor are boys, the others girls. We all think that Mercer and Velvet have the same father because they look alike. Maybe he was a merchant or some such, p'raps of fabric, and that is why Velvet was called Velvet.'

'Why did you leave England?'

'Being that I was the eldest, Mama told me I had to work to support the family, either in the coal mine or at the cotton mill. Didn't want to do either and I knew that I would never earn enough to feed so many. So…so I'm ashamed to say I ran away. I'd heard there was work to be had in Ireland, so I ran to the docks and that's where I was led astray.'

Secret had to raise his voice to be heard over the sound of an approaching carriage. He glanced back to see Joshua dawdling behind and kicking a stone. 'Y'see I misheard somebody and I thought the *Great Britain* was sailing to Dublin. I expected it to be a day or two's sail to Dublin, but after three days I looked out from my hiding spot and there was water all round. No land in sight anywhere.'

'By which time, it was too late,' Fidelia said. 'No going back'.

'That was when I saw you first.' He smiled at the memory. 'She was like an angel, Joshua, I tell you. Joshua?'

Secret and Fidelia were so absorbed in their conversation that they hadn't noticed the cart stop behind them. They turned to see Joshua lying face up and motionless beneath it, between the front and back wheels.

'Damn stupid child stepped in front of me,' the driver yelled as he climbed off the cart. 'Is he deaf or something?'

'No, he is not deaf,' Fidelia spat. 'Are you blind? Did you not see him?' She rushed to Joshua and knelt at his feet. He did not move or acknowledge her.

Secret glared at the stony-faced male passenger. 'Don't just sit there, mister. Get off and do something.'

The man made no effort to move.

'Is he dead?' Secret asked Fidelia as he knelt beside her.

'No, he's still breathing. Go and fetch Mr Billings. Quickly! Did the horse trample him, or did he go under the wheel?' Fidelia asked the driver. He was clearly in shock and stood open-mouthed, mopping his forehead with a handkerchief. 'Did you hear me?' she asked again. He did not reply. It was then, as she stood up, that she noticed the couple in the cart: the opulently-dressed woman in a garish red silk-and-feather hat, holding an infant dressed in pristine broderie anglaise and a pink sun bonnet.

The well-dressed gentleman shook his head, bothered by this tiresome interruption to their afternoon outing. 'Can we get along please driver, we shall be late to our *thé de l'après-midi*,' the gentleman said.

Fidelia could not believe her ears. The pretentiousness of the man. He clearly wasn't French.

'This boy could be lying here dying and all you're worried about is being late to afternoon tea? Have you no decency?' She glared at the man. She had never felt so compelled to inflict grievous harm against a person. He glared back. Clearly he had no conscience.

She appealed to the woman for help. 'Can you not get down off your high seat and help?' The woman froze and looked away. Evidently she was under her husband's thumb. Fidelia could see she would get no help from these people. 'You're dastagants, the pair of you.'

'Driver, get aboard,' the gentleman instructed. 'I'll not stand to be insulted by a young whippersnapper. Now get a move on or I'll not be paying you for the privilege of our patronage.'

Joshua slowly opened his eyes. Confusion lined his face. The driver was clearly in two minds as to what to do. He bent down and grabbed Joshua's feet and pulled him from under the cart. Joshua screamed in pain and passed out.

Without further ado, the driver stepped up into his seat and flicked the reins. The cart took off in a flurry of dust.

Fidelia knelt beside Joshua, his body crumpled and broken like a doll flung from an infant's cot. She brushed the hair from his forehead. Where were Secret and Mr Billings? *Hurry up!*

'Joshua, can you hear me? Please say you can hear me.'

Joshua opened his eyes, his face contorted in anguish. 'I hear you, Miss Fidelia. But I am in such pain. I think my legs are broken. If I move again, I won't be able to stand it.'

'I understand. You stay right there. Where on earth has Secret got to?' She tried to keep the panic from her voice. She looked up the street from whence they had come and saw Secret and Mr Billings running towards them.

'Mr Billings is coming. Help is coming, Joshua. My word, but I'd like to take those people to task. Too busy worrying about their afternoon outing, they were.' Fidelia wanted to keep talking, to distract Joshua from his agony.

'Miss Fidelia, what is a dastagant?' Joshua asked.

'A thoroughly horrible and intolerable person. So say I.'

'Is that one of your made-up words?'

'Yes, Joshua. Now you lie still.'

Secret dropped to his knees beside Joshua, his face filled with distress. He touched Joshua lightly on the forehead and whispered assurances that he would be all right. Fidelia noticed that Secret could barely look at the puncture above Joshua's left knee and the protruding bone. His right leg also had a peculiar bulge. Fidelia, also, was nauseated at the sight.

Mr Billings had no doubt that Joshua's legs were broken. Both were horribly deformed. With help from a gentleman who had emerged from a nearby cottage in response to Fidelia's screams, Billings and Secret carefully tended to Joshua.

The man returned to his house to fetch sticks for splints, strips of cloth to bind them to Joshua's legs; and his wife, for moral support. He had seen this done, he said, when a crew member aboard the ship on which he made passage had fallen from a yard-arm and sustained similar injuries. It was important, he said, to immobilise the fractures, especially in view of the bumpy trip ahead. His wife offered Joshua a shot of brandy to help dull the pain.

The ride back to Melbourne, and beyond Bourke-street to the Royal Melbourne Hospital, seemed twice as long as the ride to

St. Kilda. Fidelia was sure she would never forget Joshua's screaming and moaning as they lifted him onto the cart and laid him along the bench seat. Secret grimaced at Joshua's cries of pain every time the cart bumped or swayed, while Fidelia tried her best to hold Joshua still. She could do little else to help. She sat with his head in her lap and resumed the song she had begun before the accident, trying to take his mind off the pain.

We're all going to hospital
The doctor for to see
It really isn't too comical
For Joshua, Secret and me

We're all going to hospital
And not for a swim at the bath
For Joshua's wounds anatomical
If only he'd kept on the path

We're all going to hospital
So that Joshua can be mended
They'll get him all shipshape and Bristol
And he'll go on as he intended

Joshua looked up at her endearingly. He might have laughed were he not in such pain. He hoped never to endure a day without the pleasure of seeing Fidelia's face. She could see only positive, fruitful things and was never dark or ill-tempered – although she *was* mysterious. Just her presence beside him was soothing and calming. And he looked at Secret and Mr Billings. Like dear Secret, he too thought silently of Mr Billings as 'Papa' or 'Father', but he had never said it aloud. Nor had he presumed to call Mrs Billings 'Mother' or 'Mama', despite the fact that she behaved as one.

He looked at Fidelia again. He wished she were his sister. But their closeness made it feel so. No matter that they were not related by blood. They could be related by thought, by proximity, by aspiration. By love even.

Fidelia read his mind. She could see by the indefinable serenity in his eyes that he regarded her as family. Kin. She looked at Secret, whose worried face conveyed the genuine concern that a brother might show for a brother. She felt closer to these boys than she had to Permelia and Ninian. Yet never a day went by that she didn't wish her siblings were here in Melbourne with her. Living.

She looked at Mr Billings whose countenance bore all the hallmarks of a concerned father. There was a word for this, but she couldn't bring it to mind. She tried to visualise it in Samuel Johnson's pages. But that was of no use because she was fairly certain the word started with 'P'. Did Mr Webster know the word? She scanned her memory. P-p-p…

'Propinquity!' she blurted, to the surprise of all aboard the cart.

'What is that you say, Fidelia?' Billings asked.

'Propinquity. That describes us. We're like a family, yet none of us is related. It means a state of being close to somebody or to feel kinship with somebody who isn't necessarily kin.'

'It describes us perfectly then.' Billings patted her hand.

'Is it a real word, Miss Fidelia?' Joshua asked.

'Yes, of course it is.'

Joshua craned his neck to get a better view of Fidelia's face. 'How did you know what I was thinking, Miss Fidelia?'

'And me too,' Secret said.

'Now that, I call mentalling.'

'And is *that* a real word?' Billings asked.

'It is now.'

Q

Queenie Quacksalver Queried a Quidditative Questmonger,
Causing him to Querken, Quiver and Quagswag into a Quandary at
Billings Better Bookstore and Brasserie
Did she Questioningly? She did indeed!

Joshua was in a nightmare of unrelenting agony. He had never known such pain. Both of his femurs were broken and the process of setting them in plaster casts was excruciating. He was grateful for the laudanum. It dulled the pain, but it wore off quickly and he begged for more. The left leg was more badly damaged than the right. Although they didn't tell Joshua, the doctors confided in Billings that the boy might be forever lame.

Madeleine, Fidelia and Secret spent time at the hospital with Joshua every day, while Billings, Jasper and Myrtle took turns for occasional visits.

Billings and Madeleine agreed with Fidelia's observation that Secret was perpetually subdued until he was again in Joshua's presence. Fidelia didn't miss much. She envied the closeness of the boys; the way they became animated the moment they saw each other. Sometimes it was as though nobody else existed.

A week passed. While walking to the hospital, accompanied by Madeleine, Fidelia noted that Secret was fussing with something in his pocket.

'What do you have there, Secret?'

Secret looked sheepish. 'I had an idea, to cheer Joshua up.'

'Yes?'

'He doesn't know when his birthday is, so I thought we could pretend it is today.'

'A splendid idea.'

Madeleine agreed. 'Why not? I have some toffees in my purse.'

Once at Joshua's bedside, Secret winked at Fidelia and Madeleine to initiate a rousing rendition of *For He's a Jolly Good Fellow.*

Joshua was nonplussed. 'What's this all about?'

'We have decided,' Secret said, 'that today is your birthday.'

Joshua's mouth widened into an unbridled grin. 'Wonderful. I've never had a birthday.'

Madeleine hugged Joshua and presented him with the paper bag of toffees.

Fidelia was embarrassed that she had no gift, then remembered the two half crayons in her pocket. 'Sorry that they're already half used. I'll go and see later if I can scrounge some paper for you.'

Secret, Fidelia noted, appeared reluctant to reveal the item in his pocket. 'Come on Secret. I am sure you have something there.'

'It's just a silly drawing, and you know I can't draw.' Secret pulled out a folded piece of heavy paper and placed it between Joshua's hands. 'You know what it means,' he whispered in Joshua's ear.

'What is it? Show us,' Fidelia said.

'It's private. Just for Joshua to see.'

Fidelia could barely contain her curiosity. 'There should be no secrets between friends – between *family.* '

Joshua, also, was intrigued. He opened the paper close to his face, then quickly closed it again and put it under the bed cover. He knew exactly what it meant.

Madeleine was familiar with the boys' surreptitious exchanges of notes. She touched Fidelia's shoulder. 'Now now, Fidelia. You know how little boys like to keep secrets.'

After a second week in hospital, Joshua was confined to bed at home for another four weeks. To counteract the sheer boredom of it, Billings furnished him with sheets of paper pinned to a board and a collection of pencils, crayons and pastels.

'If you can't go to the studio – the studio will come to you.'

An unfortunate consequence of the accident and Joshua's prognosticated three to four-month recovery time, was that he lost his position at the government printer. He missed the daily interaction with the other employees and the urgency of the business, but he was philosophical about it.

'All things happen for a reason,' he told Secret. He wasn't sure what the reason was, but he hoped that would become clear in time. Of course he missed Secret during the daytime too and he would have missed his classes, had Fidelia not suggested that she conduct them at his bedside. Secret didn't mind this either, since it meant he could work while comfortably ensconced in his own bed.

Fidelia had it sorted. She would continue morning classes with Mrs Billings and Mrs Godwin and then come to Joshua and Secret in the afternoons.

Since it was a short walk from Billings' store to the Billings' residence in Stephen-street, Fidelia often visited Joshua at other times to keep him company and help relieve his debilitating ennui. She remembered the tedium of being confined to bed with the scarlet fever. But that had been a mere week. Nothing by comparison to Joshua's necessary detention in bed.

'What is that you're drawing now?'

'It's a kangaroo. Or a wallaby.'

'And you're drawing it from memory. You are a marvel, Joshua.' Fidelia drummed her fingers on her knee. A verse was forming in her mind.

The red kangaroo
Goes hoppity-boo
And hoppity-boo it goes.
It bounces along,
Never puts a foot wrong,
As it pushes itself off its toes.

The brown wallaby
Goes boppity-wee
and boppity-wee it goes.
It bounds in a flurry
'cos it's in a great hurry
To see where the kangaroo goes

Joshua stared at her. 'Where do these rhymes come from, Fidelia?' Fidelia had insisted some time ago that Joshua no longer be so formal as to call her 'Miss Fidelia'. 'Do they just spring from your head?'

'Yes, they do, Joshua. I don't know why or how. I think I must have taken after my father. He was forever making up verses. But your picture gave me the inspiration.'

Fidelia fell silent, thinking. 'I have an idea Joshua,' she announced suddenly. 'We're going to write a book. I'll do the writing, you will do the illustrating. What do you think?'

'An excellent idea. What is this book about?'

'It will be all about the wonderful animals here in Australia. A poem – with pictures. Let's shake on it.' Fidelia held out her hand and Joshua shook it firmly.

'Secret can see about printing it, and Mr Billings can sell them in his shop. We'll call it *Chasing Hoppity-Boo*. Yes, *Chasing Hoppity-Boo*, by Fidelia Knight and Joshua Wright. Funny, I'd not thought before about how our names rhyme. There's poetry in that.'

Joshua was excited at the suggestion and immediately opened his sketch-book. A folded scrap of paper flipped onto the floor. Fidelia picked it up and glanced at it. It was a drawing – an outline of a person with one half shaded; one not of Joshua's usual standard. Oh, it was the paper Secret had given to Joshua for his birthday.

'Give me that,' Joshua said sharply.

Fidelia handed it to him. 'Do you know what it means?'

'I do.'

'So do I.'

Once Fidelia had the notion, the words almost wrote themselves. At home on the kitchen table, she penned furiously, allowing no time to blot the ink. She couldn't help it. The words spilled off her pen faster than she could load the ink.

This would be a story for other children, to educate them about this country's peculiar wildlife. Given that Jasper was already creating realistic Australian animals in clay, a book might be a logical progression from a sales point of view. She always knew she would be an author. She didn't know she would become one when she was ten.

The grey koala
Goes dippity-dala
And dippity-dala it goes
It walks on all fours
With a shake of its paws
To see what the kangaroo knows.

The spiny echidna
Goes prickety-pidna
And prickety-pidna it goes
It bristles its spines
Into prickly lines
To stick in the kangaroo's nose

The feathertail glider
Goes wirrily-wida
And wirrily-wida it goes
It flies through the air
Like it hasn't a care
To land on the kangaroo's toes

The strange platypus
Goes swimmily-shush
And swimmily-shush it goes
It swims along silently
Then quite surprisingly
Sneaks up should the kangaroo doze

It took barely an afternoon to complete her poem. All twelve verses of it. She would have to tell Joshua tomorrow to draw a cockatoo, a goanna, a wombat, a brushtail and a ringtail possum, a galah, a frilled-neck lizard, a lyrebird and many more.

Every self-respecting parent would want to buy this book for their children. It would be one to treasure. And one to add to, because, Fidelia knew, this would be the first of many. She was already thinking about the next book.

Fidelia Knight and Joshua Wright would become household names and every household would have their books on the shelf, she was sure of it. She might have to sign autographs. She had better practise her signature.

Jasper thought it a wonderful idea and Myrtle was thoroughly engaged by Fidelia's recitation of her work. This girl never ceased to amaze them with her confidence and wisdom. In a few short months she had captured their hearts and become the daughter they had always wanted.

Myrtle was a changed woman and her metamorphosis was not lost on Jasper. She positively glowed these days. And her command of the language, her confidence and her own positivity were reflections of Fidelia's influence. As for Jasper, he was as happy as a mudlark after a rain-shower. He could hardly wait to tell Billings of the children's plans. Unless, of course, Joshua had beaten him to it.

He had. When Billings came to extinguish their lantern and make sure the boys were tucked in tight, Joshua told him of Fidelia's plan. Secret was already privy to it and though excited for them, he was envious of their talents.

'It's a topping idea,' Billings said. 'I would like to hear Miss Fidelia's poems.'

'She is amazing, Mr Billings. She spurted out this poem, right off the top of her head, like she'd known it all her life. I don't know how she does it.'

'Our Miss Fidelia is a marvel. She never ceases to surprise me. But you, Joshua, are equally talented with your drawing.'

Joshua beamed. He had seldom been praised for anything.

Secret felt excluded. 'You and Fidelia will have to spend so much time together,' he said to Joshua after Billings had left.

'I guess,' Joshua shrugged. 'Are you jealous?'

'Jealous? Of course not, but I wish I could be part of it too.'

'You can. You can help us *make* it. You could find out from Mr Ferres what it will cost and maybe he'll put you in charge of the binding.'

'I guess. It might cost a lot. How will you pay for it?'

'I hadn't thought of that. I don't think Fidelia has either. But you know how infectious her enthusiasm can be.'

They need not have worried about the outlay. Billings did not hesitate to put up the money for the first print run, regardless of cost. He was confident of a return on the first fifty sales and a profit beyond that. He planned to put money into a trust for Fidelia and Joshua, on the understanding that when they were of age, they would use the money for their own betterment or business ventures.

Like Jasper and Myrtle, Billings and Madeleine had not looked back since the children had come into their lives. They felt they had been blessed by God himself. Their lives had taken on a dimension that Billings could never have envisaged had it not been for Fidelia. There was almost nothing he wouldn't do for her, or for the boys. He had just volunteered to become a publisher. What other strings might he add to his bow?

Joshua was on his feet again, despite a lingering limp of the left leg, for the gala opening of *Billings Better Bookstore and Brasserie*'s second store in St. Kilda. The event coincided with Fidelia's eleventh birthday and it became a truly festive occasion.

Fidelia felt like a princess in the new mauve dress Madeleine had had made for her. She fingered her hair constantly to ensure the matching amethyst-encrusted comb was still in place.

Billings and his newly-engaged employees had worked day and night to stock the store, while Fidelia, Jasper and the boys had spent the two previous weekends working on the window display. What Fidelia and Joshua didn't know (and Secret had been sworn by Billings to abide by his name) was what else was to be displayed in the window.

As their carriage pulled up in front of the Barclay-street store, Secret deliberately distracted Fidelia and Joshua with the charade of a broken bootlace, until everyone, Madeleine and Myrtle included, was off the carriage.

The gathered crowd parted for the arrival of Billings and his entourage. As they passed the window on their way in the door, Joshua suddenly grabbed Fidelia's elbow.

'Look at that Fidelia. Will you look at that?!'

Billings turned – a look of mock surprise on his face. He repeated Joshua's words for effect. 'Well, will you look at that, Miss Fidelia?'

Fidelia's jaw dropped. Beneath a red banner emblazoned with

"The book every child must have"

was a neatly stacked pile of books: CHASING HOPPITY-BOO, by Fidelia Knight, with illustrations by Joshua Wright.

The best birthday present ever. And such a surprise. She hadn't expected it to be printed for at least another month. Fidelia was overcome with joy.

Once inside the store, Fidelia was almost squashed in the crush. Several times, she had to dodge the elbows of people holding her book above her head as they pushed their way to the register. Nobody knew who she was – that she was the author. In fact, nobody even knew that the author was an eleven-year-old girl and the illustrator a fourteen-year-old boy. She was merely another child to jostle past. Adults could be needlessly rude. Hands on her shoulder, shoving her out of the way. None of them wanted to miss the opportunity to purchase the new book.

She could hear the constant sound of coins tinkling in the tin box on the counter. Joshua grabbed her hand and pulled her through a barricade of bodies to a spot where there was enough room to breathe. Secret was there already – shaking his head at the scrummage. He had never seen a crowd so determined toward a single cause.

'I think,' he said to Fidelia and Joshua, 'that your book is going to be a great success. Can you believe this? And nobody even knows who wrote it. That, I believe, is the power of advertising. You didn't know that Mr Billings had placed a special advertisement in yesterday's *Age*.'

'No, I didn't,' Fidelia said. That explained why Jasper was so adamant that she not look at yesterday's edition.

Secret nudged Fidelia and pointed toward the back of the store. Lucas Billings stood at the top of the steps of the mezzanine level and tried, in vain, to hush the crowd. Nobody paid him any attention. Secret knew what to do. He pushed between the customers, made his way up the three steps, put his fingers to his lips and whistled – a crowd-startling, silencing whistle. Billings nodded his thanks. Secret returned to his spot beside Joshua.

'Welcome, welcome, welcome everybody to our second bookstore and brasserie. I do hope you will all become regular patrons. And I do hope you will all partake of that delicious-smelling coffee and our fine patisseries after making your purchases. I encourage you to purchase books, for they are the very evidence of human existence and knowledge. Every book has its own secrets and I feel sure it will be of great pleasure to all of you to help unlock some of those mysteries with a purchase here today.

'Now, I have the special privilege to introduce you to two exceptional young people. The author and illustrator of the exciting new book, *Chasing Hoppity-Boo*, which we have the pleasure of launching on its way today. I am pleased to see that so many of you have already purchased your own copy. I have been advised that we are almost sold out, so don't miss your opportunity by procrastinating. It will be, I am certain, the first of many books from this talented collaboration. Miss Fidelia and Master Joshua, come forward please.'

Fidelia was overcome.

'Take a deep breath Fidelia,' Joshua said, as he clasped her hand firmly and led her through the crowd.

Fidelia giggled at the collective gasps of the patrons as they parted to let them through.

'But they're just children,' a tangerine-bustled woman said as they passed. 'Oh for the love of God, look how tiny they are.'

Fidelia did not *feel* tiny. She felt like she had grown a foot in stature. And her chest could hardly have swelled more. As they reached the top of the steps to stand beside Billings, they were enveloped in applause so deafening, Fidelia thought she might never hear again. Did Emily Brontë or Jane Austen ever face such adulation? Not that she compared to them. But one day she might.

She saw that Joshua, too, was revelling in the moment, with a grin so wide Fidelia feared his face might crack in half. He took a bow and Fidelia curtseyed to the crowd. The applause reached a new crescendo.

Secret, by contrast, did not look happy. He was overjoyed for his friends – of course he was. So what was this bad feeling he had? He had not expected to be green. It was not an emotion he had ever felt before. But he *was* envious. He couldn't help it, foolish as it was.

He didn't begrudge them the success they had earned through their undeniable talents. It wasn't that. But they were sharing something that he wasn't a part of. He'd noticed how close they had become and he had to acknowledge his jealousy.

He felt excluded from their little project, even though he'd used his bookbinding skills to bring it into being. He had offered suggestions and been ignored. Fidelia would give him a perfunctory nod. Joshua would plain tell him his suggestion was a dumb idea; that he knew nothing about drawing. Joshua and Fidelia were in cahoots – wherever that was – and there was no room for him.

It wasn't fair. He had met Fidelia first. He was first to befriend her. He did better in her classes than Joshua. Yet she always deferred to Joshua, and Joshua to her. Joshua also, had been distant, dismissive even, as though consumed by this creative liaison with Fidelia. Secret missed the intimacy of his friend.

Secret watched as Fidelia and Joshua sat at a table to sign copies of their book. Such fawning. Such gratuitous adulation. These people hadn't even read the book yet. How were they to know whether it was good, bad or indifferent?

Secret suddenly felt claustrophobic. He had to get outside. He pushed against the human traffic in the store and finally made it to the footpath. A few paces down the street he leant against a veranda post. He folded his arms and drummed his fingers against his biceps.

Mr Billings had more time for Fidelia and Joshua of late, too, and more praise. Secret had kept this whole thing quiet. 'Live up to your name,' Billings had cajoled him. And he had. Fidelia and Joshua had had no notion of today's launch. He'd almost blurted something accidently to Joshua a couple of times, but had caught his tongue in time. Where was Mr Billings' praise now?

Secret was still dwelling on this, head down, when he became conscious of cigar smoke and shiny black brogues almost toe to toe with his own shoes. He looked up, no smile on his face.

'And why would you be looking so glum, my number one man?' Billings asked him.

'Huh? Oh. I don't know.' He scuffed one foot against the other.

'Feeling a bit left out, are you?'

Secret shrugged. 'I guess. A bit.'

'Did I forget to tell you what a marvellous job you've done? Not just on the binding of the books, but in keeping the secret.'

Billings smiled at him. Secret's mouth crinkled into an almost-smile. 'Yes, they might be getting all the attention *today*, but do you have any notion of the plans I have in store for you?'

Secret raised his eyebrows quizzically. 'No, sir. Plans? For me?'

'Indeed. What if I were to tell you that I have enrolled you to attend classes at Melbourne Grammar School? We passed it along the way here this morning. Do you recall that I pointed it out?'

Secret was dumbfounded. Unable to form words, he shook his head in disbelief.

'Miss Fidelia tells me that you have great talent that she feels unable to further.'

Secret was speechless. *A real school?*

'I have observed myself that you're much too clever to be a book-binder or printer. Fidelia believes your future lies in politics, writing or further study at university. She believes you will fulfil your potential much better with an all-round education. What do you think?'

'I'd say I was surprised. I thought she didn't think…that much of me. She's so taken up with Joshua.'

'On the contrary, Secret. She thinks the world of you. She admires your enthusiasm, your ability to grasp new concepts so quickly, your innate goodness. I grant you, Fidelia and Joshua have made a great success of their collaboration. In fact, we will embark on a second printing shortly as we have almost sold out. But each of us has to think about where our talent lies.

'I, too, see a big future for you, in publishing or the business world. But a good education is the key to a productive future. You will enter there a boy and emerge a gentleman, you mark my words. Besides, at Grammar School, you would be able to partake of all the sports – Australian Rules Football for example. I hear the boys have a fierce rivalry with the boys from Scotch College – rowing, cricket, athletics, swimming. Whatever you like.'

Sports? Secret had never even thought of such things. He had learned the rudimentary technique of kicking a football at the asylum, but had not mastered it. It had taken him some time to grasp the trickery of the odd-shaped ball – after all, balls were supposed to be round, weren't they? – as good balance was required. But he had never seen a real match, nor thought that he might one day have the opportunity to play in one.

'But my situation at the printers? Without it, how would I pay you – for board and keep, I mean?'

Billings put a hand on Secret's shoulder. 'Secret, Madeleine and I see you as our son now. We no longer expect you to pay us for the privilege of sharing our home. We only ask that you do us proud – as a natural son would. Do you think you can do that?'

Secret fought back a tear. It would not do to cry. But he was overjoyed. He had a father. And a new mother too; one much more respectable than his old one. 'Oh yes, sir. But, but what about Joshua? Will he-?'

'My Madeleine and I don't believe that grammar school will necessarily be in Joshua's best interests. He has a natural talent as an artist, which will pave a successful future for him – school or not. But you must not be jealous of the fact that he'll continue to learn from Fidelia.'

'I, I don't know what to say, sir.'

'Then just say thank you. And call me Father.'

R

Rudolph Rascalion Randomly Recited Rhymes and Rhapsodies by Rote,
So Rejoiced in Reading Rhetorick at a Rantipole Rate at
Billings Better Bookstore and Brasserie
Did he Really? He did indeed!

Secret adjusted quickly to school at Melbourne Grammar. Usually, he travelled there by coach, but often – weather permitting – he would walk or jog home at the end of the day. Fidelia's efforts, and his own ability to absorb useful information, found him in the top echelon of his class. He was well liked by the other boys. He loved history, geography, English literature and mathematics, and he was good at most of it.

But school was as much about discipline and gentility as it was about English, science and history and Secret was happy about this. He'd wanted to lose his Liverpudlian accent and this he had accomplished. He wanted to be a gentleman, refined and confident. He wanted to be like Mr Exon, or Mr McCoy at the University museum, or like Lucas Billings.

He did *not* want to be like his father. Whoever his father was. To be sure, his father was not a gentleman. After all, what gentleman would pay to lie with a woman and then discard her and walk away? What sort of man would father a child and then not *be* a father? A woman could not do that. A woman who became a mother would always *be* a mother even if, like his, she did not *want* to be a mother.

No, he would not be *that* type of man. He would be the type of man who honoured a woman, took care of her, nurtured her aspirations and gave her the freedom to pursue them. He would be the type of man who would see another man not as a threat or rival, but as confederate in decency and morality.

He wanted to be that sort of gentleman for Fidelia. One day, when she was old enough, she would see the great esteem in which he held her. Prior to meeting her, nobody else had ever thought he would amount to anything. Nobody had ever known he might aspire to become an educated gentleman of the world. She had taught him what it was for a man to have such aspirations and how to go about achieving them. But also, she had taught him what it was for a woman to have such aspirations.

Fidelia had taught him that being a woman – even though she was still only a girl – did not mean having to settle for a desultory life. Mrs Billings – *Mother* – and Mrs Godwin were testament to that. Whereas before they had been wholly subservient to their husbands and preoccupied with all things domestic, they now had a more worldly view of life and a keen desire to grasp the essence of it and make a mark on it. They had been discussing starting a proper school – not one which occupied but one room of the bookstore – and taking up the challenge of becoming teachers themselves. What they had learned in such short order from Fidelia, they could surely teach to young children. Five, six, seven-year-old children.

Secret had overhead them talking about the notion over afternoon tea one Saturday, while Papa was at Flemington watching horses run around in circles.

'We could put Fidelia in charge of educating the older children, if she were of a mind to,' Madeleine had said.

Myrtle had agreed wholeheartedly. 'A sterling idea.'

'Aside from teaching the youngsters to read and write, we would teach good manners, etiquette and deportment.'

Secret had chuckled to himself at Myrtle asking what 'deportment' meant. She'd thought it meant sending someone back to their home country.

They'd heard that a woman by the name of Emma Cook had done just that in Hawthorn. Her school, Tintern, which had opened this year, had come of Emma Cook's desire for her own daughters to be properly educated. The school was already gaining a wider enrolment.

'Why could we not emulate her success?' Madeleine had said.

Now all they had to do was convince Billings of the merits of their idea. They would need his money of course to establish such a school. Granted, they said, it might not be as fancy as the new Presbyterian Ladies College in East Melbourne and may not aspire to have sixty students; but then, that was only open to Presbyterians.

Everyone knew that Presbyterians were mostly Scottish and mostly loopy. Secret had known several Presbyterians in Liverpool. Those who had ventured south of the border to ply their trades in the port city. They were mostly quite mad. Speaking a language which tried to be English but wasn't and calling their children *bairns* and saying 'I cannae do this and I cannae do that.' He recalled a freckle-faced, red-headed boy chasing Hunter down the street, calling out 'Yer baggin' and manky and faert o' the dark. Away an' boil yer haed!' Secret didn't know what it meant but it didn't sound pleasant.

It got him to thinking about home.

He often wondered what had become of all his siblings. What must they have thought of him abandoning them? At night, when he lay awake in bed, this was what he mostly thought about. Charity with her pretty blonde curls and penchant for bringing home stray animals – starving, flea-ridden cats most particularly; Hunter, whose freckles could seldom be seen beneath the dirt that invariably caked his face; Factor, born with a withered hand that flapped uselessly at his waist, but able to do most things with his good hand without complaint; Mercer, whose dark hair cascaded to her waist like her mother's but who was slow of speech and simple of mind; Sailor, who as a toddler had demonstrated the affinity with water his name suggested and who liked to make boats from paper or bark; and Velvet, still a babe in arms when Secret last saw her – too young to have any personality, save for her tendency to squeal.

And what of Mama? Was she still selling herself on the streets of Liverpool? Bringing stinking, raucous, drunken men home to have them share her bed behind the curtain. Then waiting once again for her belly to swell. Was there a new brother or sister that he didn't even know about?

How were they faring? Did they have enough to eat, as he did? He surmised not. And nor would any of them ever learn to read and write, let alone find themselves in a grammar school, of all places. Yes, he had been lucky. Much luckier, he believed, than if he'd stayed in Liverpool to work down the mine or boarded a ship to Ireland. Ireland was still recovering from the potato famine. He was lucky that he had never known such starvation, such want. Such emptiness.

No, he guessed it was luck that found him inadvertently aboard the *SS Great Britain* and on his way to the Colony of Victoria. What a life of opportunity he now had. But one day – one day, he would go home. He would make amends to his brothers and sisters. He would be a gentleman. And they would be in awe of him. Not too much in awe, mind, lest they called him uppity.

While Secret thrived at Grammar School, Joshua thrived at his artwork. He had mastered the techniques of lithography and engraving so that his images could be replicated many times over. With thanks to Mr Billings for providing the wherewithal, he'd also learned to make picture frames so that his artworks could be sold as complete entities, ready to adorn the walls of Melbourne's more elite households. He had a steady following of customers wanting their portrait drawn, whether as a mirror image or as a caricature. Most were in awe of his ability; some thought him a novelty. Either way, he was helping the prosperity of *Billings Better Bookstore and Brasserie*.

He was glad about that. It was the least he could do for the man he now called Papa. And he knew that Papa was putting aside money for him, from his book and picture sales; a legacy that would become his when he reached the age of eighteen.

Joshua enjoyed his time in the workshop with Jasper. He especially liked Jasper's stories about life on the goldfields. He couldn't imagine such a rough and rugged existence. The asylum seemed like a palace by contrast. He hoped to travel there one day, to Bendigo, Ballarat and Beechworth. to see what lay beyond the structured confines of Melbourne. To see what was out there in 'the bush'. It sounded like a place he might like, especially given the possibility of seeing a kangaroo or a wallaby, or an *Ornithorhynchus anatinus,* in its natural habitat.

Imagine drawing wildlife from real life. What a treat that would be. To see how a kangaroo looked through all the movements of its powerful legs and tail. To see a koala actually up a tree eating gum leaves. To see how the reflections of water might play light tricks against a platypus's fur. Now, that would be something for an artist to witness.

He still studied under Fidelia's tutelage in the afternoons, though it wasn't the same without Secret beside him. The three of them were seldom together these days. The occasional Saturday outings to St. Kilda beach, where they competed to be first into the water, were few and far between. Joshua was amazed at how fast he and Secret could run upon Fidelia's directive of, 'Last one in the water must recite a poem'. Poetry, after all, was never his forte, nor Secret's for that matter.

Fidelia's efforts to encourage him to appreciate literature fell equally flat, since his reading interests tended more towards natural history. He wondered what it might have been like to meet Charles Darwin, or better, to have travelled with him on his voyages on the *Beagle.* What a life that was. And what a man of prolific opinion and wisdom.

Joshua could better liken himself to Sir Joseph Banks, at least from an artistic point of view, although he much preferred to draw animals, whereas Banks was more remembered for his depictions of plants. But Joshua admired the detail in his works and the flawless execution of his research. He could learn much from such a man. Or, in his absence, from his legacy.

He could already see improvement in his own work. In his and

Fidelia's second literary collaboration, *They Call Me Macropus giganteus,* he evinced a definitive "Joshua Wright" style.

Where did this talent come from – could his father draw, his mother? – he would never know. But he felt blessed that such a talent had been bestowed on his small shoulders. Blessed that he had an ability which could also earn him money. Blessed that others had recognised his talent and enabled him to extend himself to wherever it might take him.

And he was blessed that he had transcended the bounds of life as an unhappy orphan to now revel in a life of prosperity, brought about by a man with vision and a girl with a big heart, a wealth of knowledge, and uncanny insight.

The summer holidays presented the opportunity for Fidelia and the boys to enjoy each other's company. Carefree picnics on the lawn at Fitzroy Gardens, complete with blanket, hamper and scones, were an almost daily event. On this day, they had retired to the shade of a willow to escape the scorching sun; far enough from the creek to avoid the irksome smell.

'What are you sketching, Joshua?' Fidelia asked, lifting her head from Secret's lap. Secret leant against the tree trunk absentmindedly running his fingers through her hair.

'You two, and you can't see it until it's finished.' Joshua lay on his stomach, propped on his elbows, his sketchbook tilted against the wicker basket. 'You look like a married couple.'

He didn't mention which of them captivated him most. Fidelia was becoming more attractive every day in her girlish way, but Secret had no notion of his good looks and disconcerting magnetism.

Fidelia lifted her head. 'Joshua, you mock us. Marriage is for those who can't abide their own company; who need to share every little detail of their life.'

'Rubbish,' said Joshua. 'I think you would be hard pressed to deny your hand to Secret – or to me. One day, when we're all old enough.'

'Never. How could I choose between you? Besides, you're my brothers.'

'Not really, of course.'

'No, not really, but essentially.'

'If you never marry,' Secret said, 'you will never have children.'

Fidelia poked her tongue out. 'Plenty of children at the orphanage need a mother. Why make more when so many have no parents?'

'There's logic in that,' Secret said.

'We all know what it is to have no parents. Not a day goes by that I don't think of Mother and Father, or wonder what happened to them. And we all know what Mr and Mrs Billings and Pa and Ma were missing before we came along. That's what I'll do. When I have made so much money that I can't possibly spend it all, I will adopt five children – no, six!'

'Is there no end to your generosity, Fidelia?'

'Wealth – if you're lucky enough to have it – should be shared, Secret.' Fidelia fanned her face with a fallen willow branch. She was becoming sticky in the heat. 'Are you drawing us as caricatures, or for real?' she asked Joshua.

'Fidelia, darling, I have made that nose of yours longer than an aardvark before. Now I see wisdom in drawing it as perfect as it is.'

'You will be famous one day Joshua. And prosperous.'

Melbourne itself was a prosperous place. New buildings were raising the skyline to three or four storeys. It was as though the streets were paved with gold. Indeed, it could have been said they were; such was the legacy of the gold rush of the previous decades in central Victoria. Men had money to spend, and lots of it. They flaunted opulent homes filled with ornate furnishings and fittings, fine clothing, original artworks, epicurean diets and gambling. Alcohol too was a wealthy man's prerogative; a working man's reward. It flowed freely in the colony's many flourishing hotels, much to the chagrin of many long-suffering wives.

It was now, by an act of Parliament, compulsory for children to attend school, but such prosperity meant that people, even common people, had more choice as to where that education might be had. Not everybody could afford Melbourne Grammar or the Methodists' Wesley College or other non-secular institutions popping up about the City of Melbourne. Some simply preferred a secular education in which learning, rather than religion, was the key premise.

It was such an establishment that Madeleine and Myrtle, and of course Fidelia, aspired to open. One that did not pander to religious beliefs, nor discriminate against those of any particular theist or atheist viewpoint.

Such a notion might prove difficult, despite the passion of the women, for they were not versed in the intricacies of buying property. But, as with the many other hare-brained notions this silk-and-lace-clad female triumvirate had put before him, it took only a moment for Billings to see the wisdom of the idea.

Yes, he would put up the money. Yes, he would help them find an appropriate building. Yes, he would help with the advertising of it. What more could he do? He would never hear the end of it otherwise. And, of course, he knew it would work. He had a feel for such things.

There was he, more successful than he could ever have aspired to be. More successful even, than E.W. Cole himself, if *he* were a benchmark against which to be compared. Edward Cole did not have two stores and two more in the planning. Of course, Edward Cole was probably busy writing religious tracts, as was his bent. Billings had read some of Cole's work including *The Real Place in History of Jesus and Paul,* a treatise Billings thought convoluted and bizarre. Perhaps *he* wasn't one of the "rational Christians of all denominations" that Cole was aiming to enlighten with his views.

Billings was in the process of negotiating a lease on a new premises in Camberwell and another further afield, at Geelong. Indeed, there was no stopping him from expanding further. Perhaps Bendigo, perhaps Ballarat, perhaps that place along the Gippsland rail line he'd read about the other day…a place with the strange name of Traralgon. He would have managers follow his model of how his store and brasserie should be operated and he would grace them with visits on occasion, as his whim took him.

Yes, he would do all these things. But now, he had a school to establish. A school that would bear his name. Madeleine's name actually, but still the Billings name. Billings and Godwin – as it should be, despite Myrtle and Jasper having no financial stake in the venture. Convenient it was, that the perfect building for this enterprise should be available at exactly the right time and only a block from their Stephen-street residence.

Fidelia called it serendipity. Billings called it luck. Madeleine called it opportunity.

The rest of Melbourne called it the Billings-Godwin School.

In preparation for its grand opening, it was advertised in *The Age* and *The Argus* as:

Billings-Godwin School
for Girls and Boys
of Secular and
Non-Secular Disposition.

S

Sophronia Slubberdegullion Shamelessly Sought Solace and Sympathy, and Scoffed a Sack-posset and Sandwiches at Billings Better Bookstore and Brasserie (with Snacks) Did she Sincerely? She did indeed!

April, 1879

'I see here, Joshua,' Fidelia said, referring to an article in *The Age*, 'that they are reminding potential exhibitors in the Melbourne International Exhibition that applications should be made not later than the end of June. You had better get to thinking about it, if you want people from the whole world to see your art next year.'

'I still have time to think about it.'

'Now, don't you procrastinate, Joshua. It will be a great opportunity to be seen by some important people. You can't leave it entirely to Jasper to organise everything. Who knows where such a thing might lead you?

'It says here the exhibits will be divided into ten groups, including works of art – that's you of course – and "exhibits connected with education and the liberal arts; furniture and accessories; textile, fabrics, clothing and accessories; raw and manufactured products; apparatus and processes used in the mechanical industries; alimentary products; agriculture; horticulture; mining machinery and products."

'It will be an interesting affair indeed. But you must get your application in, then you have almost eighteen months to prepare.'

'Yes,' Joshua nodded distractedly. He glanced up from his sketch, to study the light and how it cast a shadow on her chin. 'I told you not to move. You must stay completely still or else I might have you looking like Jasper's potoroo.' Joshua wanted to capture the essence of Fidelia's spirit on paper.

He had sketched her many times before, but then he had always depicted a child. He'd noticed of late how she was changing. She was not a little girl any more. At 14, she was almost as tall as he, and was noticeably developing in the chest. Her dresses were now more feminine and she had a penchant for shiny fabrics, mostly in blues and lilacs. She carried herself with perfect deportment and was quite the young lady.

It was as well that she now had access to a monthly allowance, thoughtfully entrusted to her by Billings from her book earnings, to spend on lavish costumes. Indeed, she enjoyed going shopping with Madeleine and Myrtle to the Bourke-street fashion houses, where one could be fitted with an exclusive gown from London or Paris. Fidelia modelled herself more on Madeleine than Myrtle: the two shared a taste for elegant refinement which Myrtle had not quite grasped.

But Joshua was fond of Myrtle. Her style was unaffected and her manner more down to earth. He could rag and tease Myrtle in a way he would never presume to with Madeleine. After all, Madeleine was his mother now, and a son should always behave respectfully toward his mother.

Joshua, now almost seventeen, was bordering on manhood. His voice had long ago deepened and he had a downy spread of whiskers on his jawline. He already had the tell-tale signs of a moustache. It made him feel quite grown up, though his fair hair made it hard to see.

He was envious of Secret's more obvious moustache. He looked quite the aristocrat, despite being only a month or two older than Joshua. Secret was also handsome in a way Joshua would never be, with his piercing blue eyes and debonair attitude. He had a cultured sophistication which Joshua attributed to his attendance at grammar school.

Joshua saw the way Fidelia looked at Secret. It was very different from the way she looked at him.

Fidelia fixed her pose and stared out the window down onto Lonsdale-street. 'The view from your drawing room window is nothing like the one from mine, you know. Our drawing room, if you could call it that, is at the back of the house. Nothing to look at. But this is grand. I can see right up and down the street from up here. It's a lovely day. So many people out and about. We should take a walk up to where they're constructing the exhibition building. I've heard it's really something.'

'A topping idea,' Joshua said, 'but, in fairness, we should wait until Secret arrives home from football. He'd be upset if we went on such an excursion without him.'

'I wouldn't dream of going without him. Now, we really should be discussing the layout for *Kendall Koala*. I think we should follow the same format as *Willy Wallaby* and *Winston Wombat* to maintain the continuity.' She shuffled through the pile of books on the table.

Kendall Koala was their eleventh collaboration. All had been best sellers, yet Fidelia and Joshua were humble about their success. They had never boasted or become big-headed about it. No arrogance or conceit. Neither Billings, nor Jasper, would have allowed it. Nor had they become complacent. The next book had to be as good as, if not better than, the last. They had a duty to their readers to ensure it. Their adoptive parents, both the Billings and the Godwins, were undeniably proud of their humility in the face of increasing renown.

'Hmm,' Joshua said distractedly, 'I wish you would keep still. When you move, the light changes.'

'Goodness, Joshua. I know perfectly well that you could draw me exactly from memory, like you do your animals. I see the way you look at me, especially lately. Don't think I haven't noticed.'

Joshua flushed. He thought he'd been surreptitious in his admiration of her. It used to be her mind he admired. Now it was her body too. He was of an age when it was expected that he should notice such things. He was embarrassed that he had been caught out. Was it so obvious? Was his admiration so manifest? He didn't know what to say.

'You're imagining things Fidelia. As you say, I *could* draw you from memory. It's the light I'm looking at...for the contrast and shading'.

'Whatever you say, Joshua.'

Autumn was such an unpredictable time in Melbourne. Warm and humid in the morning; howling a gale or showering rain in the afternoon; fine again by dinner time. Any outing in this season dictated that one must dress for all contingencies, so Fidelia had taken the initiative to carry an umbrella. But it was a pleasant afternoon and she enjoyed strolling, arm in arm with Secret and Joshua, to Victoria-street. The mellow April sun had brought out many promenaders; others who'd had a similar impulse to inspect the progress of the grand building.

At first sight, it was not as imposing as Fidelia had expected, but it was certainly a hive of activity. The sounds of mallets on timber, and bolsters on stone, rang out like an orchestra tuning up for a recital. A wire fence enclosed the Carlton Gardens to keep the crowds at bay. A large tract which Fidelia estimated to be 200 feet wide had been cleared from Victoria-street up to the front of the building, affording an admirable view of the works. The eastern half of the building was well underway – the brickwork of the first level almost finished – and Fidelia marvelled at the triple windows. 'It will have so much light inside!'

'The foundations are all of bluestone,' Secret remarked, 'with brick on top'. Huge piles of bluestone were off to the left, while to their right was a veritable timber-yard of huge beams being chiselled and shaved into submission by a large party of industrious carpenters.

'It is to have a huge dome in the centre,' Fidelia said. 'It will be the tallest building in all of Melbourne and I heard that from the promenade around the dome, one will be able to see for ten miles in all directions. Can you imagine? Ten miles.'

'I don't believe it,' Joshua said.

'I heard it will be the tallest building in the colony. Certainly it will be the most impressive,' Secret said. 'Let's go up there, along Nicholson-street, and look at the front of the east wing.' He crooked his arm again for Fidelia and the three set off.

The eastern aspect of the emerging building was more ornamental than the Victoria-street frontage, with three large, square doorways and bow windows. The serpentine façade of the brickwork lent it a special elegance. It was Italianate in design and yet, strangely, it did not look out of place in this dusty, brown environment.

'It looks a bit like a cathedral to me,' Fidelia remarked.

'Oh, no,' Secret disputed, 'it's much more attractive than St Patrick's, which is so dark with all that bluestone. So austere and forbidding. I wouldn't ever want to go in there, if it's ever finished.'

'You wouldn't want to go in there because you're not a Catholic, Secret,' Joshua said.

'True. But even if I were, that place would truly put the fear of God in me. This looks more like a palace to me. Or, at least, what I imagine a palace should look like.'

'I think it is awe-inspiring,' Joshua said. 'I wish I'd thought to bring my sketchbook.'

'Knowing you,' Secret said, 'you'll draw it from memory when you get home.'

'Imagine what an event it will be next October,' Fidelia said. 'A true spectacle. We'll see all manner of things from Switzerland, the German Empire, Holland, the United States of America and even India and Fiji. It will be so exciting and – exotic. Yes, exotic. And they will be in the good company of the consummate artist, Master Joshua Wright.' Fidelia unlinked her arms from the boys and performed a curtsey.

'So you *are* going to exhibit, Joshua. I thought you'd decided against it,' Secret said.

'Why ever would you think that, Secret? Of course he's going to enter. If it's the last thing I do, I will make sure that he's there. Even if I have to fill out his application myself,' Fidelia said.

'You can't argue with that, Joshua.'

'You're right, Secret. I can't argue with Fidelia.'

The Billings-Godwin School now boasted 120 pupils. It had grown dramatically in its first three years, once word had spread around Melbourne of its reputation for providing a solid grounding in reading, writing and arithmetic, as well as history, geography and biology. As headmistress, Madeleine had become the woman she was always meant to be. Not a day went by that she didn't thank Fidelia for opening her eyes to what was possible for a woman. Myrtle also had blossomed into a woman she would not have believed existed within herself four years earlier.

While they established the structure and backbone of the school, attended to its day-to-day affairs and propounded the virtues of refinement and discipline, it was Fidelia who the students aspired to emulate. All the students – even the boys – were in awe of Fidelia's capacity to foster and inspire a love of learning. After all, this girl had been a published author at the age of eleven, had ten volumes to her credit, and still found the time to read two hours a day and help out, when needed, at *Billings Better Bookstore and Brasserie*.

Most tried hard to follow her advice – 'be *all* that you should be'. To the girls she would say, 'Be Cordelia – but don't get hanged!'

Some of the children were convinced that Fidelia had more hours in her day than they did, while others acknowledged the merits of never wasting a moment in idleness or lethargy.

Jasper had long outgrown his studio in the rear of *Billings Better Bookstore and Brasserie*. He now worked from an address in Russell-street, under Billings' patronage. He had more freedom now to pursue his craft.

Billings had provided the means, but it was a philanthropic gesture. He no longer needed to earn income from his friend's artistry, although he maintained space in his stores as an outlet for Jasper's creations. Jasper was so busy nowadays that he'd employed an apprentice to perform the more mundane tasks – slip-casting, cleaning up, loading the kiln and the like. This left Jasper with more time to work on his moulds and his one-off sculptures, for which he had a long waiting list.

He was currently working on a commission for his friend, Frederick McCoy. McCoy had, two years previously, published a poster identifying five dangerous snakes of Victoria: the Death Adder and the Brown, Tiger, Copper-headed and Black snakes.

McCoy thought they might look dramatic replicated in clay. Jasper was not so convinced. They all looked much the same to him, but he humoured the scientist and acquiesced to the commission. It was McCoy's money, after all.

He enjoyed lively debates with McCoy; their views on Darwinism diametrically opposed. While Jasper saw great wisdom and logic in Darwin's observations, McCoy ascribed to the view that *he* could produce geological confirmation of the phases of creation outlined in *Genesis*.

The more animated, verbose and riled McCoy became, the thicker his Irish brogue became until it rendered his conversation incoherent to Jasper. Jasper would stand back and laugh, hands on hips, until McCoy realised, once again, that Jasper had got his goat. Sometimes Jasper wondered whether McCoy's flaming red beard might spontaneously combust. McCoy always, ultimately, saw the humour in his vehemence and apologised for sermonising.

Lucas Billings was an exceedingly busy man, but not so busy that he couldn't take the time to plan where his next shop might be or what enterprise he might propose next. Sydney was a likely prospect, but Madeleine had her doubts. She felt that such a venture might keep him away from home too long. Already she seldom knew where he might be at any given moment. Ballarat, Geelong, Bendigo, Traralgon, Wangaratta, Warragul, St. Kilda, Camberwell, Bourke-street.

Sometimes even he didn't know where he was supposed to be,

but he revelled in the travelling and the wondrous sights along the way. He only knew that wherever he was, he was welcome; such was his capacity to see the good in others and draw it out of them. He had the uncanny knack of determining a person's worth within moments of meeting them – and he was seldom wrong. His many employees were fiercely loyal and most aspired to reflect the integrity, empathy and genuine compassion that he showed them. He was also a generous man. He could afford to be. Despite his self-made affluence, Lucas Billings was not one to shun the hoi polloi or place himself on a pedestal.

Indeed he was as happy to be seen in the company of street merchants or stable-hands in one of Melbourne's seedy hotels as he was to be seen in the elite circles, sharing high tea with others of the *nouveau riche* or *tête-à-têtes* with this political dignitary or that renowned author at the Melbourne Club. He believed that every person had an interesting point of view – something worth listening to – and he was a good listener. This was undoubtedly why all his employees, customers, associates and acquaintances felt at ease with him. His demeanour was always fatherly and equable.

His only vice, if it were to be called a vice, was that he had little time for people who underestimated their own value. *Intresiacs* he called them. He had borrowed the word from Fidelia. He'd overheard her referring to Joshua as such, not long after the boys had come to live with him, and then heard her explain to Joshua what it meant.

He wondered how many of the other interesting words Fidelia used were known to anyone other than her. It was hardly surprising, though, that she was already an author. Such a mind for an author, to create words where none existed for the specific purpose. He wondered what the future would bring for her.

The one thing he knew was that it would be a successful and important future, carried out with typical Fidelia aplomb.

T

*Theodosia Tomboy, Tired of her Tenebrous Tyrannical Tutor,
Thought a Tincture might Topple her Tormentor at
Billings Better Bookstore and Brasserie (with drugs)
Did she Truly? She did indeed!*

October, 1880

Fidelia had never seen so many people in one place, nor heard so many different tongues. Snatches of familiar French here, murmurs of indecipherable Germanic phrases there. Clusters of people caught in deep discussion blocked the thoroughfares in places and it was hard to know in what language to beseech them to make way. It was like fighting against a strong current and made it nigh impossible to see any of the displays properly. Fidelia was glad she was taller now than when she had first visited the museum, else she might not see a thing.

The Melbourne Exhibition Building today was a microcosm of the whole world and Fidelia did not wish to be anywhere else. Save, that was, for the twelve eight-and-nine-year-old children who were accompanying her today. Despite their excitement at seeing as much as possible during their three-hour excursion, the children suffered from a collective deficit of attention and were becoming tired and tiresome.

Madeleine, Myrtle and the new teachers, Felicity and Ava, all had their own entourages of children to contend with. This was a major outing on the Billings-Godwin School calendar. A once in a lifetime opportunity for some of the children.

They had marvelled at Fijian dancers, giggled at Dutch women in their funny lace head-dresses, smelled the German beer being served by gruff-sounding men in lederhosen, gaped at peculiar machines and implements designed for obscure agricultural purposes and admired many traditional crafts. It was an assault on the senses. Noisy, fragrant, tempting, tactile and enervating. But exhilarating as well.

The tumult did little to dampen Fidelia's curiosity about the world. Indeed, it was inflamed, ignited like a burning torch, illuminating the wonders of the universe which had been placed before her eyes.

She hoped the children were experiencing the same sense of awe. She hoped this would convince them that Melbourne was not the whole world, nor anything more than a tiny speck on a vast, unfinished map.

The building was impressive; a great light-filled cathedral with ornate vaulted ceilings and central naves joining at the majestic central dome. Fidelia and the children looked up into the dome with astonishment.

'It is the largest building in the *whole* of Australia,' Fidelia told the children.

Fidelia knew, from Joshua's directions, where he and Jasper would be located, but it was taking an eternity to find them. At last, she saw their booth, adorned with framed lithographs, rolled up unframed prints, shelves full of animal figurines and piles of their books. An easel, located to the side, carried a sheet of blank paper, ready for Joshua's next portrait commission.

Joshua was busy with customers. Fidelia could see him placing a book into a bag and handing it to a woman dazzling in peacock blue. Her monstrous hat, which looked like it had inadvertently captured the inhabitants of an aviary, threatened to topple from her heavily coiffed head as she bent forward.

Such ridiculous attire, Fidelia thought. So outlandish and unnecessary. Why did some women seek to look like a walking zoo or botanic garden? Was it merely to draw attention to themselves? To be more ostentatious than the next woman?

Between her hat and her voluminous bustle, the woman took up the space of two people. Some women simply had more money than sense. Fidelia would never be like that. For sure, she would one day have a lot of money, but she wouldn't poke it in people's faces like the lady in the hat did. And she would not be seen dead in such a daft get-up.

Jasper was also busy, holding up two of his sculptures so that a rough-looking man, undoubtedly European, could admire them from all angles. As Fidelia approached the stall, she instructed her charges to stay together in a group. The peacock woman was holding the hand of a small girl. The child's blonde curls bounced under a pink bonnet as she jigged up and down. Something about her fleetingly reminded Fidelia of Permelia. The child was moving along, tapping her hands on each pile of Fidelia and Joshua's books.

'What's this one? What's this one?' she asked Joshua in a childish drawl. Joshua, now deep in discussion with two impeccably-dressed gentlemen, was too busy to reply to her incessant questions.

Fidelia intervened. 'This one,' she said, 'is called *Never Bother a Belligerent Badger* and this one is *Chasing Hoppity-Boo* and this one is *Willy Wallaby* and then we have *Winston Wombat and Kendall Koala…*'

'Yes, I've bought her that one,' the woman said impatiently, resenting Fidelia's explanations. 'Not that she was asking you. If the young man could see fit to answer her questions, or if the author were here–'

'I *am* the author,' Fidelia said. She put her hand out to shake the woman's hand.

The woman ignored it. She eyed Fidelia up and down like she were some museum specimen in a glass cabinet. 'Hmph.'

'What's this one?' the child interrupted, pulling another book from a pile and holding it up to Fidelia.

'That one, dear, is our latest book in the series. *Pleasant Possum.*'

The child squealed with delight. 'My daddy's name is Pleasant. Mummy, can we get that one too?'

'Now, that's remarkable sweetie. My daddy's name was Pleasant too, but he–'

A strange, choking sound disrupted her flow. Fidelia looked at the child's mother.

She looked like she had been hit by the Geelong train.

Fidelia tossed and turned. Tangled in her sheets, sleep was not forthcoming. *My daddy's name is Pleasant.* What was it about the child's words and the woman's demeanour and their sudden vanishment into the crowd?

There one moment, gone the next. Like a sideshow magician had waved a wand and flooffed them to another dimension. Magicians may have been there, at the exhibition. Fidelia would find out. Tomorrow. But just mentioning Father's name – *my daddy's name is Pleasant* – had him stuck in her mind.

Not a day went by that she didn't think of him, but she seldom actually spoke his name, as if doing so would make his absence more real. More intolerable. She still thought of him being in the custodial arms of mermaids. Entering an ethereal existence of shimmering shadows. It was how she saw him at night as her dreams assuaged her reality.

Hearing the name *Pleasant* emanating from the lips of another child was disconcerting. Of course, many men were named Pleasant; it was not uncommon. And it was curious that the child had reminded her of Permelia. But it was the woman's reaction that was most discombobulating. Why did she behave so?

Fidelia could not summon a mental picture of the woman – her face had been so anonymous under that canopy of a hat. Nor could she put her from her mind. Something about the whole episode was peculiar, yet Fidelia couldn't put a finger on what it was.

What was she thinking? The child's father could be any of a thousand Pleasants. Her own Pleasant Fidelius Knight was long since gone to God and she was the only remaining evidence that he ever even existed. Not that she could prove that. Half a dictionary was still all she had to prove his being and, for that matter, her own identity. Even that was tenuous.

When she finally slept, she dreamt about Father, alive and well and living in Melbourne. And all she had to do was find him.

The Melbourne International Exhibition was a triumph. The chance to see so much talent, artistry, imagination and industriousness under one large roof was not to be missed. It was as well that it was running for seven months. That gave Fidelia, Madeleine, Myrtle and Secret the opportunity to visit several times.

It was hard work, though, for Joshua and Jasper to man their display day in, day out, but Billings offered his staff, on a rotating roster, to relieve them for an occasional morning or afternoon.

For Joshua, the art world seemed to be at his feet. In his limited snatches of time away from his booth, he tried to see all the artworks displayed. It was as though the Louvre and every other European art gallery had been divested of their collections to be showcased in Melbourne. Joshua could only marvel at the tapestries, the oil paintings, the lithographs and engravings; most especially those featured in the French exhibition. Art spoke a universal language. One need not know French, or German or Dutch to admire the work of their countries' artisans.

He was particularly taken with the streetscapes of Paris and also the portraits. The artist Herkommer entranced him with portraits of Alfred Tennyson and Wagner; Eugène André Champollion intrigued with his *Arabs Playing with a Vulture;* and Joseph-Félix Bouchor delighted with his oil painting, *Farmyard in Brie.* But it was a painting by La Guillermie that Joshua knew he would have to show Secret. It was entitled *Gulliver in the Island of Lilliput.* Joshua still liked to tease Secret about being a Lilliputian, even after all these years.

He could learn a lot just by looking at these works, but Joshua got to thinking about how much more he might learn if he could go there – to Paris, Amsterdam, Berlin. To visit these artists' studios, learn their techniques. He had already made acquaintance with several members of the French delegation and a few had come to admire and comment on his work.

One man in particular, a rotund gentleman with a neat moustache and Macassar-oiled hair, was very taken with Joshua's portraits and animal sketches. He patted Joshua on the shoulder. *'Un triomphe pour un si jeune,'* he commented.

Joshua didn't know what he was saying, but sensed it was positive from the tone of his voice. The man handed Joshua a calling card.

> Edouard Prilibert
> Pourvoyeuse des beaux-arts
> 61 Rue de Montmorency
> Paris

'Cherchez-moi si jamais vous veniez à Paris. Je serai heureux d'être de l'aide,' said the man, presumably Mr Prilibert, shaking Joshua's hand warmly.

Joshua shook his head at the man, indicating that he hadn't understood. It was evident Mr Prilibert did not speak English. Joshua offered him a pencil and paper and the man wrote down his message. Joshua hoped Fidelia might decipher it.

'He's an art dealer, Joshua.' Fidelia studied the calling card and then the slip of paper. She sipped from a cup of tea as they sat by the window in the Billings' drawing room. 'He may be an artist himself. He says here that if you should ever go to Paris you should look him up. He would be happy to assist you.'

'Goodness me. I think he must have liked my work.'

'I think everybody likes your work, Joshua. Who would not, after all?'

'But it means my work has artistic merit – rather than just being nice to look at.'

'I guess it does.'

'Do you think I could ever go to Paris?'

'Of course you could. We're not at the end of the earth here, you know. You should have more than enough money, from your royalties, when you turn eighteen.'

'Oh yes, of course.' Joshua's eyes widened at the revelation.

'I went there once, you know, with Father. I was only seven. It was spectacular. The Champs Elysees, the Arc de Triomphe de l'Étoile, the Louvre – ah! the Louvre – the Notre Dame de Paris. Father showed me everything. And we ate and ate. The pâtisseries, Joshua. Well, you could not go past them without wanting to try something new. Ah, *mille-feuilles* – a thousand leaves – pastry with custard and icing. Impossible to eat, but equally impossible to not. You would love it, Joshua. You must go. As an artist, there's no argument that you must go to Paris. You would want to visit Montmartre. It is, I believe, where many artists and writers and musicians now congregate. An environment conducive to creativity. I would go there again in a heartbeat. Perhaps when I am a little older.'

'We could go together,' Joshua suggested.

'I suppose we could. But remember, Joshua, you're older than me and you wouldn't want me tagging along. I am still a child, after all.'

'Child? Poppycock and balderdash. You are the most sophisticated girl I know.'

'Aren't I the *only* girl you know?'

'No, of course not. But I would be happy to escort you anywhere, Fidelia. Anywhere at all.'

The few months of the exhibition was a wondrous time, but now it was over and all the delegates from parts local and foreign were gone.

And so was Joshua.

Gone.

Fidelia wanted for him to go. She was so excited for him to go. To experience the life a young artist – and for that matter, a young man – needed to experience to make his way in the world. The opportunity had been too good to pass up. The jolly and enigmatic

Monsieur Prilibert had offered to escort Joshua to Paris on his return trip. He promised to introduce the boy to *'tous les artistes importants'* and to act as guardian for a stay of six months or more. Billings had kindly given Joshua an allowance of twenty pounds, in advance of his eighteenth birthday, to pay for his passage and living expenses.

But Fidelia found herself lost, at a loose end, glum, melancholy, *calabrous*. Yes, that was how she described herself – *calabrous*. And only she knew what it meant. She hadn't thought how much she would miss her regular interaction with Joshua – their playful banter. Even the way he had looked at her sometimes. Was she reading too much into his expressions, his demeanour around her? He would always change his posture when she entered a room, from slouching to upright, hung head to bright smile. And he thought she never noticed.

Secret never behaved like that, but then Secret always looked debonair, genteel. It wouldn't do to compare them. She never had before. Before they had just been Secret and Joshua. Soon they would be Mr Jenkins and Mr Wright.

Soon they would be young men looking for wives. Fidelia doubted that any young woman would be good enough for either of them. How would she feel if either of them married? *Jealous?* Yes, she might be. Yet neither seemed in the least bit interested in the notion. But what if she had to choose between them? What if they both vied for her affection? It wouldn't do.

She would never choose between them.

Which meant she would never have either.

Joshua was the more Bohemian of the two and Fidelia could imagine him fitting right into the Paris art scene. He would become a part of it, entrenched in its beauty, its reality, its truthfulness.

Secret would not fit so well. He would be more aloof, more of the observer, the connoisseur, the bourgeois, the hedonist. Secret would do well at whatever he wanted to do, probably without really trying. And now that grammar school had ironed his Liverpudlian accent out of him, he sounded quite the toff. He could pass well in any society and was, Fidelia grudgingly admitted, now almost as erudite as her, especially when it came to Greek and Roman history, a particular passion. She liked to josh him, referring to him as Apollo, who was, after all, the God of light, music, poetry, prophecy and manly beauty. He was well versed in Latin too, and it was taking Fidelia some effort to catch up to him. She would need a much better knowledge of Latin, given that it was the root of much of the English language, if she were ever to consider becoming a lexicographer like Father.

Which of the boys would become the more successful? The more prosperous? Joshua had already made a name for himself in his chosen field. He was, and would always be, an artist, an imitator of life, a mirror of the world. He would return from his sojourn in France a changed man. For the better or worse?

Fidelia could only speculate and wonder how he was faring in *La Ville Lumière* – the City of Light. She hoped he was being enlightened.

U

Ulysses Ubiquarian Uttered Unbeseeming Ululations,
Upsetting Users and Ushering Umbrage at
Billings Better Bookstore and Brasserie
Did he Utterly? He did indeed!

1881

'Melbourne would be the best city in the whole world – more impressive and vibrant than London or Paris even – if it didn't positively pong,' Fidelia told the class. She walked between her pupils' desks and sauntered to the window.

'Pong, Miss Fidelia?' young Benjamin Wilson queried.

'Pong. It's *my* word for "to smell bad" – a malodorous smell.'

'Oh yes,' Mabel Fairclough agreed, 'it is certainly stinky. But isn't that natural?'

'It shouldn't be, Mabel. I'm going to take it upon myself to raise the matter with those political men up there in Spring-street. I will write them a letter. We should not all have to be so careful where we step as to avoid somebody else's excrement. Do you not agree?

'Now, I want you all to write down as many synonyms for 'pong' that you can bring to mind. Come along, pencils on paper. And then we shall learn about King Henry the Eighth and his six wives.'

'Six wives?' Benjamin was astonished. 'He was a busy man indeed. How could he remember them all?'

'*Bonitas mihi*, they weren't his wives simultaneously, Benjamin. I am sure no man could keep up with that.'

'*Bonitas*? What does that mean, Miss Knight?'

'Goodness me, Benjamin. It is Latin for goodness me.'

Fidelia was pleased that she was able to toss the odd bit of Latin into her English and history classes, now that she was learning it herself. It had been her idea to attend Tintern for two or three hours a week to learn more of the language. Latin was, after all, the root of many of the European languages and the etymology of many current words derived from it. A good knowledge of it was therefore imperative for somebody whose interests lay in linguistics and the derivation of words.

She had commenced at Tintern four months ago. Sharing in lessons as a pupil, with several other girls her own age, was a strange experience, though one she had always dreamed of, and the regular cab rides to Hawthorn gave her a new perspective on how fast Melbourne's inner suburbs were growing to keep up with its booming population.

After congratulating her pupils on coming up with *stink, reek, stench* and *effluvium*, among others, Fidelia steered the lesson from English to history.

'Now, Henry the Eighth was the second Tudor king of England and most noted for breaking with the Papacy of Rome, creating the Church of England and beginning the Reformation. But he is perhaps remembered more for his six wives and his respective treatment of them. To simplify, or help you remember them all, I will sing you a song.'

Fidelia had composed the song in her head the evening before, as a way to remember all those Tudor wives.

Six wives he had, did Henry the eight
Three Catherines, two Annes and a Jane
But how to get them in order by date
Just follow and all will be plain

The first was Catherine of Aragon,
Who he wed for alliance with Spain
They married in June of 1509
She bore Mary; later briefly to reign
But after 24 years he tired of her face
As he'd started to look at another
The marriage annulled; she in disgrace
As she'd earlier married his brother.

He'd been secretly coveting Anne Boleyn
Whose sister Mary had prior beguiled him
They married in secret; she had child within
And Elizabeth she bore unto him.
But just three years would she remain queen
As the court did conspire against her
They plotted and schemed in all manner obscene
Until, on the green, they beheaded her

On the very next day he married Jane Seymour
For whom desire a while he had shown
Not too long later she did him the honour
Of bearing a male heir to the throne.
But Prince Edward the Sixth would not ever know her
As just two weeks later she died.
But she became the sole spouse of this Tudor
To have him later interred by her side.

Two years later, a new queen was sought,
Far and wide the net cast for a plan.
Artist Holbein dispatched to Duke of Cleves' court,
To paint sisters Amelia and Anne.
Anne was the chosen, though not liked by the king
'Flanders Mare' was the name he resolved.
Yet he went ahead and gave her his ring,
Six months later the marriage was dissolved.

He had his eye on Anne's lady in waiting,
Kathryn Howard, in two weeks, was wife number five
Their betrothal was indeed a short mating,
She was young and made him feel alive.
But she was not so enamoured of him
And sought other companions to bed
Of her infidelity, he had a view dim
And so he cut off her head.

Wife number six was named Katherine Parr,
Henry her spouse number three.
She was first Lady Burgh, and then Lady Latimer
She outlived them both, so to wed she was free.
Clever and erudite; a Protestant fast
She became the first authoress queen,
She nursed her husband 'til the day that he passed
So remained the Dowager Queen.

Fidelia wrote the verses onto the blackboard and instructed her students to copy them. She sat back at her desk and began the latest in a long line of letters to various parliamentarians. She was seeking their support for ideas, admonishing them for some foolishness or another, congratulating them on a masterful piece of legislation or urging them to action over issues of public health or such like. Usually, she received no reply, but on the few occasions she did, the letters reeked of platitudes and derision. Imagine if those assigned to write these responses knew that they were addressing a mere sixteen-year-old! It did not stop her from writing. Perhaps one day she would receive a reply worthy of her own correspondence. It was a pity that she could not become a parliamentarian herself. To be disenfranchised merely because of one's gender was ludicrous.

Fidelia now regularly read *Hansard* – that book which she had first seen all those years ago at the Government printer, the day she was reacquainted with Secret. She anxiously awaited its arrival at the Athenaeum Library every quarter and devoted an afternoon to its perusal. She quickly learned that, after reading *The Age, The Herald* or *The Argus*, it was the next best thing for keeping abreast of all important developments in Melbourne.

Hansard also gave her keen insight into the workings of men's minds. They, she decided, were as labyrinthine as the alleys off Cheapside – winding here and there with no clear direction. She had been lost in Cheapside once; had strayed from Mother's side and thought never to see daylight again. She had meandered forlorn and waif-like over rough, cobbled, muck-filled vennels and twittens, despairing of ever finding the comfort of Mother's hand.

Yes, men's minds meandered and they too were often muck-filled and cold as hard cobbles. Men were so full of bluster and froth. A woman saw things in a different, more practical way, so why were their opinions so frowned upon, so anathema to men? It sometimes made Fidelia's blood boil. She was glad that men like Billings and Jasper did not have such poor opinions of women. Parliament needed men like them. Men who might deign to give women a voice and see merit in their existence. Men who would foster and encourage them and not present hurdles to their advancement.

Billings had long ago seen the wisdom of education for women. He knew it was pure logic that if women were not educated and could not read, he would have half as many customers. His sales figures demonstrated that female customers accounted for more than fifty percent of his sales. Whether that meant women read more, or merely shopped more, he could not say, but he knew it would be foolish not to respond to the fact, or build on it. It was common sense. He always advised Fidelia to promote her strengths and defeat her weaknesses.

She had followed his direction. He was a mentor nonpareil. She need look no further for a role model. Jasper was a paragon of goodness too. She always sought his opinion, and Myrtle's, about anything of the slightest significance. They were, to all intents and purposes, her parents and she valued their guidance greatly. She no longer sought to compare them to her true parents.

Such a comparison was unfair. She was certain, as certain as the sun would rise every day, that they loved her as much as Father and Mother had. And for that, she was blessed.

Fidelia was convinced that the reason seven pupils were missing from class today, having been struck down with the typhoid fever, was somehow related to the foulness of the streets. She made this the crux of her letter to the Premier of Victoria himself, Sir Bryan O'Loghlen. Perhaps this new premier would be more responsive than the last and would see the logic of her reasoning.

Or not.

When a reply came, penned by some parliamentary lackey, it referred to her suggestion that human and animal waste might be carried away from the city by a subterranean network of conduits – as had been happening in London before she had left – as 'ludicrously expensive. A flight of fancy. A whimsy. Was she a doctor, a scientist, an engineer?'

Fidelia had expected as much. But she was still convinced that the malodorous stench – or more pertinently the filth from which the stench emanated – in the streets was responsible for the typhoid, the dysentery and probably every other stomach upset in the metropolis.

She had read that an English gentleman by the name of John Snow had proved that cholera outbreaks were connected to foul water. So why would that not apply to typhoid? She had seen children playing in the streets then wiping filthy hands on trousers and pinafores and touching their faces. Surely there was a connection. Darwin and his ilk had referred to it as miasma and blamed the pervasive smells of London and other large cities for spreading disease.

It was no surprise to her that her beloved home was often heard referred to as *Smelbourne*. Flattering? No. Accurate? Indeed. One could not walk the streets on an otherwise pleasant morning without shnerkeling or holding a handkerchief to one's nose or fearing that one might carry the stench indoors on their boots.

The written rebuke made her all the more determined. She wrote again, outlining her hypothesis.

The reply?

Fidelia seethed at the gall of it. It suggested that her *outlandish* proposition might be better heard should she stand for parliament and present it herself, directly.

'But given that you are a woman, and a woman has not the right to vote, let alone stand for office, I see that that would not be possible. Therefore, you might, madam, be better off leaving such matters to the gentlemen members of parliament.'

The letter concluded with the statement that 'no further correspondence will be entered into'.

Fidelia showed the letter to Billings. 'Should I not take umbrage at such remarks from a man who does not even know that you should not end a sentence with a preposition? And he referred to my suggestion as "outlandish". What do you think, Mr Billings?'

'I think your idea has great merit, Fidelia. A similar thought has occurred to me, you know. But this is a problem the world over. Who can know the solution? Although I have read that the city of Hamburg in Germany has instituted a sanitation system not unlike that which you suggest. I might raise the matter with some gentlemen I know at the Melbourne Club. An engineer and a medical man. See whether I can't spark some lively discussion on the issue. Would you mind my doing so?'

'Of course not. If it were to result in some positive plan, I should be most pleased. And might I suggest, while you have their audience, that you raise the matter of women's rights – to vote, to hold office, to maintain property rights.'

Billings patted her on the shoulder. 'Now that, dear Fidelia, might truly curl a few moustaches.'

'It seems inequitable to me that in a few short months, I will have enough money to buy my own house and yet if I were to marry, I would lose my rights to that property to my husband. What incentive would I ever have to marry? Better to stay single, I say. And yet that would be the more frowned upon. Imagine a young woman wanting, deliberately, to remain *femme sole*. Do you understand what I mean?'

Billings ran his fingers through his beard. 'I do indeed. It is quite inequitable. Yet I fear what my associates might think if I were to champion your cause.'

'Mr Billings,' Fidelia said indignantly, 'since when have you worried about what other people think?'

'You are right, of course. And I do hope you're not serious when you question your desire to marry. Marriage is a blessed institution. Besides, I have it on good authority that a certain young man might have such a proposal in mind.' Billings raised one eyebrow, but he was not about to elaborate.

No. It could not be. Was it Secret? Joshua? Neither? Another suitor of whom she was not even aware?

Joshua was still coming down to earth after arriving home three weeks ago, having stayed in France many months longer than planned. He *was* a changed person. Interesting, animated, dynamic, articulate, fascinating. He held Fidelia spellbound with his stories of the people he had met, the sights he had seen, the artworks he had beheld, the opportunities he had seized. His accounts of life in Montmarte, his forays into the French countryside and his brief visit to London, made her envious. And he spoke French so well, almost better than she did. He was almost unaware of his assumed French accent.

Most exciting were his satirical drawings published in *Le Caravari* and *Punch*. Fidelia envied his worldly view of continental life. She suggested that he might find an outlet for such commentaries and cartoons of an Australian flavour in *The Bulletin* magazine.

He showed how much he'd missed her when he had swept her off her feet and swirled her in a full circle around the Godwins' kitchen upon his surprise return. Fidelia had been almost overcome with joy. She hadn't realised how much she'd missed him until he returned.

But then there had been talk of Marie-Hélène. She featured so prominently in Joshua's accounts that Fidelia was certain he was besotted with the young dancer with whom he had shared lodgings in Montmartre. And so it was unlikely that *he* would have intimated at a proposal. But he also spoke freely and affectionately of Étienne, a fellow young artist with whom he had shared numerous escapades. So perhaps his dalliance with Marie-Hélène was of a platonic nature.

What about Secret? Secret had been so attentive of late. Obsequious even. Especially since Joshua's return. She had noticed a change in his demeanour. Much bravado and talk of his achievements. Did he want to be her husband? Was he thinking of intimacy? Was he competing with Joshua for her affection? Or was he merely competing with Joshua? Trying to impress *him*? Fidelia could not be sure. Secret had also missed Joshua deeply, and their affinity seemed heightened nowadays, perhaps a product of that melancholy which had come with separation. But a greater rivalry between them was apparent too, each trying to outdo the other in thought and action.

It seemed unlikely that Secret would be busying himself with thoughts of matrimony. Surely he had more important things on his mind, now that he was embarking on his own publishing enterprise. It would not do to mix entrepreneurship with romance. One or other would ultimately suffer. To speculate was folly. Besides, Secret and Joshua were like her brothers. It would be unseemly to marry either of them.

What other young men of her acquaintance might be vying for her hand? Surely not Thomas Westerfold, the new salesman at Billings. While handsome and prone to a charming turn of phrase, he was most definitely not suitable husband material. His irritating habits of constantly smoothing his hair and running his index finger back and forth under his nose were altogether too bothersome and irksome. He also suffered a slight stutter, although Fidelia noticed it emanated only when he was speaking to her. He had much too nervous a disposition to be taken seriously.

Or was it Jonah McBride? She often spoke to the lad at the Athenaeum. While in no way easy to look at, he was exceptionally well versed in matters political and sociological. He had touched her hand in a quite familiar fashion on more than one occasion. Fidelia was at a loss.

'Oh, do not tease me so Mr Billings. Who is this would-be suitor? No, do not say, for I say, regardless of who he might be, I am absolutely not ready for marriage. I have a life to live, children to teach, books to write, etymologies to unravel, causes to pursue, travel to – contemplate. Why, I would even consider studying at the university, now that it will accept women scholars. I am not of a mind to merely become somebody's wife. I will not be so ordinary.'

'And how did I know that you would say those very things?'

'Because you read me like a book, Mr Billings.'

'Perhaps, but you are a book with a convoluted plot and a perpetually uncertain dénouement.'

Fidelia smiled. 'I will take that as a compliment'.

'As it was intended.'

Fidelia could see that Angus Freeman was not concentrating on her discussion about *Macbeth*. Head down, he was intent on something else and oblivious to her approach. She slapped his hand lightly, forcing him to move his hands from the object of his attention. She picked up the book.

Cole's Funny Picture Book. She had seen them before, of course. These volumes created by Mr Cole himself. They were indeed engaging for children, but school time was not the time for them.

'I shall divest you of this distraction from the matter at hand, Master Freeman. If, and only if, you are of good behaviour for the remainder of the day shall I consider returning this to you.'

Having resumed her seat at the head of the class, and while her students were intent on their essays, Fidelia flipped through the book. It was easy to see why it was so popular and how it served the dual purpose of engaging children's interest in reading and attracting customers to his store. Cole was selling these by the thousands.

They were but a marketing ploy, but evidently a successful one. This was an idea to emulate, as she had done before with Billings' advertising and merchandising campaigns, which Cole had unwittingly assumed came from Billings' pen. She could suggest it to Joshua. Not with a view to plagiarism or imitation, since imitation was mere artless flattery, but as a means of superior educational enrichment. Such a periodical, in a magazine format, might be a productive earner for Secret's fledgling publishing house. And it might provide her with a teaching tool for the benefit of her charges.

Joshua had happily assumed the role of Secret's creative partner and head of printing and binding. He had the freedom to pursue his own art while ensuring that every volume that emerged from *The Secret Press* was of enduring worth.

Secret had made a pact with himself to never publish anything by an unknown writer without Fidelia's perusal and approval of the work. It wasn't that he didn't trust his own judgement, more that he valued Fidelia's opinion, in terms of a manuscript's appeal to women as well as men. She always knew, by the end of a first chapter – sometimes a page or merely a paragraph – whether a manuscript had merit or whether it would take too much time, effort and editing to refine.

Fidelia loved to be involved with the publishing business, but Secret's demands on her time were leaving her with little free time of her own. She advised Madeleine and Myrtle that she would be curtailing her teaching time so as to devote more time to *The Secret Press*.

Billings suggested that, given her penchant for airing her political views and having them fall on deaf ears because of her gender, she might produce her own pamphlet. She gave the idea some thought. She could write editorials under an assumed name and express her political views as a man might. Who would be any the wiser?

Secret was doing this for his latest discovery, a woman named Mary Fortune, whose detective stories, written under the pseudonym Walter Wainright, were his biggest sellers. Copies were almost selling themselves, so curious was the reading public about gruesome crimes and educated detective work. And the readers all the time imagined that a bearded gentleman, cigar in hand, had penned the works between studious sips of brandy. In fact, Mary was likely to pen her stories in the brief lulls of sobriety when her mind and neat copperplate penmanship were in a more lucid state.

Fidelia took an immediate liking to the feisty Irishwoman, some thirty years her senior and rough as a reused grain sack, but could not initially understand why she had chosen to write under a man's name.

'To be heard, girl, to be heard,' Mary responded, still showing traces of her Belfast accent. 'No man will read something penned by a woman unless they don't know it's a woman. So if you want to be a writer for *everyone*, it's a shame, but you must be a man.'

Only now, after months of misogynistic rebukes from those trouser-wearing, pipe-smoking individuals at Spring-street, did Fidelia understand Mary's approach. A young woman who wrote children's books would not be taken seriously as an opinionated pamphlet editor. Writing poetic books suitable for children was one thing – writing words of political significance with a view to imparting change was another entirely.

So now, as she studied *Cole's Funny Picture Book,* Fidelia began to see the wisdom of having more than one identity. Several *noms de plume* might be judicious. For Joshua also.

In that moment, Delphi Day was born. Delphi Day would express opinions that Fidelia Knight should never be seen to contemplate. He would satirise those plum-headed, beer-swilling Spring-street incumbents and goad them into topical public debate. He would hold them accountable for their dubious decisions and conceited aggrandisement. And Joshua, although he didn't know it yet, would lampoon them in pictures. Perhaps she could give Mary another voice with new *nom de plume.* They would take up the cause of women's franchises. Surreptitiously of course. Subliminally even.

Yes, picture books for children to enthuse over and a pamphlet for serious-minded adults to broaden their political and cultural views, were now firmly on Fidelia's agenda. Fidelia was about to become a journalist.

Had this been in her scheme of things? It had not. But the last thing Fidelia Knight wanted to be was predictable.

And how she loved a challenge.

Secret thought both were champion ideas. His concern was for the detractors who would surely beat a path to his door should Fidelia's views become too inflammatory or controversial. While amenable to assuming the role of printer of *The Voice of Reason*, he suggested it might operate from a separate address, not apparently connected to *The Secret Press*.

Mary was enthusiastic. She relished the task of reporting crime-related events and was not averse to donning a morning suit or frock coat and trousers, her hair piled up into a top hat and a moustache – cleverly fashioned from her own hair and applied with animal glue – to complete the disguise, to render herself an unobtrusive witness to events. Many saw her with paper and pencil in hand. Nobody ever *really* saw her. Nobody knew she was *The Eye*, incognito. Her reports, though prone to melodrama, were succinct and incisive and soon gained a loyal following.

Fidelia laughed at the brazenness of the woman. She could learn a lot from Mary Fortune. A lot about making one's way as a woman in a man's world. A lot about marshalling her resources, focusing her views and never taking 'no' for an answer.

She did, in short order, learn from Mary Fortune, that their aliases, Walter Wainwright and Delphi Day, when appropriately attired in manly garb, could venture into the public bars down Bourke-street to eavesdrop – or *earwig*, as Mary called it – on the local tattle. Provided they avoided engaging other customers directly, lest they betray their identities, they were able to glean valuable information on all manner of goings-on about Melbourne. A pair of quiet drinkers with lagotic ears that could detect salacious conversation at ten paces.

It became a regular Friday afternoon affair, though they wisely never imbibed at the same hotel two weeks consecutively. With so many hotels, they could choose whether to spend their time among well-heeled professionals or merchants opting for a late afternoon tipple after work at one of Bourke-street's high hill establishments, or whether to join the labourers' swill at a less salubrious locale. A low place or tied house. Only once or twice did they pluck up the courage to venture into one of the low dens of the back slums and mix it with the drunkards, vagabonds, thieves and prostitutes. It took a week for Fidelia to stop shnerkeling at the memory of the smells.

And only once did they enter the front bar of the *Australia Hotel*, where the male patrons were unnaturally absorbed in unseemly close *tête-à-têtes*, oblivious to anything going on around them. Fidelia thought it odd, though strangely, it made her think of Secret and Joshua. Might they be comfortable here? Mary was more percipient.

'All I can say 'bout them is that they'd not be interested in you, and especially not if they were apprised of your true gender.'

They partook of ale at the *Menzies*, imbibed brandy at the *National Hotel* and sampled Guinness at more than one popular Irish haunt.

Fidelia called it entertainment; Mary called it research.

They eagerly awaited the opening of the soon-to-be completed *Grand Hotel*, opposite Parliament House on Spring-street. The hotel's building work was impressive indeed, opulent and imposing. It was sure to become the preferred watering hole for those Jacks-in-office – and what revelations might part from their lips once alcohol was imbibed.

V

Vertiline Vamper Valiantly Vouchsafed a Virtueless Vagabond,
Vehemently Veiling his Virulent Vulgarities outside
Billings Better Bookstore and Brasserie
Did she Verily? She did indeed!

1883

The Secret Press made no secret of its mission to publish top quality works by established and budding novelists, poets and writers of nonfiction. Naturally, among its first editions was Fidelia's latest work – a memoir about her passage to Australia entitled *Travelling by Knight.*

Secret often wondered how she could fit so much into her days. Teaching, publishing pamphlets, writing memoirs, furthering her own studies, travelling to Tintern for her Latin classes, and being ready at the drop of a hat to help anybody with anything. She was a marvel. He wished he had even half of her enthusiasm and motivation.

Of course, Secret had planned to become the sole publisher of Fidelia and Joshua's previous body of work and they had naturally obliged. Reprints of their dozen or so titles were still in great demand and guaranteed Secret a reliable income during his business's infancy.

But Secret was also proud to count Edwin Exon, his former guardian at the orphan asylum, among his stable of authors. Exon had gladly granted Secret the rights to re-print his *Lost Flower Found* collection of poems, since his original publisher had long since fallen by the wayside. Fidelia's suggestion that a poetry reading by Exon at Billings might attract more sales had been a master stroke. Forty-eight copies of his work departed the store in the hands of happy customers in one afternoon.

The event led to a series of author readings and Billings' cash drawer constantly rang with the sounds of clinking coins. Once again, Billings was in awe of Fidelia's Midas touch. No wonder he, Madeleine and their adopted boys were now living in an elegant terrace in a tree-lined East Melbourne street. The Godwins were enjoying almost equal good fortune, savouring a much more agreeable lifestyle in a newly-built home one street away.

Jasper Godwin's latest sculpture was ambitious. It was as well that his two apprentices, Jack and Clara, shared his passion for the craft and his eye for detail. To contemplate a life-sized giraffe in clay was one thing, to accomplish it, another. It had been weeks in the planning and more weeks in creating the formwork. But now Jasper was on the verge of declaring it impossible. Impossible in clay. Too heavy, too large for his kiln unless made and fired in segments, and too fragile. Long, spindly legs and a precariously long neck were fraught with potential weakness. He threw his hands up in frustration.

Then he recalled Joshua's descriptions of the wondrous marble statues at the *Palais du Louvre*, many of which, he had explained, were originally modelled in plaster of Paris. He thought of Joshua, bedridden in stiff plaster casts those five years ago. The plaster was solid stuff when dry and eminently suitable for the task. Its use had not previously occurred to him, but since this commission was to be housed under cover at the Royal Melbourne Zoological Gardens, it would serve the purpose admirably while being considerably lighter. Also, it could be painted rather than glazed, enabling a more realistic outcome.

Jasper could see the necessity of engaging Joshua's artistic expertise in clothing the creature in its beautiful tessellated pattern.

It took Jasper no time to master the technique of mixing gypsum and water to a slimy consistency and applying it to long strips of gauze to bulk out the giraffe's metal sub-frame and give it fleshy form. It was a messy business and he, Jack and Clara looked perpetually like powdered spectres.

Joshua had never had to climb a scaffold to apply paint to any work. But to reach the creature's head required a climb of fifteen feet. Not as daunting as for Michelangelo painting the Sistine Chapel, but disconcerting for somebody just discovering an unsteadiness of movement at height.

The Billings, along with Myrtle and Fidelia, were astonished at the sight when implored to visit Jasper's workshop to view the near-completed sculpture.

'It's splendid,' Fidelia gasped, 'and so realistic. So tall and elegant – and intelligent looking. I can almost see the African savannah mirrored in his eyes'.

'I'd have thought a giraffe more daft than intelligent,' Myrtle observed.

'Is it not intelligent of an animal to grow so tall, so as to reach the tops of the tallest of trees where no-one else can feed?' Jasper asked his wife.

'Isn't that why God created birds?'

'Well, my dear, I can't argue with that logic.'

'It's spectacular,' Secret said. 'Imagine riding it through the streets. What sights you would see from up so high.'

Billings silently admired the huge sculpture. He ran his fingers through his beard, as he did when musing. Secret's words had him thinking.

'I have a marvellous idea,' he announced.

November 6, 1883

Melbourne Cup Day was destined to be a day of pomp and festivity. It was also the biggest day to date in the life of the distinguished Edward William Cole. As promulgated in his advertising leading up to the occasion, all those Melbournians not of a bent to watch horses vying for supremacy at Flemington would certainly come to the opening of his grand new book arcade in Bourke-street. Cole knew how to draw a crowd and his sparkling new store was already being hailed as the largest establishment of its kind in the world.

The crowds appeared at dawn. Hundreds upon hundreds of people jostling for the chance to be the first to enter the wondrous new emporium. Some had tasted from a Spanish menu within its walls, before Cole had taken over the lease and redesigned the interior to create first floor balconies which overlooked the ground floor.

Policemen patrolled the front of the store, truncheons at the ready to keep the peace if the crowd become unruly. The crowd was but a heartbeat from doing so. Bustles and parasols gave the women, at least, some breathing space, while men pressed shoulder to shoulder as if girded for battle. Patience stretched and humour quashed.

'It'll be unusually quiet at Billings today,' Fidelia said to Mary Fortune as they waited patiently on the outskirts of the crush. 'I do feel decidedly conspicuous in this get-up, Mary. I have never resorted to such chicanery merely to attend a public event. These trousers are most pricklesome and I swear this moustache feels like it might be alive.'

'Oh nonsense, girl. You want to witness this event, but you daren't be recognised, especially not by Mr Cole. So, I say, what choice have you? Come now. It'll be fun.'

'Did I ever tell you about how I used to sneak into Cole's store at night to read his books? I thought he might catch me once, though at the time I didn't know who he was. Quiet as a snail, I had to be.'

'Goodness me girl, you've led a captivating life, so you did. And I thought I was a brazen child.'

'I didn't have anywhere to live at the time. I'd been working for a family by the name of Fleet up in Russell-street, until Mr Fleet thought he might like me as a night companion.' Fidelia had never told anybody this before.

'Surely you don't mean Lester Fleet. Oh my good God.'

'Do you know him? Lester's a silly boy.'

'Boy? No, I know of Mr Lester Fleet. In his forties, dark hair, slovenly–'

'That sounds like Mr Fleet. I never knew his name was Lester too. But how do you know him?'

'Do you not remember reading of the wee girl found in Little Collins-street some time back? Bashed blue and assaulted – you know – carnally. Left for dead?'

Fidelia did recall. She had felt the girl's pain and grief upon reading a report in *The Age*. She had imagined what it might be like to have been so defiled. She nodded.

'Lester Fleet did that. I heard it all at the trial. Fleet's a guttersnipe of a man with a cowering, snivelling wife and a milksop of a son. He'd already given a harlot the back of his hand earlier in the night, up there in some Stephen-street house of ill repute. She testified against him.'

'What happened to him?'

'Why, he's serving time – good time – up there at Pentridge.'

'Mary Fortune, you have made my day. That is, without comparison, the best news I have heard in a long time.'

'Sure, it makes you a lucky girl that he never did for you too.'

'You're right about that. And that was only because I ran away. But it surprises me not one iota that he'd have done it to some poor girl, some time.'

'Doubt she was the first. Men as that as can't keep their hands to themselves. They ought to be…well, prison's where they ought to be.'

A ripple flowed through the crowd. Anticipation. Shushes repeated. Necks craned. People on tiptoes. The doors were about to open. Bodies pressed forward.

But then, heads turned. Eyes were diverted up Bourke-street. Something had attracted the attention of those on the east flank of the congregation.

'What in the name of Saint Crispin is that?' a bespectacled gentleman exclaimed.

Fidelia and Mary followed the gaze of those around them. Fidelia almost bent double in laughter and Mary soon followed.

'Oh, he is a master of timing,' Fidelia said.

'And of upstaging, I might say.'

Two horses pulling a dray approached the crowd. Atop the dray was an eighteen-foot tall *giraffa camelopardalis*, convincing as the real thing. Astride the giraffe sat Secret, shining in red and blue silk, like a Melbourne Cup jockey. Mouths dropped. Astonished exclamations and expletives were uttered. The crowd parted to make way for the impossible sight. Billings sat, legs dangling from the tray of the cart, with a smile more smug and mischievous than Lewis Carroll's Cheshire cat. Jasper led the horses through the crowd.

'Off to the zoo,' he said to those with querulous expressions. 'Off to the zoo.'

'Curse the man,' Cole said, arms folded across his chest. Two red-jacketed employees stood either side of him. 'Does he not know the bounds of propriety? Must he always try to steal my limelight, rob my breeze? Did you see the man gloat?'

'Never mind sir, he will be past in no time and the sideshow will be over,' one employee said.

'A sideshow. Exactly. That's exactly what Billings is. A mere sideshow to my main event. And this, a mere folly. I will not have him irk me so. Now let's get these doors open and show this crowd what a *real* bookstore should be.'

It was almost impossible to see anything, such was the crush inside Cole's Book Arcade. It reminded Fidelia of the opening day of Billings – such a shame she had been too sick to enjoy that; or the opening of Billings in St. Kilda – during which she had been overcome with nerves and anticipation. Now, she was just a furtive customer feigning masculinity and trying to look inconspicuous.

Cole's new bookshop was similar to his other store, but bigger, grander, shinier. And more books than she had ever seen in one place.

Musicians lent a festive atmosphere to the occasion but their notes were inaudible over the chatter of excited customers and the background murmurs of readers cogitating over purchase dilemmas. Laughter reverberated around the vast space as patrons marvelled at quirky mechanical toys set off to enchant the children.

Fidelia was in awe. This was a spectacle. She wanted to drink in every detail. Billings would expect a comprehensive account from her later. She would hate to report to Billings that his shop had been left behind; that Cole's was bigger, brassier, bolder. And much better stocked. She looked up at the light-filled atrium, flanked by the balustraded mezzanines. People were up there browsing through row upon row of books or peering over the railing at those below, like passengers aboard a sailing ship waving their farewells.

As she eyed a moustachioed Mary, who was feigning perusal of a gardening manual while surreptitiously surveying the crowd, she became aware of something tickling her neck. She turned her head slightly. A lilac feather brushed her face. It trailed from a preposterously ostentatious hat and tickled her cheek each time its owner moved her head.

Something about the sensation was familiar. Something about the woman was familiar. Auburn curls and hazel eyes. A stare to melt glass.

Then Fidelia saw the child. She might have been looking at Permelia, such was the likeness. Blonde curls wisping from under her crimson bonnet.

It all came back to her. Three years ago at the exhibition. *The little girl with the father named Pleasant.* Fidelia could not take her eyes off the child. The child stared back, put her hand to her mouth and giggled. She pointed toward Fidelia's left ear. Fidelia put her hand to her ear and realised that her hair had slipped from under her hat. She quickly tucked it back in. Pulled a face such as a young man might when trying to raise a smile.

The girl giggled again. The woman eyed Fidelia, grunted and moved on. 'Come Eudora, come away from that fellow. We must look at the dictionaries for your father'.

A father named Pleasant who liked dictionaries? Surely that was a coincidence. Fidelia was intrigued. 'I have a task for you,' she whispered to Mary. 'How are you at following somebody, without them knowing you are following them?'

'I do it all the time. Amazing what you can learn from following someone.' Mary slipped the paper-wrapped book she'd bought into her suit pocket.

'Good, then I would like it if you would follow that lady and child. Keep a close eye on them and tell me where they go. Follow them home after, if you would, and see what you can find out.'

'What's this all about, now?'

'I have this notion that they might know the whereabouts of my father. That indeed, he might be alive and here in Melbourne.'

'Good gracious, girl. I thought you said he was long drowned at sea.'

'Yes, I did. And so I thought. But this is the second time I've seen this woman and child and the second time the child has given me cause to— Oh, look, they're going. Best get after them. Here's threepence for a cab should you need it.'

What if Father were still alive? What if he had been right here in Melbourne all this time?

It wasn't possible that she'd mourned a man all these years for no good reason. Except that he had been lost to her, which was tantamount to being dead, if one thought about it.

But why would he have abandoned her? Was it not enough that he had lost his dear Jessamine and her baby, that in his grief, he would voluntarily abandon his only remaining child? He was not a selfish man. Fidelia couldn't countenance the idea.

But if this man were not her father, who was he?

This man named Pleasant who liked dictionaries and had a daughter who looked like her sister.

It didn't bear thinking about. But she had to know.

W

Walter Whimsey Wailed Wickedly of Wasps, Wizards and Witches,
And Waved Weirdwardly at Waygone Warlucks Waiting in
Billings Better Bookstore and Brasserie
Did he Wholeheartedly? He did indeed!

Mary instructed the driver of the hansom cab to follow the woman's cab ahead of them but to remain unobtrusive. The driver thought it a merry lark. They turned left into Exhibition-street, formerly Stephen-street, and continued up to Victoria-street before veering off along Rathdowne-street, past the Carlton Gardens and the exhibition building. Presently, they turned left into Faraday-street and the cab ahead reined in to the left.

'Keep on a wee way,' Mary instructed her driver. As they passed the stationary cab, she saw the woman and her daughter alight the vehicle. They walked straight into a two-storey terrace house, resplendent in filigree wrought-iron lace work and a rampant, blooming wisteria the colour of the woman's outfit. They closed the heavy black front door behind them.

Mary told the cab driver to stop. She wondered what pretext she could use to knock on the door and garner information about the family. She clasped the book she had bought at Cole's, still wrapped in brown paper and tied with string, and alighted from the cab. She was not certain her disguise would stretch to passing herself off as a man in conversation. If the man of the house was at home, she could find herself confronted by him with no good explanation for her intrusion. She paced, thinking.

Perhaps she could engage the little girl in conversation. Little girls were notorious for not keeping secrets. What a pity that she didn't know the family's surname.

She entered the gate of number 161, admiring the tiny, manicured garden, pansies and Sweet William in bloom alongside the wisteria on the path to the front door.

Once on the porch, Mary shrank back as she read the brass plaque on the wall.

P.F. Knight Esq

Surely not! *Pleasant Fidelius Knight?* Perhaps this really *was* the home of Fidelia's father. Mary hadn't thought it at all likely.

Before she could decide whether to knock or ring the bell, the door swung open. A maid, dressed in white pinafore and cap, a besom in hand, stepped out, blinking at the brightness of the daylight.

'Oh, me goodness, sir. Why, ye did give me a start. Can I 'elp ye with somethin'?'

'I want to speak to the gentleman of the house, Mr Knight, if I might.' Mary spoke in the deepest voice she could muster.

'Naw. He ain't in, mister. Gone t' the Cup. Y'know the big fancy race? Not sure when t' expect 'im back.'

'Perhaps Mrs Knight? I bring a special delivery, you see.'

'Now, she just come home. She's quite spent I'm afraid. Gone upstairs t' bed for a nap. But I could pass the parcel on, if ye like.'

'I do appreciate that. But I am under strict orders to deliver this personally. Tomorrow maybe?'

'He'll be at work tomorrow. Over at the university, ye know.'

'Of course. And what does he do at the university?'

The maid shook her head. 'Somethin' with a long name.'

'English,' came a small voice from inside the house. Mary peered around the maid and through the open door. A blonde girl with dimpled cheeks emerged. 'He's a lexicographer. He teaches English and linguistics.'

'That's interesting, now,' Mary said. 'And what's your name?'

'My name is Eudora.'

Mary smiled at the girl, who bore a striking resemblance to

Fidelia. It now seemed highly probable that her father was also Fidelia's father.

'I saw you in the bookshop,' the girl said coyly. 'Just before. Do you work there?'

Mary wasn't sure how to respond. 'Sometimes. Let's say I run errands sometimes. And I love books.'

'I have a big book. Daddy gave it to me.'

'Do you, now? Would you show it to me?'

The girl ran down the hallway. She returned momentarily, labouring under the weight of a huge, leather-bound volume.

The wait for Mary to return seemed like eternity. Fidelia wished she had gone with her. She *should* have gone too. But she had promised Billings she would wait at the shop for an important delivery while he was off with Jasper. Besides, she was not prepared for a confrontation. She needed more information to go by.

She sat behind the counter alternately clenching her hands and twiddling her thumbs. She had removed the prickly moustache and divested herself of the sack-suit, returning to the relative comfort of her feminine garb. Not one customer had entered the store since she had returned two hours ago. Fidelia suspected this trend might continue for some time.

She hoped that Cole's new enterprise would not herald the demise of *Billings Better Bookstore*. She knew how hard Billings had tried to emulate Cole; to better him. But nobody was interested in *Billings Better Bookstore* today. Today, Cole's was the better bookstore. Many would say it always had been, but that never daunted Mr Billings.

It was a sad truth, but at this moment, Fidelia had more pressing concerns. What was Mary up to? Was there a chance she would see Father again?

Secret's arrival at the shop was a welcome respite. She told him about the episode with the woman and child at Cole's. He was dubious.

'Yes Secret, I know it sounds implausible, but if you had seen this girl you'd understand. Why, she was almost identical to my sister Permelia. It was the same girl and woman I saw at the exhibition years ago. Remember? I could not get them out of my head for weeks. I kept holding on to a thread that Father might still be alive.'

'I wouldn't get your hopes up on that score, Fidelia,' Secret said earnestly. 'I cannot believe that your father would betray you – desert you. Why would he do that?'

There was something he'd always wanted to tell her. Something he knew. The time had never been right. Now was not necessarily the right time either.

He put his hand on Fidelia's and looked her in the eyes. 'I will help you find this man Fidelia, once Mary returns with some intelligence for us. I'll come with you and we will resolve this conundrum.'

'You know, it has just occurred to me, what if, for some reason, Father was told that *I* had died aboard the ship – or that I had, I don't know, fallen overboard – just as I was told that he was gone? I was separated from him a week before the end of the voyage. Perhaps–'

'But who would do such a thing? And why?'

Fidelia hung her head. 'I guess you're right. But that would explain Father being here in Melbourne and never trying to find me. Maybe he thought I was dead.'

Secret tried to take her mind off it by telling her of the escapade transporting the giraffe to Parkville. It had been quite a morning. Fidelia held her breath as he explained how the long-necked giant had almost toppled off the dray. It could have been a disaster. It had taken quite some effort and ingenuity to manoeuvre it into place. Jasper had been most pleased at the installation and Billings had given him a jolly good pat on the back. So pleased were they to have the job done in short order, Billings had suggested to Jasper that they abscond for the afternoon and ride over to Flemington for the cup.

Fidelia was surprised at this news. She had never thought of either man as a gambler, but Secret put her mind at rest. 'Father said he had a good tip for the cup race, a horse by the name of Martini-Henry. It's come all the way from New Zealand. Father thought it might be auspicious to wager on it, given that his own middle name is Henry.'

'Is it? I never knew that. Let us hope he hasn't squandered his hard-earned money on a no-good nag.'

'After this morning's events, I told him he should back the horse named Commotion,' Secret said.

Commotion appropriately described Fidelia's reaction to Mary Fortune's revelation on her return to Billings. Fidelia sat wide-eyed as Mary recounted her discovery.

So Father *was* alive. Alive and teaching at Melbourne University. How many times had she been to the museum and not known he was somewhere there, so close? And evidently, she had a little sister. An eight-year-old sister who did not die aboard the *SS Great Britain*. An eight-year-old sister named Eudora.

The dictionary the girl showed Mary was the proof: the *L to Z* volume of *Samuel Johnson's Dictionary of the English Language*. The other half of her soul. The other book-end of her father's life.

'She told me that she stands on the book when she washes her hands at the wash stand in her bedroom,' Mary said.

Much as Fidelia had sat on her volume to elevate herself. But who was the girl's mother? Who was this imposter in the impossible hats? What did it mean?

'This Eudora might be my sister, but that woman is certainly not my mother.'

'Perhaps your father remarried,' Mary suggested.

'So it might appear.'

Secret said nothing.

Joshua arrived. Mary and Secret filled him in on the afternoon's revelations. *Fidelia's father was still alive!*

Fidelia could feel tears welling. 'But why did he abandon me?

And she has had him as father all these years. I've had no sister, no family. I don't know whether to love him or hate him. Or her. How could I love a sister I don't even know?'

Secret had never seen Fidelia so distraught. 'Best, I think, that we confront him on the question. Mary and I will come with you.'

'And I,' said Joshua. 'I wouldn't miss this. I hope for your sake, Fidelia, that he has a compelling reason for what he's done. When shall we go?'

'Tomorrow.' Fidelia's tone did not invite debate. 'I would see him at the university, without the distraction of that woman and the girl. Do you think he'll know me? Remember me?'

'Of course he will,' Secret said reassuringly. 'Who could forget a face like yours? And a vocabulary like yours?'

Perhaps he was wrong about what he had seen aboard the *SS Great Britain* all those years ago. A scenario in which Pleasant Knight was alive and well was definitely preferable to the alternative. He really should tell her not to get her hopes up, but sometimes it was difficult to tell a person you loved the truth.

Secret pondered all night. The more he thought about it, the more he hoped he was wrong. He would know either way tomorrow. And Fidelia would know whether she was truly an orphan, bereft of any true kin, or whether she had a little sister and, indeed, a father.

He told Joshua about his misgivings, without telling him the whole story. Joshua had tried to reassure him. They talked at length after extinguishing their lamps, as they did every night. Telling each other their innermost thoughts, dreams and aspirations.

They had no secrets. Not since they had learned of each other's affections for Fidelia. They had ironed out what could have become a fierce rivalry; agreeing that neither would ruin the friendship the three of them shared with a marriage proposal. After many long nights of discussion, they agreed that Fidelia might be too much to handle as a wife and that probably neither of them was truly worthy. Better that she remain a friend, an ally, a mentor and a paragon of their platonic admiration than the object of their emotional self-destruction. It could only be expected that they would love Fidelia. Everybody loved Fidelia.

Besides, they enjoyed each other's company and any *affaire du coeur* or thoughts of marriage would set them on separate paths. Any marriage for them would be a mere response to public expectation and tradition. They agreed that they were not ready for such a proposition. They wanted nothing to jeopardise their fellowship.

'So if this man is not Fidelia's father, but some imposter,' Joshua started, 'what would he stand to gain from impersonating another man?'

'An entrée to a prestigious position and the elite of Melbourne society.'

'Who would have such gall?'

'Any desperado wanting to rise above his lot. An opportunist. A cad. A ne'er do well.'

'I can't believe anybody would do—'

'Then you've never seen a desperate man, Joshua. How do you think half the population of this country came to be here? For some petty crime or other that saw them transported at His or Her Majesty's pleasure over the past hundred years or so.'

'I guess.' Joshua preferred to think that such skulduggery existed only in the realms of fiction.

The pall of cloud hanging low over Melbourne matched their mood as Fidelia and the boys made their way to Melbourne University. Mary had declined the invitation to accompany them, as she needed to be present for the verdict of a murder case at the magistrates court.

Nobody spoke. Fidelia's heart beat to the rhythm of the horses' hooves. The animals' snorts at the coldness of the morning echoed her emotions. Buildings melded into a grey blur as they passed; grey as Fidelia's expression. She should be excited, but the uncertainty of what might soon unfold felt inauspicious. A light drizzle dampened their moods further as they alighted the carriage in Swanston-street and made their way on foot through the university grounds. Fidelia lifted her skirt to avoid dirtying it in the runnels between the cobblestones.

She had never been so nervous and despite having Secret and Joshua for moral support, she felt alone. A dour secretary bade them sit and wait. Mr Knight was not available at present but she might persuade him to find ten minutes for an audience before too long.

Secret took charge and told the woman they wished to discuss the concept of a new dictionary with Mr Knight, given that he was an expert in such matters. That circumvented her interrogation of these unannounced interlopers.

Fidelia held Samuel Johnson close to her chest. Even after eight years, he was still her most valued possession. It was appropriate that he accompany her on such a significant occasion. He was proof of her identity, should Father be in any doubt. Would he recognise her? Would he be overwhelmed with joy to see her? She realised, more than once, that she was holding her breath.

Half an hour passed and Fidelia thought she would burst with anticipation. Anticipation mixed with excitement and dread. A feeling she had never known before.

Secret placed his hand on hers, a gesture of comfort. He could sense her tenseness. 'Breathe, Fidelia, breathe.'

She exhaled audibly.

Finally, the heavy oak door bearing the shiny brass plaque engraved with the name, Mr P.F. Knight, Dean of English Language, opened and the secretary appeared.

'Mr Knight will see you now. He can only offer you ten minutes, mind, so you had best be explicit in your deputation.'

She opened the heavy door and ushered them through, Fidelia entering first. She locked eyes with the man sitting behind the desk.

This man was not Father.

He was entirely the wrong shape, age and bearing.

Yet he was familiar. She wanted to cry and shout and scream in frustration and anger all at once. She looked at Secret and Joshua. They could tell from her face that this man was an imposter.

Joshua returned to the anteroom and beckoned the secretary into the office. A witness would be required for the impending confrontation.

Fidelia stepped forward. 'So, you are Pleasant Knight? Pleasant Fidelius Knight?'

'Indeed I am. How can I be of service?' The man spoke warily. He stood slowly and adopted an intimidating stance. He eyed Samuel Johnson, still held firmly to Fidelia's chest. His eyes flickered with recognition.

'If you are, as you say, Pleasant Fidelius Knight, you would recognise me – even after eight years – as your daughter.'

She watched the colour drain from his face. 'You know, the daughter that you abandoned aboard the *SS Great Britain* upon arrival in Melbourne.'

It was clear the man was dumbstruck. Unable to utter any word at all.

'So, either you are a man totally derelict in his responsibility as a father, or you are an imposter, guilty of subterfuge, impersonation, kidnapping and goodness knows what other heinous and dastardly crimes. Perhaps you would care to explain to me what happened to my father, the *real* Pleasant Fidelius Knight.'

'Goodness me,' the secretary exclaimed, her hand on her mouth.

'Which is it?' Secret asked, trying to muster a deep and authoritative voice.

'I have no idea what you are talking about. I have but one daughter and she is, at this moment, at school.'

Fidelia took a deep breath to quell her mounting rage. 'And what is her mother's name?'

'Her mother? Her mother, er, my wife's name is Jessamine. Jessamine Mary.'

Now she knew she had caught him in a lie. 'I have seen your wife and she is most definitely not Jessamine Mary Knight.'

'You are deluded, child. What are you hoping to achieve by coming here?'

Fidelia ignored his question. 'And where was she born, this Jessamine Mary Knight?'

The man stared at her. Clearly, he didn't know what answer to give.

Fidelia was glad that Secret had suggested they come via the police station this morning, to summon assistance for their mission.

'Secret,' Fidelia turned to him, 'I think you could fetch that constable now'.

X

Xavier Xerxes, a Xenodochial Xenagogue, used Xyston and Xiphos
to eXtricate himself from a Xanthippe aboard his Xebec,
in an eXotic display at
Billings Better Bookstore and Brasserie
Did he Xenially? He did indeed!

Fidelia could not believe the nerve and obstinacy of the man. He was still trying to pass himself off as Pleasant Knight, while claiming no paternity of her. The threads of his preposterous story did not draw together into a neat, credible package. The more she looked at him, his exaggerated mannerisms and his blustering protestations, the more familiar he seemed. She did not recall having seen him aboard the *SS Great Britain*; her recognition seemed more recent. Perhaps it was merely that he bore a strong resemblance to somebody else.

'This man is not my father, Constable. He is not Pleasant Fidelius Knight. And yet I am almost certain that Eudora, the girl he claims is his own flesh and blood, is my sister, the one I thought stillborn on board the ship to Melbourne eight years ago. She is the mirror image of my late sister, Permelia. Such a likeness could not be coincidence. I thought it three years ago when I first saw her at the exhibition, and now that she is older, I am all the more convinced. And Eudora is exactly the right age.'

The constable took notes on a pad before addressing the man. 'So you tell me categorically sir, that you are Pleasant Fidelius

Knight and that the woman that Miss Knight here saw yesterday, your wife, is Jessamine Mary Knight?'

'I do indeed.'

Even in front of the constable, a pillar of the law, he lied.

'Now tell me, how can that be? Miss Knight says that you are not her father and that your wife is not her mother.'

'Of course we are not and why she should claim such a thing is beyond me. We have one child and that is Eudora. Perhaps she is trying to hoodwink you, Constable, for her own questionable gain.'

Fidelia handed Samuel Johnson to Joshua and placed her hands firmly on her hips. 'How dare you? You, sir, are masquerading as my father. You are the hoodwinker here.'

'I do not claim to be your father, girl. As I said, I have but one child and—'

The man's eyes were diverted to Joshua, who held Samuel Johnson a little higher, in defiance. The man could not keep his eyes from it.

'Tell me, Mr Knight,' the constable said, 'how you came to be here in Melbourne, and more specifically, in this position at the university'.

'Why, I took up the position eight years ago, at the invitation of the university board.'

The constable drummed his fingers on his notepad. 'Hmm, and how did you make passage, sir? Aboard which ship?'

The man looked at the floor. 'Er, not sure that I rightly recall.'

'Was it the *SS Great Britain?*'

'Could well have been. I cannot recall.'

'That appears a convenient lapse of memory.'

'I suspect,' Fidelia said, 'that he is also having trouble remembering where Jessamine was born.'

'Of course not, child. She was born in the United States of America.'

'As was my mother, Constable. But he would have known that if he had ever met her. The woman I saw yesterday has an English accent, not American at all.'

The constable probed further. 'You maintain that you are Pleasant Fidelius Knight? Then I ask you sir, to tell me to where your letter of offer for this position was addressed.'

The man was taken aback. Fidelia was not sure what the constable was getting at. The constable pulled an envelope from the inside pocket of his coat. He showed it to Fidelia. Her eyes widened in disbelief. She took it and studied the address.

Mr P.F. Knight Esq.
14a Rochester-street
Blackheath

She had never seen this before. 'Where did you get this, Constable? This was our home in England.'

'Can you tell me your former London address, sir?'

The man was flabbergasted, though he tried to disguise it behind his hands, which now covered his lips. He rolled his eyes towards the ceiling as though trying to recall a vague memory.

'Blackheath it was sir.'

'The exact address?'

The man waved his hands as though it would help him think. 'We lived at various addresses. I cannot bring to mind where we were when the letter arrived.'

'But you do recall receiving it? Maybe then, you could explain to us where I found this.'

The impostor shook his head. Wide eyes betraying his loss for words.

'I found this inside the second volume of *Samuel Johnson's Dictionary of the English Language*. The one in the possession of your daughter Eudora, sir. You might have known that, had you placed it there.'

'But how did you–'

'I was at your residence earlier, along with two other constables who are interviewing your wife as we speak. I'm fairly certain that she's telling them an entirely different story.'

Fidelia nodded knowingly. 'They will almost certainly have

learned by now that that woman was not born in America, as the real Jessamine Knight was. In New Haven, Connecticut, to be precise.'

The man sagged in his chair. His game was up. He looked at his secretary. Fidelia noted that she could not return his gaze. She looked more than a little hostile.

The man shook his head in defeat. 'All right. You are correct. I am not Pleasant Knight.'

'Now, perhaps, you'll tell us who you really are,' the constable said, 'and what you know of the fate of this girl's parents.'

'And how it is that you have passed yourself off as a master linguist and lexicographer all these years,' Fidelia added.

'My name is Norman Bartholomew—'

'Bartholomew!' Fidelia gasped. 'That was the man who took me to the orphan asylum. But that wasn't you. Are you telling us more lies?'

'No, I am not, missy. My brother, Mr *Francis* Bartholomew, escorted you after the sad loss of your parents.'

Fidelia thought his tone disingenuous; this hornswaggler with his counterfeit sympathy.

'Tell us what happened,' the constable said.

Bartholomew steepled his fingers in front of his mouth. He did not speak for some time, evidently rehearsing a plausible story in his head.

'My wife Helena and I, along with my brother Francis were, as you are obviously aware, aboard the *Great Britain* making passage to Melbourne to embark on a business proposition.

'A week or so before our arrival, my wife Jess…er Helena, was summonsed to your parents' stateroom. She had some experience as a midwife and a steward told her of the birthing difficulties your mother was experiencing. You, I believe, had already been removed from the stateroom, to protect your innocence, you understand, when Helena arrived. The child was duly delivered but complications followed and, I'm sorry to say, Helena, despite her best efforts, was unable to stem the loss of blood.'

Fidelia had always pictured this in her mind. She imagined it night after night. Wishing she had been there to hold her mother's hand and give her comfort as her life ebbed away. Now, eight years on, she was detached. Unmoved. Bartholomew would have her believe her mother's life had ended with little drama.

The constable thought the story plausible so far. 'I take it the child did not die.'

It was a rhetorical question, but Bartholomew nodded almost imperceptibly.

'Are we to take it then, that you took this child as your own? That you did, in fact, kidnap the baby?'

Bartholomew bowed his head. 'That is true.'

'So, we have you on a count of child stealing. What became of Mr Knight?'

This was the question that everybody in the room wanted answered: and *two* people in the room *knew* that answer.

'I cannot say precisely. I merely heard that later that evening Mr Knight leapt off the stern of the ship. He was obviously grief-stricken at the loss of his wife.'

Tears welled in Fidelia's eyes. Despite believing that this had happened, she'd never wanted to hear it.

He had me and a new-born daughter to care for. And he abandoned us both. Me and Eudora, my sister.

The constable looked set to accept Bartholomew's explanation.

Secret did not. He placed his hand on Fidelia's arm and tilted his head down, unable to meet her eyes. 'How about you tell us the truth, Bartholomew.'

Bartholomew's head snapped up. 'And who are you to be asking?'

'My name is Secret Livingston Jenkins. I was aboard the *SS Great Britain*. And I saw, and heard, what happened on the night in question.'

Bartholomew was wary, but his bluster had all but evaporated.

Fidelia gasped. 'You saw something…and you never *told* me?'

'I am deeply sorry, Fidelia, but I always thought it best you didn't know. Sometimes the truth is more shocking than the belief. Believe me, it's been a difficult secret to keep and a heavy burden that I now lay upon you. But this man is guilty not only of kidnapping, but of murder. I suspect that his wife is guilty of manslaughter, if not murder also.'

Secret turned to the constable. 'You might want to ask Mrs Bartholomew the story of the bottle of laudanum.'

'Why, that's preposterous,' Bartholomew started. 'What would I have to gain from–?'

'Everything. A prestigious position awaiting you in Melbourne, a semblance of prosperity, a healthy daughter to pass off as your own. How were you going to achieve this aim if Fidelia's mother had not had difficulty with the birth? What is wrong with your wife, Bartholomew? Is she barren? Or are you not enough of a man to father a child? Is that why you pushed Fidelia's father overboard?'

Fidelia stared at Secret, her mouth agape.

Bartholomew was nonplussed at this barrage of questions and accusations. 'You had better mind what you are saying, young man. I'll have you on a charge of libel.'

'Don't you mean *slander*, Bartholomew?' Secret retorted. 'Surely a renowned linguist should know the difference. I have not, as yet, put my accusations in writing so they cannot be classed as libel. But just you wait.'

'Now, now,' the constable said, 'I suggest that we all keep our heads.'

'Oh, I haven't finished with this man yet, Constable.' Secret caught Joshua's elbow and ushered him forward. Joshua had not the slightest idea why.

'Joshua, my friend, do you recall the afternoon some years ago when we were to go swimming at St. Kilda Beach?'

Joshua and Fidelia were bewildered by this seemingly unrelated question.

'Of course I remember. It was the day I got hit–'

The realisation hit him and Fidelia at the same moment.

'Huh,' Fidelia gasped, 'that's why you look familiar. Not from the *Great Britain,* since I remember you not at all; and not because of a likeness to your brother; but from a horse and cart. Joshua, lying broken on the road, in agony, his legs crushed.'

The image of the top-hatted man, his startled wife awash with red feathers and a child in broderie anglaise and a pink bonnet wavered before her eyes. *The child was my sister.*

Fidelia realised that she really hadn't studied the faces of the people in the carriage that day. Nor had she drawn a parallel between that woman and the woman at the exhibition, or in Cole's Book Store, despite her obvious proclivity for garish, ostentatious hats. It should have dawned on her sooner.

'And you drove off! You broke both his legs and left him for dead. What kind of man would do that?'

'I am sure I don't know what you're talking about,' Bartholomew protested.

'I know it was you,' Secret said. 'I remember that mole on your nose.'

The constable rubbed his hands together. 'My word, you have some explaining to do, Mr Bartholomew. How entertaining this will be for the magistrate.'

Eudora Knight did not know what was happening. Mother was always there to greet her when she arrived home from school. But today, Pansy the maid opened the door looking dour and crestfallen. Eudora sensed something was wrong before she entered the drawing room, where three strange uniformed men perched on her parents' chairs, and a young woman and two young men stared at her as though she might evaporate any moment.

Her first instinct was to cry, but she had learned long ago that crying did not elicit the response she wanted from others. Father would tell her to 'grow up'. Mother would tell her to 'be quiet and stop simpering'.

Crying was unproductive. As was anger. Or sulking. Instead, she was intrigued. She looked at each of the six people in turn. It was clear none of them was about to explain their presence.

'Would one of you strange, unfamiliar people care to elucidate this intrusion into my family's domain?'

Secret and Joshua grinned at each other. 'There is no doubting at all that she's your sister, Fidelia. What other eight-year-old would ask such a question?' Secret said.

'I am eight-and-one-third,' Eudora corrected. 'What are you talking about? I have no sister. I am an only child. Where are my parents?'

A lump rose in Fidelia's throat. 'Actually, Eudora, you do have a sister. I am your sister. My name is Fidelia. I'm sorry to tell you that your parents – your *real* parents – died many years ago, on the day you were born. These people whom you know as your parents–

How was she to say this?

'They are impostors, I am sorry to say. It's likely that they are going to jail for a long time'.

Fidelia expected tears. A tantrum, perhaps. Some indication of shock or anguish. None of these emotions registered on Eudora's face.

Instead, the child smiled. 'That explains a lot.'

'What do you mean?'

Eudora shrugged. 'I have never been able to fathom how I came to be born of such people. Their views, their treatment of other people, their feigned superiority, their whole demeanour, is anathema to me. I have always felt like a foreigner, an alien even, in my own home. I just know I don't belong here.'

Fidelia couldn't help but grin. She took Eudora's hand. 'Do you love Samuel Johnson?'

'Oh yes, indeed I do. He is my saviour, my companion, my mentor, my confidant.'

'Then let me tell you about Father. Let me tell you about the real Pleasant Fidelius Knight.'

Y

Yudelia Yemeles Yodelled at Yon Yawning Youngling
And Yearned Yarely for Yellow Yarn at
Billings Better Bookstore and Brasserie (with haberdashery)
Did she Yes? She did indeed!

February, 1884

The trial was a long, drawn-out affair. Time stood still as regular daily routines were exchanged for the ennui of endless days of silence on the hard, wooden benches of the Supreme Court of Melbourne. Though it was uncommon for two people to be tried together, the judge deemed it judicious, given that the evidence to be presented pertained to two related murders, potentially committed by the two accused as part of a conspiracy to assume the identities of the victims.

Despite the tedium of much of the evidence presented by the Crown, Fidelia was enthralled. She was impressed that these wig-wearing men of silk could remember so much information. She was impressed also at how the counsel for the defence was able to present such plausible variations of the truth. Plausible to those who knew no better, but not to her or to Secret. She was intrigued that the defendants, Mr Norman and Mrs Helena Bartholomew, had such an unwavering recollection of events which happened almost nine years ago. Their memories were so convenient, so contrived. So dubious.

She became absorbed in the eloquent and persuasive words of the barristers. Their mastery of the language held her spellbound.

They were like politicians, though not so self-serving. They seemed more inclined to learn the truth than some of the pompous sorts up at Spring-street.

Fidelia was hoping to gain a place at the university but she still could not decide between languages and linguistics – which Father would have hoped for her – or politics. But studying politics would be pointless, since she could not become a politician. She couldn't even vote, let alone contest a seat in parliament. Maybe she could become a lawyer, a barrister. Couldn't she? And if that opportunity were not open to her, she would fight for it.

Why shouldn't a woman do what she wanted, study what she wanted, *be* what she wanted?

Because men were afraid of women, she decided. And they should be. Women were much more likely to foster goodwill, reach peaceful decisions, take a compassionate view of things. Besides, women were much better judges of character.

If Fidelia found much of the proceedings tiresome, Mary Fortune could not disguise her boredom. She occasionally whispered in Fidelia's ear some observation about a lawyer or witness, likening them to a weasel or pirate or some such, that caused Fidelia to stifle an inappropriate giggle or nudge her friend in the ribs. Although, upon some enlightening disclosure to the court, Mary would nudge Fidelia to indicate its importance to the proceedings. It appeared to Fidelia that by having her eyes closed and feigning sleep, Mary was, in fact, absorbing every detail which would add colour and clarity when she set about reporting on the trial for her column. She was a rough diamond, was Mary Fortune, but to Fidelia, she was the sharpest gem in the room.

The case presented to the court by the defence was that the defendants had unwittingly become involved in a series of events totally beyond their control. Aside from Mrs Bartholomew rendering her best assistance during Mrs Jessamine Mary Knight's labour, she was not in any way to be held to account. The defence's contention was that Helena Mary Bartholomew was not guilty of manslaughter and that Mr Norman Arthur Bartholomew was not guilty of murder.

They also contended that the couple did not kidnap the child known as Eudora Lavinia Knight, but adopted her out of the goodness of their hearts, given that she would otherwise have been an orphan. They conveniently overlooked the fact they had not deemed it fit to 'adopt' Fidelia as well.

The prosecution knew better. Much of the information it had gleaned about the backgrounds of the defendants had come courtesy of the astute detective work by one Mary Helena Fortune and one Secret Livingston Jenkins.

Secret felt compelled to uncover as much evidence as possible about the Bartholomews' sinister intentions. Even he had been astonished at what he'd learned. He became a crucial witness for more reasons than one. He had also located another witness, whose testimony would be explosive.

He had decided, however, to divulge this information only to the prosecution and not to Fidelia, in case the witness didn't show. He didn't want to get Fidelia's hopes up. What if the jury didn't believe his testimony? What if the prosecution established him as a liar? Besides, he knew that the revelations that would come to light in court would play to her love of dramatics more than if he told her himself.

The first revelation when Norman Bartholomew took the witness stand was that he was in no way a stranger to Pleasant Knight, as he'd claimed to be. In fact he had been a student, albeit a lacklustre one, of Mr Knight for some two years prior to Mr Knight's emigration to Australia.

Through a delicate thread of strategically placed questions, Mr Cromwell, for the Crown, compelled Bartholomew to admit that he had, indeed, sought passage to Melbourne with the intention of following the Knights.

'I put it to you, Mr Bartholomew, that it was your intention to ensure that Pleasant and Jessamine Knight never reached Melbourne. And it was your intention, you and your wife Helena, to usurp the roles of Pleasant and Jessamine Knight and pass yourselves off as them once you reached the shores of this fair city. And I put it to you that Jessamine Knight's difficult labour offered you not only the opportunity to set your plan in action, but also the opportunity to claim the child, Eudora, as your own. Given that, and I stand to be corrected, you were unable to have a child of your own. What do you say, Mr Bartholomew?'

'I say that your accusations and assertions are preposterous and entirely unfounded. It was pure coincidence that we happened to be on board ship together. And I say that, had it not been for my wife's intervention, the child also would have died.'

'You say that, despite the fact that we can establish, beyond a doubt, that your wife had no experience, whatsoever, of midwifery or birthing a child. And that, rather than being summoned to Jessamine Knight's stateroom for the delivery by a steward – as you claim – Mrs Bartholomew in fact offered herself up as a qualified midwife at your behest. And you say that, despite the fact that you have impersonated the Knights here in Melbourne for nine years.'

Murmurs echoed around the courtroom, as they had done each time either of the defendants was unable to give a satisfactory explanation.

Fidelia was glad she had insisted that Eudora not attend. She would have been bored and fidgety. Besides, there was much that she was better off not hearing, not knowing. At least, not until she was old enough to understand.

Discussions about the potency and dosages of laudanum and paregoric were singularly wearisome. That was, until she realised where the prosecution was leading with this line of enquiry.

In her testimony, Helena Bartholomew said that she had administered 'a teaspoon or two' of opium to Jessamine Knight 'to ease the pain'.

Cromwell took her to task over the matter. 'I ask you, Mrs Bartholomew, whether it was tincture of opium or camphorated tincture of opium that you fed to Mrs Knight?' He intimated that a qualified midwife would know the difference.

Helena Bartholomew shook her head almost imperceptibly. 'I believe it was camphorated tincture of opium'.

Cromwell nodded. A deliberate, telling nod. 'For the benefit of the court,' he motioned to the jury, 'and to save us the time of calling an expert witness on the matter, as this is a known and immutable fact, camphorated tincture of opium – also known as paregoric – is one-twenty-fifth the strength of opium tincture. It is relatively safe to administer such a dose in the instance of pain associated with childbirth.

'On the other hand, opium tincture, otherwise known as laudanum, is so potent that two to three teaspoons of the substance could be fatal, particularly to a person not habituated to such opiates. In a person already weakened by childbirth and blood loss, the potency would be compounded.'

Cromwell let the information sink in. 'So I ask you again, Mrs Bartholomew. What was the substance you administered to Mrs Knight?'

Helena now seemed certain. 'Camphorated tincture of opium. I am sure of it.'

'Are you now?' Cromwell could barely hide his scepticism. 'And this "camphorated tincture of opium" that you administered to Mrs Knight, where did it come from?'

Helena was nonplussed by the question. 'Why, the steward gave it to me. He said it came from the ship's medical supply.'

Cromwell fixed Helena's gaze. 'I put it to you that you are lying. I put it to you that, in fact, you had your own bottle of laudanum, which you carried with you to Mrs Knight's stateroom. I put it to you that you deliberately dosed Mrs Knight with three teaspoons of laudanum, *not* camphorated tincture of opium, and then watched her die.'

The courtroom was silent; in a collective state of shock. Fidelia wanted to leap from her seat and clutch Helena Bartholomew by the neck. '*You killed my mother!*'

She really hadn't meant to speak out loud. She was quickly silenced by the judge. Jasper put his arm around her and Secret leant across Jasper to grasp her hand in comfort.

'I did no such thing,' Helena said. 'You have no proof!'

'As it happens, Mrs Bartholomew, I do,' said Cromwell. 'I have two witnesses, both present here today, who will testify that they either saw you with the bottle of laudanum or heard you speaking to your husband about it.'

'Nonsense,' she exclaimed. Despite her denial, she stared wild-eyed at the prosecutor. She knew he had her number.

Fidelia thought the woman looked like Medusa, and half expected to see snakes emerge from her curls. She whispered this to Mary, who did not do so well at stifling a titter.

Mary knew that Fidelia was unaware that Secret had found the steward who had attended to the Knights during their passage and on that fateful night. She braced herself for the coming testimony as the next witness was called. She knew the distress this testimony would cause Fidelia and, in an out of character gesture, she patted Fidelia's hand.

'This could be alarming, sweetie,' she whispered.

David Bracegirdle was the ace up the prosecution's sleeve. As he took the stand, Fidelia was sure she recognised him. He had the unmistakable red curly hair of the young man who had escorted her from her parents' cabin that night. Here he was now, older of course, but offering her some salvation or, at least, some enlightenment.

By way of introduction, the prosecutor told the court that Bracegirdle had been so enchanted by Melbourne upon arrival in 1874, he had returned two years later as a permanent resident. He had, since then, worked as a porter at the *Menzies Hotel*.

A neatly-groomed Bracegirdle told the court that he recalled the evening well and had relived it many times in his head.

'I have lived with the guilt that I should have done something, said something, at the time, but I was in fear of the repercussions. Afraid of what Helena Bartholomew, and worse, Norman Bartholomew, might do to me.'

He regretted his silence, he told the court. And he regretted that he had never done the right thing by Miss Fidelia Knight, the little girl he had shepherded from her parents' room on that night. That action was not, he testified, at the behest of the captain, nor indeed the surgeon, of the *SS Great Britain*.

'It was at the behest of Mr Francis Bartholomew, Chief Steward, and *my* superior officer.' Bracegirdle glared at the defendant as he spoke.

This was the detail that Secret had gleaned when he had sought the crew manifest from the *SS Great Britain* for the voyage of winter, 1874. More pertinent was the fact that the chief steward's brother and sister-in-law, currently on trial, were *not* listed among the passengers. This led him to the conclusion that they had either stowed away, under some clandestine arrangement with Francis Bartholomew, or they had boarded the ship under false names and with false travel documents. Either way, their presence aboard the *SS Great Britain* reeked of intrigue and subterfuge.

Mr Francis Bartholomew, the court was told, would be tried at a later date for conspiring to commit murder and for being an accessory after the fact. He was, it transpired, currently languishing in Her Majesty's Prison Pentridge on an unrelated charge of fraud.

Bracegirdle testified that he had not, at any time, taken laudanum or paregoric to the Knights' stateroom and that Mrs Bartholomew had had her own bottle in her pocket.

'I asked her what it was and she said, "never mind, it'll help her with the pain". She didn't use a teaspoon. I watched her pour the liquid into a glass and force Mrs Knight to drink it.'

'She drank it from a glass, you say.' Cromwell ensured that the whole courtroom heard and understood his iteration of the testimony. 'You say that Mrs Bartholomew did not, in fact, mix a few drops from a syringe into a glass of water?'

'No. She poured it straight from the bottle into the glass and Mrs Knight drank it, straight from the glass. I presumed it was alcohol of some sort.'

'What happened to the bottle after that, Mr Bracegirdle?'

'I took it while Mrs Bartholomew wasn't watching. I'm not proud of myself but I thought it might help numb the pain of a toothache. I had a chronic toothache and the surgeon on board the ship was threatening to pull it. I was having none of that. It wasn't until I got back to my quarters that I read the label. Laudanum. Tincture of Opium it said, with *Poison* written clearly underneath. About twenty-five drops, the bottle said, was the usual amount for pain relief for a person aged in their twenties.'

'And after that? What did you do with the bottle?'

'I kept it. Worked well, it did. Fixed my toothache good and proper. I didn't learn the fate of Mrs Knight until the next morning. Even though I suspected that it might have been the laudanum that did it, I was too ashamed of the fact that I'd stolen it to tell a soul. And for that I am deeply remorseful.'

Helena Bartholomew rolled her eyes to convey her assertion that Bracegirdle was lying; tried to catch the eyes of the jurors in doing so. 'You can't prove it. It's his word against mine.'

'Silence please,' the judge admonished her, 'You cannot speak unless you are in the witness stand, Mrs Bartholomew'.

'If it pleases the court, I offer this exhibit as evidence.' Cromwell produced a small corked bottle with a pinkish-red label and awaited the drama of its impact on the court. 'Mr Bracegirdle, is this the bottle that you took from Mrs Knight's stateroom?'

'Yes sir, it is.'

'How is it that you still have it after so long?'

'I only ever used it sparingly; a mere drop here or there. There's still some left in the bottle.'

Cromwell read from the label. 'I advise the court that Mr Bracegirdle is correct. Opium tincture, as contained in this bottle, is twenty-five times as potent as camphorated tincture of opium. While it might be appropriate to administer the latter by the teaspoon, to do so with opium tincture could prove deadly. I will put it to Mrs Bartholomew, under cross examination, that that was exactly her intention.'

Helena Bartholomew shook her head wildly. 'No, no. It isn't true.'

The judge silenced her again.

Fidelia was astonished that this very bottle could have murdered her mother. And that somebody had kept it all these years. *Bless his heart.* But her joy was short lived.

Under cross-examination, the defence argued that the bottle should be inadmissible. 'There is no proof that it had belonged to Helena Bartholomew or that it was her intention to murder Jessamine Knight.'

Secret smiled at this. He was the next witness for the prosecution and his testimony would put paid to that detail.

Fidelia's heart sank as Secret recounted to the court what he had seen and heard that fateful night. How could he have never told her? She didn't know whether she should love him or hate him for it. But she knew him well enough to know that he had kept it secret for her sake.

He had been up on deck late on that evening, getting fresh air as he was feeling nauseated by the smell in the crew's quarters. His attention was drawn to the stern of the *SS Great Britain* by the sound of somebody sobbing. He was certain it was a man and he thought it unusual that a man should sob. It must have been some dire circumstance to make a man behave so. He was about to approach the man and offer some consolation when he realised that two other people were on deck. A man and a woman, by then engaged in a heated exchange.

'What were they saying to each other?' Cromwell said.

'I heard him say, "Is it done then?" and she replied, "It is. Easier than I thought". I didn't know to what they were referring but I could tell by the conspiratorial tones of their voices that it was something dreadful.'

'And what happened next?'

'Then I heard him ask her, "what did you do with the bottle?" and she became quite agitated and said, "Oh my goodness, I have left it in their state room". He became vexed with her and told her to get it and bring it back to throw overboard like he had told her to do. I didn't know what it was, of course, but it sounded like something too hot to handle.'

'They definitely spoke of a bottle?'

'Definitely.'

'And then?'

'And then I heard him say to her that he would "deal with the other problem". I hid behind the hatchway cover, hardly breathed because I didn't want them to know I was there. She went off down the companionway and I watched him walk to the stern towards the crying man. I presumed he was going to render assistance.'

'Did it appear to you that the two men knew each other?'

'Yes, indeed. The first man, the distraught one, turned and I heard him say, "Norman, what on earth are you doing here?"'

'He addressed him by name?'

'He did, sir.'

'And you are certain it was "Norman" he said?'

'Absolutely certain. And then the unthinkable happened. The second man – Norman – without further ado, placed his right hand between the other man's legs and his left arm on his shoulder and lifted him up and hoisted him over the rails. Off the back of the ship. It happened so quickly I didn't even have time to react, though I could not have covered the distance quickly enough to have intervened.'

The courtroom resounded with a collective gasp. The jurors, all twelve, looked appalled. Their previously inert faces crumpled into shock, disbelief and pity.

Secret grimaced at Fidelia. 'I am so sorry, Fidelia. There was nothing I could do.'

Fidelia's eyes stung with tears but she nodded to him in understanding. Now that she knew the truth, she would never hold anything against him. She understood why he had never told her. But now it was essential that the truth be known. And he would help see justice done to this murderer. Let him hang. As for Mrs Bartholomew, she belonged with her husband on the gallows.

Father had not killed himself. He did not abandon her and Eudora. She had known all along he would never have done that.

But in the absence of fact, one invents one's own fiction and over time adopts it as truth. The reality, though brutal and painful, was somehow easier to bear. Fidelia could only speculate as to what Father's last thoughts were as he plummeted to his doom in the frigid waters of the Indian Ocean. She thought again of the mermaids. It had been a while since they had entered her head.

> *For they are creatures of the deep, my child*
> *Creatures of the deep,*
> *They are creatures of the deep, my child*
> *And they'll swimmingly send you to sleep*

Cromwell asked Secret what he did next. Secret explained that his first reaction was to approach the murderer, but he was too afraid, lest he might, as a witness to the terrible event, suffer the same fate. So he did nothing.

His shame and regret were constant companions. He told the court that he did not, at the time, know the identities of any of the three people and he had retired to his quarters immediately. He did not know whether the woman had returned with the bottle. Nor did he know the significance of the bottle, only that it was to be banished into the sea.

'Aside from having seen that man, Mr Knight, being thrown overboard, I never learned what was going on; the significance of it. Not until I met Miss Knight, some time later.'

'Now tell the court why you never spoke of this to anyone on board the ship.'

'But I did sir. I told the Chief Steward, Francis Bartholomew. I told him the next morning.'

'And what did Francis Bartholomew do?'

'Aside from giving me a slap about the ear and telling me to mind my own business, he...he told me he would look into it. Those were his words, "I'll look into it", but as far as I know, he did nothing. Now I realise why.'

The court knew most of the story now, as did Fidelia and her adopted family. But the proceedings were not yet concluded. The defence had summonsed several character witnesses, though their testimonies had become tainted by what they now knew about the Scaramouch that was Norman Bartholomew.

The most telling, and to Fidelia the most interesting, was Arthur Pendleton, Dean of Humanities at Melbourne University. Mr Pendleton told the court that from the moment he had first met Norman Bartholomew, the man he knew as Pleasant Knight, he had found him a flawed character.

'Not at all the person who I expected to come to us with such estimable credentials. Though relatively well-versed in the particulars of the English language – I realise now, from the real Mr Knight's expert tutelage – he was distinctly rough around the edges. Not the refined gentleman whom I had anticipated meeting.

'I found him to be a braggart, subject to endless rodomontade, a man full of promises that never eventuated. His students found him congenial, but I attest to the fact that I never thought him right for the position. His lack of acumen in his chosen field might account for the painfully slow progress of the lexicon which had been the faculty's primary focus of his tenure. Always he had an excuse, and after almost nine years, we have seen little progress on the project. We had hoped to emulate or rival the work being done by Meriam Webster in the United States and by our esteemed counterparts at the Oxford University. Now, of course, we find ourselves without a helmsman for this important project, an Australian dictionary.'

Fidelia liked this man immensely. His comportment, articulacy and confidence reminded her of Father. She wished they could have met. They would have been firm friends. Mr Pendleton had a similar calibre of language and, given that she deemed herself a good judge of character, Fidelia could tell he was a kind man. A generous man. She would meet him one day, she vowed, once she had taken a place at the university.

She could not have imagined that he would seek her out at the end of proceedings that very day.

Mr Pendleton had heard a lot about her. The police had spoken highly of her. Most especially, he had learned about her love for words, her aptitude as a teacher, her passion for learning. She was her father's daughter: the erudite daughter of a man he wished he'd had the pleasure of meeting.

'I feel sure he would have been pleasant in more ways than one,' Pendleton said to her.

Fidelia smiled at his pun. She told Pendleton that indeed her father had lived up to his name.

Pendleton pressed a card into her hand and told her to visit him at the university at her earliest convenience; after the conclusion of the trial, of course. He wanted to speak to her about the lexicon project.

She could not have been more flabbergasted. Nor could she have been more flattered.

It took the jury a mere three hours to reach their two verdicts. The jurors unanimously found Norman Bartholomew guilty of the murder of Pleasant Fidelius Knight and guilty of conspiracy to murder Jessamine Mary Knight.

They found Helena Bartholomew guilty, not of the manslaughter of Jessamine Knight, but of the more heinous charge of murder. It was, the jury deemed, premeditated. Both were also found guilty of the kidnapping of Eudora Lavinia Knight.

Despite her desire for it to be so, Fidelia felt unusually ill at ease when the judge donned his black cap and decreed that the two should be hanged by the neck at Her Majesty's pleasure at HM Prison Pentridge on a date to be determined. It was a fitting outcome. Justice would be served.

Fidelia thought that the only person, aside from the conspiratorial brother, Francis Bartholomew, who would grieve their deaths was her little sister.

Eudora Lavinia Knight would become an orphan for the second time in her short life.

Z

Zylphia Zoographer Zealously Zearched for Zibets and Zebras
for her Zodiack Zoophorus,
She found them in the Zoology Zone at
Billings Better Bookstore and Brasserie
Did she Zestily? She did indeed!

March 21ˢᵗ, 1884

On Fidelia's nineteenth birthday, she could have been busy attending to her own wardrobe in readiness for the afternoon tea party planned by Jasper and Myrtle. Instead, she revelled in running Eudora's golden hair through her fingers as she modelled it into a cascade of ribbon-laced braids. Fidelia recalled watching Mother braiding Permelia's hair and from the day Eudora had come to live with them, she had emulated Mother's handiwork on her young sister's lustrous hair.

She felt like both mother and sister to the girl. She felt as though her life were more complete. She was pleased also that Jasper and Myrtle had not hesitated in welcoming Eudora to their home. Fortune had smiled upon them all. She could not have been happier.

It was hard not to liken Eudora to Permelia, but her memories of Permelia had faded, as had those of Mother, Father and Ninian. Instead, Fidelia was left with impressions that lingered on the periphery of her vision like will-'o-the-wisps. Certain things reminded her of them. She only had to look at the two volumes of Samuel Johnson, now side by side on the bookshelf in the drawing room, to think of Father and the legacy he had left his two daughters. Her precious Samuel Johnson; her only constant in life, now complete. The two halves making a whole. Like she and Eudora.

Father would have been proud of them. She told Eudora so.

'I wish you could have known him, Eudora. He could inspire like no other person I have ever known or ever will.'

'I wish I had known him too. I can only imagine how different my life would have been. Was he handsome?'

'Handsome as Adonis, though not so complex; sightly as Romeo, though not so tragic; personable as Mr Darcy—'

'But not so wealthy or aloof, I should guess.'

'Yes. You are astute Eudora. He was everything a man should be.'

'Like Mr Godwin?'

Fidelia hugged the back of Eudora's head. 'Yes, not unlike Jasper. You can call him Jasper, you know.'

'I like Mr Jasper. But he told me I should call him Papa.'

'Given time, I suspect you will *love* Mr Jasper – Papa – as I do. He did not *have* to be my father. He *wanted* to be. And I have known such happiness being his daughter, as I am sure you will.'

'I am glad you found me, Fidelia.'

'I am glad, happy, delirious, pleased, delighted, overjoyed, and elated too, that I found you, Eudora.'

'Gleeful, thrilled. And cock-a-hoop. Don't forget cock-a-hoop!'

The party had begun, yet the crowd was incomplete.

Secret was impatient. 'I wish Papa and Mama would hurry up. We can't really start without them. I know it's a long trip from Bendigo, but they did promise they would be back in time. I hope no mischief has befallen them.'

'Secret, pessimism does not become you,' said Fidelia, always the positive one.

Mary tutted. 'Ah, Secret. They'll be here shortly, now.'

A moment later, the Billings arrived, Madeleine resplendent in cherry pink, and Billings dapper in a fine suit and bearing more than one gift. He was soon surrounded by the eager youngsters, their mouths collectively agape like nestlings awaiting juicy worms.

'Wait, wait, wait. Our birthday girl must, of custom, be first.' Billings handed Fidelia a tiny box. 'A treasure for a treasure.'

Fidelia could scarce pull the bow quickly enough. Inside was an exquisite cameo necklace on a fine gold chain. 'Oh, Mr Billings. I love it. Mrs Billings, would you do the honours?'

Madeleine pulled the necklace from the box, fastened it at Fidelia's nape. 'You were right Lucas, it suits her admirably and complements her outfit perfectly.'

'Now,' said Billings as he pulled a slim, cigar-sized box from his pocket. 'A little something for Secret. Not because it's his birthday but because it is, I believe, something long amiss.'

Secret was perplexed as he removed the lid. He put his hand to his mouth to stem his glee. 'Oh, Papa. How did you know?'

'A certain birthday girl apprised me of the fact.'

Secret put the whistle to his lips and blew, his fingers taking no time to recall the musicality of its notes. It had been a very long time since he had played one; not since he'd accidently dropped it overboard from the *SS Great Britain,* somewhere off the coast of Africa.

Billings beamed. 'And it's not mere tin, young man. Only pure silver for my son. Would you regale us with some old tunes a little later?'

'Oh, yes indeed. I hope I can remember some.'

'And now for young Eudora. A little trinket for a cherub.'

Eudora's eyes lit up. 'For me?' She hastily tore the brown wrapping from the gift to reveal a tiny ceramic ornament of a dictionary. 'Mr Billings. It is so beautiful and so…appropriate. Thank you so much.'

'So there you have it,' Billings said swiping his hands together. He eyed Joshua, who was doleful. 'Ah, Master Joshua. You think I have forgotten you? For you, I have perhaps the best present of all.'

Billings pulled out a long paper cylinder, well concealed under his jacket. 'I should tell you of our ulterior motive for our little jaunt to Bendigo. I did some investigating on your behalf.'

'Oh, quite the detective he was,' Madeleine chimed in, 'He'd have put you to shame, Mary.'

'As I was saying,' continued Billings, 'I sought to learn something of your parents, Joshua. A young man needs to know such things. He needs to have a history. And this, I believe, will speak volumes about the cradle of your talent.'

Joshua could barely contain himself. 'Can I see?'

'All in good time. It took me a mere visit to the *Bendigo Advertiser* to learn of the illustrious history of your parents. They were most highly esteemed in the district. Your father, Clarence Earl Wright, struck gold in the diggings and in short order became a major property owner, producing top quality beef and gathering an enviable reputation as an altruistic gentleman. Your mother, Lily Augustine, was a beauty and – and herein lies the answer to your wondering – a prolific and gifted artist.'

'Oh!' Joshua looked ready to burst with both sadness and joy.

Billings produced a photograph from his pocket and held it up for all to see. 'Joshua, I present you your parents, on their wedding day. Also,' he unrolled the scroll of papers, 'a few remaining samples of your mother's artistry and a copy of their joint obituary which I am certain will reveal as much of their history as could be known.'

Joshua's mouth formed a huge 'O', which Fidelia feared might be permanent if the wind changed.

'But there's more.' Billings pursed his lips in a deliberately long pause. 'Further enquiries, through a Bendigo solicitor, led us to your aunt, Arcadia Birtwhistle – your mother's sister.'

'I have an aunt?'

'Indeed. An aunt and six cousins. But I am sorry to say that it was she who handed you over to the orphanage. She had been widowed a few months before your parents' deaths and could not afford to take care of you. Understandable, I guess, with six other mouths to feed.'

'Can I meet them?' Joshua asked excitedly.

'It is already arranged. You are to come with us next weekend.'

'Golly gosh.'

'Still, that is not all. According to your parents' will, their home was bequeathed to Mrs Birtwhistle–'

'So Joshua doesn't inherit his home?' Secret looked shocked.

'Unfortunately not.'

'Well, that's not fair,' said Secret.

'Instead, he inherits the balance of his parents' estate.' Billings paused again for effect. He smiled at the sea of expectant faces before him. 'The money has been held in trust for you all these years. It was due to you on your 21st birthday, but unfortunately, the solicitor was lax in his efforts to find you. It's a tidy sum, Master Joshua. Something in the order of five thousand pounds.'

Though still reeling from Lucas Billings' revelations about his parents, and his imminent wealth, Joshua and an equally animated Secret begged Fidelia to accompany them to the opera at the *Prince of Wales*, but Fidelia had other plans after her birthday soirée.

'I have no time for something as frivolous as opera. I will be attending a suffrage meeting to hear Henrietta Dugdale speak. I suspect she is a woman after my own heart.'

'You would spend your birthday at a political meeting?' Secret said.

'Why not? I can go to the opera any time. And yes, I would, because naturally I want to report on it, but also, I might well become a disciple. You can't do anything about anything if you don't *do* anything.' She nodded in satisfaction at her own profound wisdom.

Secret pulled a face. 'I guess I can see logic in that. Tomorrow night for the opera then?' He plucked a tomato sandwich from the tray proffered by Myrtle.

'What's a suffrage meeting?' Joshua asked.

'Hopefully, Joshua, a means by which women can make their

feelings known about being completely disenfranchised. It is absolutely abominable that I can earn my own money, own my own property and even now go to university, yet I cannot vote or stand for Parliament to change these archaic, chauvinistic and frankly misogynistic rules.'

Joshua nodded. He did not feel inclined to enter a debate with Fidelia.

'I am sure you are set to hear much more about it. You should come too. You could sketch a cartoon to run with my article. Myrtle and Madeleine are joining me, isn't that so, Myrtle? Mary is still thinking about it.'

'Indeed we are,' Myrtle replied. 'I heard Miss Dugdale speak at a temperance meeting the other night and she made jolly good sense to me. Jolly good. I may be not much of an adherent of temperance but I am certainly a staunch supporter of more rights for women. But I won't be making a late night of it, what with us setting off early in the morning for Ballarat.'

'You're going to Ballarat?' Secret asked.

'Yes. Jasper's decided, on a whim, that he wants to visit our old digs. Though for the life of me I don't know why. We're going by train and will have a short stop in Geelong on the way.'

Jasper overheard the conversation. 'Let's just say, I have to see a man about a cart'.

Myrtle looked blank and shrugged.

Mary finished the sandwich she was eating. 'I'll have a hard time keeping my mouth buttoned, but you've persuaded me that I should hear what this Miss Dugdale has to say.'

'But would only women be there?' Joshua said. 'I would feel most obvious and out of place.'

Fidelia grinned. 'If Mary can pass herself off as a man, I see no reason, why you–'

'Oh no. No, absolutely not!'

'Go on, Joshua, it might be fun,' Secret goaded. Then he turned to Fidelia. 'And I thought you would be celebrating your proposal of marriage, along with your birthday.'

Joshua was astonished.

Fidelia was mortified. 'Secret Jenkins! How did you know?'

Fidelia had hoped nobody would find out. She was not about to accept the proposal of Linden Brown, a quocker-wodger known to have a penchant for mollynogging in those brothels down in Little Lonsdale-street, just because he had been impressed with her letters to parliament. He was at least twenty years her senior and smelled of cigars and stale beer and, besides, reminded her of Lester Fleet. He had 'accidently' bumped into her on too many occasions and she recoiled from his bothersome presence. What had possessed him to think he could ask for her hand? She would rather sleep in a pit full of snakes than contemplate a wedding night – and beyond – with the likes of him.

His was the second proposal she had fended off in the past month. The other was from Netherby Goodfellow, who, in Fidelia's opinion, did not live up to his name. She did not want to become known as Fidelia Goodfellow, nor, more pertinently, Mrs Netherby Goodfellow. It would be too hard a name to measure up to and she had not the slightest desire to attempt it. Nor did she have any desire for the man himself, if desire should be a prerequisite for marriage.

Imagine having to take breakfast with the lily-livered sod in the mornings and having to lend an ear to his oleaginous windbaggery. It simply didn't bear thinking about. Besides, he was not her intellectual equal and while she did not want to appear snobbish about such things, it would not augur well for a satisfying future. She would perpetually want to correct his grammar and ensure that his tenses were correct and his verbs agreed with his subjects. No. She did not want to be a tutor *all* the time.

'I confess,' Secret said, 'Jasper told me, just as I arrived. He thought it a comedy that such a rogue would ask for your hand.'

'How should I ever countenance such an idea? To become betrothed to a man I do not want? Or love? I will not marry just because convention expects it of me.'

'The solution is simple,' Secret announced. He looked around to ensure nobody else was privy to their conversation. 'Marry me.'

'You? What?' Joshua said, incredulously.

Secret winked at him.

'Follymop,' Fidelia said. 'You don't want to marry me. You'd rather marry Joshua.'

Secret baulked, dismayed but in awe of her perceptiveness. He wondered how long she had known. He was sure that he and Joshua had never betrayed their secret.

'Which is exactly why, given that you do not *wish* to marry, you should marry me,' he persisted. 'I could make you appear respectable – of course, I am not saying you're not – and you, me. If it happened that Joshua needed to lodge with us; that would not be seen as unacceptable or untoward.'

'What are you suggesting Secret?' Fidelia digested his words.

'Exactly what I said. For as long as it suited you, you could be my wife and continue to do all the things I know you want to do – travel, write, become a politician, lexicographer, professor or jolly lepidopterist – whatever captivates you next. And if it happened that our dear confirmed bachelor friend Joshua needed a permanent address, then–'

'That could solve a number of problems,' Fidelia said. 'And it means we would never have to be separated – unless, of course, we want to be.'

'What do you think, Joshua?' Secret asked.

Joshua had tried to look stunned at Fidelia's innuendo, but the gesture was wasted. He loved Fidelia completely, but as a sister. She was the only girl who might ever have swayed him and Secret towards the fairer gender. It was Secret with whom he sought intimacy. Always had been. Fidelia evidently knew it. He could not argue the point.

'But how could you tell?' Joshua whispered to her.

'I have always seen how you look at each other – like you're mentalling each other's thoughts. Those sneaky winks you thought I'd never seen. It's all the clearer now that I see you both standing there in your matching foppish attire. I might suggest that you keep such niminy-piminy for when you're alone together, rather than raising public suspicion. I, as you know, have an open mind, but others don't.'

'Sounds spiffing to me. And Secret is right, Fidelia. Such a marriage would put paid to all those unwanted suitors of yours.'

'But how *long* have you known?' Secret asked.

'You remember the drawing you gave Joshua for his imaginary birthday – at the hospital? The shaded figure which I knew represented the two halves of one soul?'

'Oh,' Secret said, wide eyed, 'that long?'

'Yes, that long. But I can see wisdom in your proposal. There is, however, one thing of which none of us has thought.'

'And that is?' Secret said.

'Eudora.' Joshua predicted. He pointed at the child, who was busily stuffing a cream-filled pastry in her mouth. 'You wonder how could we live in such a questionable and *faux* moral arrangement with Eudora in the house?'

Fidelia nodded. 'Yes, poor Eudora. Is it not enough the poor girl has known a pair of murderers as her parents these ten years?'

'I believe that girl has at least some of your guile and nous, Fidelia,' Secret said. 'A legacy of your parents. I think we should give her credit for being adaptable to a somewhat unusual ménage. We would love her as a sister, or a daughter, or a niece or – or the way we love you, Fidelia. I would not be perturbed about her moral vulnerability.'

'You are so good to me, Secret Jenkins.'

'You deserve nothing less than our complete and utter devotion,' Secret said. 'You have helped us realise our dreams, excel ourselves, be all that we want to be. I don't believe either of us would want to live without you, Fidelia Knight.'

'Then I am juffled.'

'Is that a real word, Fidelia?'

Fidelia cocked her head coquettishly. 'It is now.'

EPILOGUE

February 9, 1885

Fidelia strode down the passage, though confident steps belied her true apprehension. The knowledge that Father would have smiled with pride, today of all days, bolstered her nerve. It should have been him striding these prestigious corridors. He never got to see them. All those who had studied in these rooms had not had the privilege of knowing him, of absorbing his wisdom and wondering at the playful glint in his eye. Pleasant Fidelius Knight had been clever and shrewd, and oft times rakish. She smiled at the thought of him.

'For you, Father,' she said out loud. She carried her beloved Samuel Johnson with her. Both volumes. They had a new home now.

She followed the directions the registrar had given to her and now approached the sixth door on the left. No knocking was necessary. The engraved brass plate on the door welcomed the new occupant.

F.P. Knight-Jenkins
Lexicographer

Fidelia was not prepared, however, for what awaited her as she stepped inside.

The room was larger than she imagined from its unassuming portal. Light filtered through an east-facing window and cast an ephemeral glow across the faces of the six people who greeted her.

She recognised only Mr Pendleton and yet the strangers were applauding her. Welcoming her to her new domain and showing their unbridled support for her appointment.

The walls around her were lined with shelves bearing every conceivable reference work, cyclopaedia and resource a logophile such as she would aspire to peruse and memorise. And so many lexicons and dictionaries bursting with new words to cram into her vocabulary. It was a library unto itself, like Father's, where she had spent so much time as a child.

It was hers. And among these like-minded people, these kindred souls, she would work to compile the first Australian dictionary.

For the time being, at least.

Who knew what would take her fancy next?

APPENDIX

The poems of

Fidelia (and Pleasant) Knight

Be Kind to the Animals

Never bother a belligerent badger
Or hobble a hirsute hare.
Don't squabble with a squeamish squirrel
Or betray a bombastic bear.

Never fetter a foolish fieldmouse
Or molest a malevolent mole.
Do not dare goad a garrulous grouse,
Or vanquish a vehement vole.

For these are creatures of the wild, my dear
Creatures of the wild.
They are creatures of the wild, my dear,
Always treasure them, my child.

Never ridicule a right royal raven,
Nor fluster a ferocious fowl.
Do not defile a delicate deer
Or obstruct an opprobrious owl.

Never offend an obsequious otter
Nor gall a giddy-brained goat.
Do not reproach a rapscallion rabbit
Or sequester a stultiloquent stoat.

Never mislead a mettlesome mallard
Nor hoodwink a hardscrabble hog.
Do not wheedle a woebegone weasel
Or fuddle a fopdoodle frog.

For these are creatures of the wild, my dear
Creatures of the wild.
They are creatures of the wild, my dear,
Always respect them, my child.

CREATURES OF THE DEEP

Never frustrate a floundering flathead
Or scuttle a serpentine snail
Do not torment a treacherous turtle
Or waylay a wallowing whale

Never pique a preposterous porpoise
Or embitter an eremitical eel
Do not castigate a camouflaged clam
Or stymie a sarcastic seal

For they are creatures of the deep, my child
Creatures of the deep
They are creatures of the deep, my child
And they'll swimmingly send you to sleep

Never saddle a sardonic seahorse
Or pickle a penurious plaice
Do no diagnose a doddering dolphin
Or wrestle a wriggling wrasse

Never gratify a grovelling grouper
Or keck at those kind-hearted krill
Do no circumscribe a cachexic cod
Or sequester a second-hand shell

For they are creatures of the deep, my child
Creatures of the deep
They are creatures of the deep, my child
And they'll swimmingly send you to sleep

BE KIND TO THE AUSTRALIAN ANIMALS

Never winnow a woebegone wombat
Or kidnap a kind kangaroo
Do not denigrate a dastardly dingo
Or punish a peeved potoroo

Never besmirch a bewildered bilby
Or rattle a rambunctious rosella
Do not lampoon a licentious lyrebird
Or kidnap a knavish koala

For they are creatures of the bush, my dear,
Creatures of the wild,
They are creatures of the bush, my dear,
Always treasure them, my child.

Never poke a parsimonious possum
Or question a quarrelsome quoll
Do not kowtow to a keen kookaburra
Or offend an obstreperous owl

Never goad a glowering galah
Or wrangle a wizened wallaroo
Do not belittle a blind bandicoot
Or cajole a capricious cockatoo

Never murder a maladroit magpie
Or enrage an ebullient echidna
Do not dare poke a petulant platypus
Or gloat at a gormless goanna

For they are creatures of the bush, my dear,
Creatures of the wild,
They are creatures of the bush, my dear,
Always treasure them, my child.

MISTER QUANDARY MAN

Why do you look so perplexed,
My dear Mr Quandary man?
Have you no thought in your head,
Or good word to be said,
Is your mind like a pineapple flan?

Why do you look so bewildered,
My dear Mr Quandary man?
Is it not your intention
To show some invention?
You must try it, try if you can.

Why do you look so befuddled,
My dear Mr Quandary man?
If you're stuck on a task
You have only to ask
And I'll do what I can, if I can.

Why do you look so confounded,
My dear Mr Quandary man?
It is not becoming
To have fingers a drumming
And a look like you haven't a plan.

Why do you look so bamboozled,
My dear Mr Quandary man?
I can tell you are kind
But you must use your mind
And show me some dash and élan.

What's Hiding Under Your Bustle?

What's hiding under your bustle?
Maybe something you'd ne'er think to find
Is it a small man bent double
Seeking refuge from trouble
And tailing you closely behind?

What's hiding under your bustle,
In that empty, voluminous space?
There's room enough there
For a small pied-à-terre,
With terrace and spiral staircase

What's hiding under your bustle,
Under all of that satin and lace?
'Tis a whale out of water
Or somebody's daughter
Trying to keep up the pace

What's hiding under your bustle
In that network of fabric and wire?
It could easily screen
The home of the Queen
With room for Saint Paul's Church's spire

What's hiding under your bustle?
There's ample and plentiful room
For a barrel of rum
And a timpani drum
And a witch riding off on a broom

What's hiding under your bustle
In that absurdly daft contraption?
A short-necked giraffe
Bent almost in half
And suffering painful contraction.

CHASING HOPPITY-BOO

The red kangaroo goes hoppity-boo
And hoppity-boo it goes.
It bounces along,
Never puts a foot wrong,
As it pushes itself off its toes.

The brown wallaby goes boppity-wee
and boppity-wee it goes.
It bounds in a flurry
'cos it's in a great hurry
To see where the kangaroo goes

The grey koala goes dippity-dala
And dippity-dala it goes
It walks on all-fours
With a shake of its paws
To see what the kangaroo knows.

The spiny echidna goes prickety-pidna
And prickety-pidna it goes
It bristles its spines
Into prickly lines
To stick in the kangaroo's nose

The feathertail glider goes wirrily-wida
And wirrily-wida it goes
It flies through the air
Like it hasn't a care
To land on the kangaroo's toes

The strange platypus goes swirrily-shush
And swirrily-shush it goes
It swims along silently
Then quite surprisingly
Sneaks up should the kangaroo doze

Six Wives He Had

Six wives he had, did Henry the Eight
Three Catherines, two Annes and a Jane
But how to get them in order by date
Just follow and all will be plain.

The first was Catherine of Aragon,
Who he wed for alliance with Spain
They married in June of 1509
She bore Mary; later briefly to reign
But after 24 years he tired of her face
As he'd started to look at another
The marriage annulled; she in disgrace
As she'd earlier married his brother.

He'd been secretly coveting Anne Boleyn
(Whose sister Mary had prior beguiled him)
They married in secret; she had child within
And Elizabeth the First, she bore unto him.
But just three years would Anne remain queen
As the court did conspire against her
They plotted and schemed in all manner obscene
Until, on the green, they beheaded her

On the very next day he married Jane Seymour
For whom desire a while he had shown
Not too long later she did him the honour
Of bearing a male heir to the throne.
Sadly Prince Edward the sixth would not ever know her
As just two weeks later she died.
But she became the sole spouse of this Tudor
To have him later interred by her side.

Two years later, a new queen was sought,
Far and wide the net cast for a plan.
Artist Holbein dispatched to Duke of Cleves' court,
To paint sisters Amelia and Anne.
Anne was the chosen, though not liked by the king
'Flanders Mare' was the name he resolved.
Yet he went ahead and gave her his ring,
Six months later the marriage was dissolved.

He had his eye on Anne's lady in waiting,
Kathryn Howard, in a fortnight, was wife number five
Their betrothal was indeed a short mating,
She was young and made him feel alive.
But she was not so enamoured of him
And sought other companions to bed
Of her infidelity, he had a view dim
And so he cut off her head.

Wife number six was named Katherine Parr,
Henry her spouse number three.
She was first Lady Burgh, and then Lady Latimer
She outlived them both, so to wed she was free.
Clever and erudite; a Protestant fast
She became the first authoress queen,
She nursed her husband 'til the day that he passed
And so remained the Dowager Queen.

GLOSSARY

A

Abecedarian – *adj* – arranged alphabetically; rudimentary, elementary

Antediluvian – *adj* – of, or belonging to the time before the biblical flood; ridiculously old-fashioned

B

Bacciferous – *adj* – bearing berries

Balbriggan – *noun* – a knitted cotton fabric used for stockings and underwear

Balistarius – *noun* – a crossbowman

Blobberlip – *noun* – a blabbering, incoherent child (FK)

C

Cabochon – *noun* – a gem that has been polished, but not faceted

Cachectick – *noun* – having an ill habit of body

Cachexic – *noun* – variation of Cachectick; weakness and wasting of the body through chronic illness

Calabrous – *adj* – despairing of never seeing someone again (FK)

Cankerdoodle- *noun* – a man who appears full of his own self-importance (FK)

Childspeak – *noun* – nonsensical speech (FK)

Circumscribe – *verb* – restrict (something) within limits

Coscinomancy – *noun* – the art of divination by means of a sieve

Cover-slut – *noun* – an apron or pinafore

D

Daggledtail – *noun* – bemired: dipped in water or mud

Dallop – *noun* – a tuft or clump

Dastagant – *noun* – a thoroughly base and unlikeable person (FK)

Definiens – *noun* – definition

Deltiology – *noun* – the study and collection of postcards

Desiderium – *noun* – an ardent desire or longing especially, a feeling of loss or grief for something lost

Designation – *noun* – the act of choosing someone to hold office

Dewbesprent – *adj* – sprinkled with dew

E

Effodient – *adj* – digging up, burrowing

Epergne – *noun* – an ornamental centrepiece for a dining table, typically used for holding fruit or flowers

Eremitical – *adj* – of, or relating to, an eremite; a hermit or recluse, especially one under a religious vow

F

Facetiae – *noun* – humorous sayings; pornographic literature

Fandangle – *noun* – useless or purely ornamental thing

Fascinous – *adj* – caused or acting by witchcraft

Flexanimous – *adj* – having power to change the mind

Follymop – e*xclamation* – meaning 'don't be ridiculous' (FK)

Fopdoodle – *adj* – a stupid or insignificant fellow; a fool

Franchise – *noun* – the right to vote; rights of citizenship

Fustilugs – *noun* – a ponderous clumsy person: a fat and slovenly woman

G

Gabion – *noun* – a basket or container filled with earth, stones, or other material and used in civil engineering works

Gamp – *noun* – an umbrella

Gilly-gaupus – *noun* – an awkward, clumsy or silly person (Scottish)

H

Habiliment – *noun* – Fr. Dress, clothing, garments

Hamshackle – *verb* – to tie (an animal) by a rope binding the head to one of the forelegs

Hardihood – *noun* – boldness, daring

Hardscrabble – *adj* – involving hard work and struggle

I

Infandus – *adj* – unspeakable, unnatural, shocking, abominable

Illuminati – *noun* – people claiming to possess special enlightenment or knowledge of something

Insouciant – *adj* – showing a casual lack of concern

Intresiac – *noun* – a person who underrates their own value or talent (FK)

Inveigle – *verb* – persuade (someone) to do something by means of deception or flattery

J

Jackalént – *noun* – a starving man, a simple, sheepish man

Jardiniere – *noun* – an ornamental pot or stand for the display of growing plants

Jibber-jabber – *noun* – rapid and excited speech that is difficult to understand

Jiggumbob – *noun* – an indistinct thing, thingamajig

Jongleur – *noun* – an itinerant minstrel

Juffled – *adj* – immensely pleased (FK)

K

Keck – *verb* – feel inclined to vomit; retch

Ken – *noun* – one's range of knowledge or understanding

Kickshaw – *noun* – trinket, cheap worthless article

Kippage – *noun* – an excited or irritated state, commotion, confusion

Knick-knackery – *noun* – collection of knick-knacks

L

Lapidescent – *adj* – tending to petrify: in the process of turning into stone

Loquacious – *adj* – talkative, long-winded

M

Madgehowlet – *noun* – an owl

Magniloquent – *adj* – using high-flown or bombastic language

Mentalling – *verb* – reading another's mind (FK)

Meretricious – *adj* – apparently attractive but having no real value

Mettlesome – *adj* – (of a person or animal) full of spirit and courage; lively.

Mollynogging – *verb* – frequenting the company of loose or immoral women

N

Nepenthe – *noun* – a drug described in Homer's *Odyssey* as banishing grief from a person's mind

Ninnyhammer – *noun* – a fool or simpleton

Noggin – *noun* – a small quantity of alcoholic drink, typically a quarter of a pint

O

Obambulate – *verb* – to walk about

Obequitate – *verb* – to ride about

Oleaginous – *adj* – rich in, covered with, or producing oil, oily; exaggeratedly and distastefully complimentary; obsequious

Opine – *verb* – state one's opinion

Opprobrious – *adj* – (of language) expressing scorn or criticism

P

Palaeography – *noun* – the study of ancient writing systems and the deciphering and dating of historical manuscripts

Pandect – *noun* – a complete body of the laws of a country

Parvenu – *noun* (derogatory) – a person of humble origin who has gained wealth, influence, or celebrity

Penurious – *adj* – poverty stricken

Phrontistes – *adj* – derived from Phrontistery – a thinking place or study

Pied-à-terre – *noun* – (*Fr*) a small apartment or house

Polrumptious – *adj* – rude, obstreperous, obnoxious

Pong – *noun/verb* – an unpleasant smell (FK)

Q

Quacksalver – *noun* – one falsely claiming to possess medical or other skills; a quack

Quagswag – *verb* – to move unsteadily from side to side or up and down; shake, quiver

Querken – *verb* – to cause to gasp or choke

Questmonger – *noun* – one who conducts inquests; one who profits by initiating lawsuits

Quidditative – *noun* – of, relating to, or constituting the essential nature of something

Quocker-wodger – *noun* – a wooden puppet controlled by strings; a pseudo-politician, one whose strings of action are pulled by others

R

Rantipole – *adj* – characterised by a wild unruly manner or attitude

Rascalion – *noun* – an archaic form of rapscallion – a mischievous person

Rhetorick – *noun* – Samuel Johnson's spelling of rhetoric

Rodomontade – *noun* – boastful talk

S

Sack-posset – *noun* – a custard-like drink often made of curdled milk and wine or beer

Slubberdegullion – *noun* – a filthy, slobbering person; a sloven, a villain

Soignée – *adj* – dressed very elegantly; well groomed

Soodle – *verb* – to walk slowly

Sprauncy – *adj* – smart or showy in appearance

Sternutation – *noun* – the act of sneezing

Stultiloquent – *adj* – given to, or characterised by, silly talk; babbling

T

Tenebrous – *adj* – dark, shadowy or obscure

Tête-à-tête – *noun* – a private conversation between two people

Twitten – *noun* – a narrow path between walls or hedges

U

Ubiquarian – *noun* – one who appears to be everywhere at once

Unbeseeming – *adj* – unbecoming; not befitting

V

Vamper – *noun* – a seductive woman who uses her sex appeal to exploit men; coquette

Vennel – *noun* – an alley between buildings

Vouchsafe – *verb* – give or grant (something) to (someone); reveal or disclose information

W

Warluck – *noun* – obsolete form of warlock

Waygone – *adj* – exhausted from long travels

Weirdwardly – *adj* – almost supernaturally

Windbaggery – *noun* – lengthy talk or discussion with little or no interesting content

Woebegone – *adj* – sad or miserable in appearance

X

Xanthippe – *noun* – wife of Socrates; a scolding or ill-tempered wife; a shrewish woman

Xebec – *noun* – a small three-masted Mediterranean sailing ship with lateen and square sails

Xenagogue – *noun* – one who conducts strangers; a guide

Xenial – *adj* – hospitable, friendly

Xenodochial – *adj* – friendly to strangers

Xerxes – *noun* – warrior; hero among rulers

Xiphos – *noun* – a double-edged, one-handed Iron Age, Grecian short-sword

Xyston – *noun* – a javelin or spiked stick

Y

Yarely – *adj* – nimble, lively

Yemeles – *adj* – careless, negligent

Z

Zibet – *noun* – an Asiatic civet cat

Zodiack – *noun* – archaic spelling of zodiac

Zoetrope – *noun* – a 19th-century optical toy consisting of a cylinder with pictures on the inner surface that, when viewed through slits with the cylinder rotating, give an impression of continuous motion

Zoographer – *noun* – one who describes or depicts animals and their forms and habits

Zoophorus – *adj* – supporting or having a carved animal figure

Author's Note

When I was set to leave school, too many years ago to mention, I was accepted to study languages and literature at Monash University. But more entranced with instant gratification – and the pay packet that accompanied it – I opted to take up a cadetship on my hometown newspaper instead. Thus, I became a journalist and not a linguist. Alas, journalism allowed no scope for my love of unusual, archaic words; those lost to the English language by the editorial dictates of newspapers and publishers. Those edicts of 'don't use long words when a short one will do,' and 'write for a 13-year-old readership,' have effectively banished many wonderful words to the realms of obsolescence.

This book has dusted some of them off.

The idea for *Billings Better Bookstore and Brasserie* came mid-flight from Sydney to Melbourne, following the inaugural Historical Novel Society Australasia convention in 2015. Inspired by the words of the convention's many panelists, I re-visited a notion I'd had some years earlier.

I'd come across a quirky advertisement for Melbourne's Coles Book Arcade, which occupied the entire right column of the front page of *The Herald* on March 3, 1875. The advertisement's alliterative verses, compiled by the eccentric Mr Edward Cole himself, struck a chord. Upon researching Edward Cole, I came across Lisa Lang's wonderful *Utopian Man,* and promptly dispelled the idea of embarking on a comparable fictionalised account of his life.

Instead, I invented a rival bookstore and created Fidelia Knight, a young girl with an equal, if not superior, love of words, books and all things educational. Edward Cole was thus relegated to a minor role, along with the story's other real characters – Edwin and Frances Exon, Frederick McCoy and Mary Fortune – and those merely alluded to; ie, John Ferres, Emma Cook and Henrietta Dugdale.

My book would not have come to pass without Samuel Johnson and his 1755 *Dictionary of the English Language*. Having downloaded the entire dictionary, I found myself lost for hours scrolling through its definitions. That one man could have almost single-handedly compiled the first dictionary of note left me awe inspired. Though long dead by the era of my work, I was compelled to pay homage to Dr Johnson and bring him to life, albeit anthropomorphically, through Fidelia's attachment to his dictionary. The online *Phrontistery* and the Facebook page, *Grandiloquent Word of the Day* also provided a wealth of hitherto unknown-to-me words.

Writing such a work entailed studying the etymology of many of the obscure words used, to avoid anachronisms. Several words I considered using had to be discarded as they weren't coined until after my timeline.

Interestingly, the word 'pong' originated in the early 20th century, but has no known etymology – and so I claimed it for Fidelia. Who's to say she didn't invent it?

Given that this story is intrinsically *about* words, I make no apology to those readers who have one hand on the book and another on a dictionary. That's why I have included a basic glossary.

Like Fidelia, I beseech you to expand your vocabulary.

Research for a historical novel is both painstaking and fascinating. It requires hours of cross-referencing to ensure historical accuracy, and even then, it's often difficult to ascertain the veracity of information and its sources. I ponder how much more difficult it was for authors and historians to effect research prior to the advent of Trove, which proved to be an eminently valuable resource.

Finding contradictions sometimes leads to creating one's own version of the truth; the adoption of poetic license. Therefore, any historical inaccuracies herein, are of my own making – and I own them. I am no more a historian than I am a linguist.

Researching 1870s Melbourne led me on many offbeat tangents – some of which appear in *Billings* as diversions, others of which are stored in my memory bank for future reference.

I hope, however, that I have portrayed Australia's greatest city – and some of its larger-than-life denizens – in a vibrant and favourable light.

Acknowledgements

As mentioned in my author's note, I commend the Historical Novel Society Australasia (HNSA) for inspiring this work and for the encouragement and support it gives to authors to bring history to life.

From the moment I wrote the first word of *Billings Better Bookstore and Brasserie*, I visualised how I wanted the cover to look. Author/ artist, Judith Rossell, must have seen what was in my mind's eye. Her artwork, from initial sketch to completed design, is a triumph. I thank her whole-heartedly for realising my dream from my words.

To editor extraordinaire, Narrelle M Harris, I say thank-you, thank-you, thank-you. From the get-go, she was as passionate and enthusiastic about *Billings* as I am. Her expertise in dialects, structure and narrative voice were invaluable. I thank her for helping me to fill in the plot holes; those things that were clear in my mind, but which may, to a reader, have been as cryptic as the crosswords I compile for fun. I thank her for helping to make this book what I'd always intended it to be.

Thanks also to the eagle-eyed Helen Burke, proofreader *par excellence*.

To my Wednesday 'Sanity Session' writing class girls (present and past) – Anne Cost, Merna Hanson, Gayle Scott, Rosie Abbott, Denice Grosdanis, Lee Moon, Leanne Dyson, Linda Collins, Laurel Warhurst, Jess Roberts, Sandy Mattingley, Marg Beazer, Mary Young, Judy Mann and Carol Marsden – thank you for your unflagging faith in me and your precious friendship. Thanks also for tolerating my sporadic readings of snippets of *Billings* and pretending to have an inkling of what it was all about.

I thank my late mother, Liz Cameron, for fostering my love of writing, reading and music, for always believing in me and for her invaluable feedback on snatches of this, and other, stories. I wish she was still here to read the finished work.

Writing is a lonely, self-indulgent pastime, absorbing of mind and body, and often foreign to those who don't partake of it. I therefore praise my husband, Steve, for never complaining about my apparent vagueness (while listening to the characters in my head, instead of him), the unwashed dishes, belated meals and inspired dashes to the computer to get some description or snatch of dialogue down before I forget them.

Most of all, I thank Lindy Cameron, founder and virtual one-woman-band of Clan Destine Press, for believing in *Billings* from go to whoa and for encouraging me every step of the way. I knew from the start that it would take a brave publisher to take *Billings* on board – for the reasons outlined in my author's note – and I therefore commend her *Xena Warrior Princess*-never-say-die attitude. She is a *kindred* soul in the strictest sense of the word

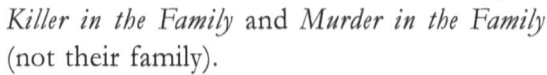

Fin J Ross

Fin is a journalist and creative writing teacher who runs a boarding cattery in East Gippsland and breeds British Shorthair cats.

She is the co-author, with her sister, of the true crime anthologies,

Killer in the Family and *Murder in the Family* (not their family).

Her first novel *AKA Fudgepuddle* is the journal/memoir of the oh-so-true adventures of a demanding cat called Megsy.

Fin has won eight category prizes (over five years) in the annual Scarlet Stiletto Awards for crime and mystery short stories. The competition has been run by Sisters in Crime Australia since 1994.

In her spare time Fin compiles cryptic crosswords.